STAR TREK

THE NEXT GENERATION®

SKETCHBOOK *THE MOVIES*

GENERATIONS™ & FIRST CONTACT™

POCKET BOOKS
New York London Toronto Sydney Tokyo Singapore

JOHN EAVES & J.M. DILLARD

An *Original* Publication of POCKET BOOKS

POCKET BOOKS, a division of Simon & Schuster Inc.
1230 Avenue of the Americas, New York, NY 10020

Copyright © 1998 by Paramount Pictures. All Rights Reserved.

STAR TREK is a Registered Trademark of Paramount Pictures.

This book is published by Pocket Books,
a division of Simon & Schuster Inc.,
under exclusive license from Paramount Pictures.

ISBN: 0-671-00892-7

First Pocket Books trade paperback printing May 1998

10 9 8 7 6 5 4 3 2 1

POCKET and colophon are registered trademarks of
Simon & Schuster Inc.

Graphic Design: Laurie Goldman, Red Herring Design

Printed in the U.S.A.

For orders other than by individual consumers, Pocket Books grants a discount on the
purchase of **10 or more** copies of single titles for special markets or premium use. For
further details, please write to the Vice-President of Special Markets, Pocket Books,
1633 Broadway, New York, NY 10019-6785, 8th Floor.

For information on how individual consumers can place orders, please write to Mail
Order Department, Simon & Schuster Inc., 200 Old Tappan Road, Old Tappan, NJ 07675.

What would you say if Production Designer Herman Zimmerman called you up one day to ask, "So, would you like to come work on a new *Star Trek* movie?"

If, like John Eaves, you happen to be a loyal *Star Trek* fan from 'way back, your response would likely be the same as his: a thrilled "Of *course!*"

Unlike most of us, however, John is an enormously talented artist—and due to that fact, the above question and answer weren't part of a fannish daydream, but actually occurred in 1993. The film in question (or "feature," to use Hollywood jargon) was *Star Trek Generations*, the first motion-picture outing for *The Next Generation* crew. Based on Eaves's prior work on *Star Trek V: The Final Frontier*, Zimmerman had called him back to work as the illustrator for *Generations*. *Star Trek: First Contact* followed, during which time Eaves gathered together his sketches on the two films. His goal—and mine—is to give readers a glimpse of the creative process that goes on inside the *Star Trek* feature art department during the frenzied months of filming.

What follows is told mostly from John's point of view, as illustrator—but bear in mind that *Star Trek* is not the creation of one single person, or artist. (John will be first to tell you that; he went through the rough manuscript marking out his own name and replacing it with those of his coworkers at every opportunity.) Each object—be it a ship, set, character, or special effect—is the work of many gifted and hardworking souls. By necessity or accident, some of them have been overlooked during the telling of this story; but certainly in this case, their labor "of the few" has led to the vast enjoyment of the many.

—Jeanne M. Dillard

THE ARTIST

This book is meant not as a technical reference or definitive guide, but rather as a family scrapbook—a family that included not only those in the *Star Trek* feature art department who worked tirelessly to bring *Generations* and *First Contact* to life, but also those of you who enjoyed the films. In that spirit, I've collected certain "moments" in time—recorded by pencil, ink, computer, or film—that took place during the creation of the aforementioned movies, and which I would like to share with you.

Like all scrapbooks, this one is far from complete; it's impossible to record every minute, every image, every contribution by every individual. Even so, I hope that this spare sampling gives you a taste of the enormous outpouring of creativity that occurred on the Paramount lot.

So relax. Take your shoes off, and let Jeanne Dillard's words guide you through the images, as I recollect the adventure I shared with so many others on the making of *Star Trek*.

—John Eaves

PART 1

STAR TREK
GENERATIONS

THE U.S.S. ENTERPRISE

NCC-1701-B

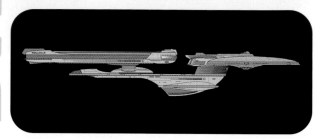

The very first assignment for *Generations*' art staff was to design the *Enterprise*-B, the ship on which Captain Kirk would meet his heroic demise (er, make that his *first* heroic demise) when a deadly energy "ribbon" destroys the reactor room where Kirk is working. Little had been established about the B—except, of course, that it came chronologically between the A (*Star Trek IV, V,* and *VI*) and the C (*Star Trek: The Next Generation*'s "Yesterday's *Enterprise*")....

According to Michael and Denise Okuda's *Star Trek Encyclopedia* and *Star Trek Chronology*, the *Enterprise*-B had been established as an *Excelsior*-class starship. (Designed by ILM's Bill George, the *Excelsior* made her first appearance in *Star Trek III: The Search for Spock*, as the ship that came to a sputtering halt while in pursuit of our favorite starship crew. Later, she appeared under Captain Sulu's command in *Star Trek VI: The Undiscovered Country*.)

Generations' producers, on the other hand, felt the *Excelsior* had been seen too many times in previous films; they wanted a brand-new design for the *Enterprise*-B. This presented a challenge: how to maintain continuity and *Trek* "historical accuracy" while giving the audience a "new" ship.

Mike Okuda felt the challenge could be met.

JOHN:

The *Excelsior* has always been my favorite of all the starships. Bill George's design conveyed power, elegance, and beauty, so when the task fell to me to modify the ship, I was both thrilled and concerned.

Fortunately, Mike Okuda came over to the feature art department [where John's office was located] to discuss changes that would significantly alter the ship's appearance while keeping her original lines. That was the first time I had worked with Mike, and that in itself was a treat; his focus and direction for the modifications were extremely helpful. So together, we set to work on the details.

First, I took an ILM photo that showed the *Excelsior* in Spacedock, did a rendering, and started putting add-ons on the ship. When I met with Mike, he pointed out that we needed to design an area that protruded from the ship, so that the energy ribbon could whip out a section while leaving most of the ship intact.

So we built a section of decks extended out from the main body, which tapers gently on the bottom and flares out dramatically on the top. We also did a detail sketch of the area around the deflector dish, designating one area as the reactor room. The addition of the decks gave the B's belly section a look similar to that of a P.B.Y. Catalina (a flying boat of the 1940s). The added girth increased the overall size of the vessel, while still retaining the original *Excelsior* design. We made a few other design changes, such as taking two fins off the top of the saucer, and putting in two major impulse engines, one on either side of the existing impulse engines (we figured these stronger engines would be needed when the saucer detached). As for the nacelles, we added a cap to them, plus a dorsal fin on top and a running fin on the outer edge.

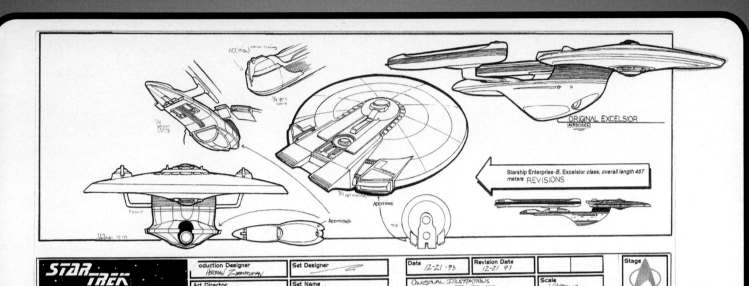

STAR TREK
THE NEXT GENERATION: THE FEATURE

Production Designer	Set Designer	Date 12-21-93	Revision Date 12-21-93		Stage
HERMAN ZIMMERMAN					
Art Director	Set Name	CONCEPTUAL ILLUSTRATIONS	Scale		
SANDY	ENTERPRISE OVERHAUL	JOHN EAVES	VARIOUS		

ORIGINAL EXCELSIOR

Starship Enterprise-B, Excelsior class, overall length 467 meters REVISIONS

▼ A CGI (COMPUTER-GENERATED)
B BY ARTIST DOUG DREXLER

▲ AN EARLY SKETCH OF THE *ENTERPRISE*-B AND
HER NOBLE PREDECESSOR, BILL GEORGE'S
EXCELSIOR. (NOTE THE FILM'S WORKING TITLE.)

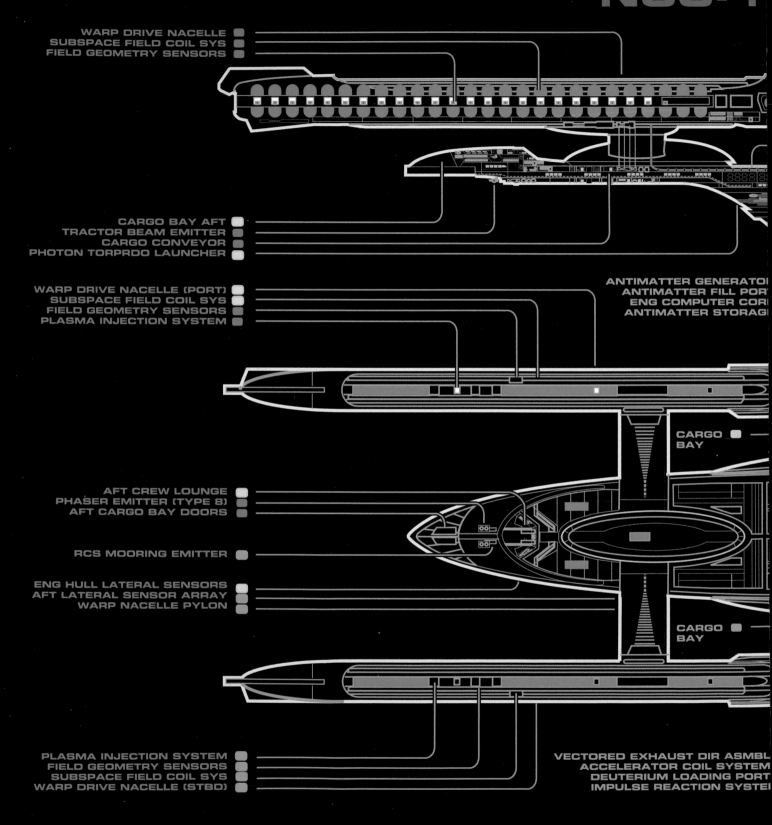

WARP DRIVE NACELLE
SUBSPACE FIELD COIL SYS
FIELD GEOMETRY SENSORS

CARGO BAY AFT
TRACTOR BEAM EMITTER
CARGO CONVEYOR
PHOTON TORPRDO LAUNCHER

WARP DRIVE NACELLE (PORT)
SUBSPACE FIELD COIL SYS
FIELD GEOMETRY SENSORS
PLASMA INJECTION SYSTEM

ANTIMATTER GENERATO
ANTIMATTER FILL POR
ENG COMPUTER COR
ANTIMATTER STORAG

CARGO
BAY

AFT CREW LOUNGE
PHASER EMITTER (TYPE 8)
AFT CARGO BAY DOORS

RCS MOORING EMITTER

ENG HULL LATERAL SENSORS
AFT LATERAL SENSOR ARRAY
WARP NACELLE PYLON

CARGO
BAY

PLASMA INJECTION SYSTEM
FIELD GEOMETRY SENSORS
SUBSPACE FIELD COIL SYS
WARP DRIVE NACELLE (STBD)

VECTORED EXHAUST DIR ASMBL
ACCELERATOR COIL SYSTEM
DEUTERIUM LOADING PORT
IMPULSE REACTION SYSTE

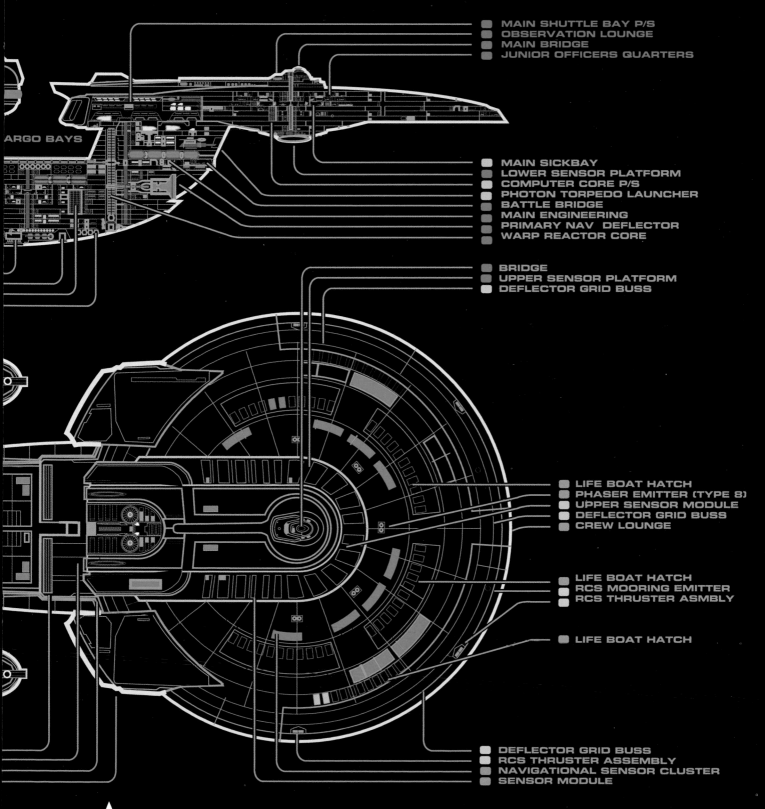

ERPRISE
01-B

CARGO BAYS

MAIN SHUTTLE BAY P/S
OBSERVATION LOUNGE
MAIN BRIDGE
JUNIOR OFFICERS QUARTERS

MAIN SICKBAY
LOWER SENSOR PLATFORM
COMPUTER CORE P/S
PHOTON TORPEDO LAUNCHER
BATTLE BRIDGE
MAIN ENGINEERING
PRIMARY NAV DEFLECTOR
WARP REACTOR CORE

BRIDGE
UPPER SENSOR PLATFORM
DEFLECTOR GRID BUSS

LIFE BOAT HATCH
PHASER EMITTER (TYPE 8)
UPPER SENSOR MODULE
DEFLECTOR GRID BUSS
CREW LOUNGE

LIFE BOAT HATCH
RCS MOORING EMITTER
RCS THRUSTER ASMBLY

LIFE BOAT HATCH

DEFLECTOR GRID BUSS
RCS THRUSTER ASSEMBLY
NAVIGATIONAL SENSOR CLUSTER
SENSOR MODULE

CGI "BLUEPRINTS," ALSO BY DREXLER.
Courtesy of the artist.

The finished sketches won approval from Herman Zimmerman and Rick Berman, and were then sent to Industrial Light & Magic, specifically to Visual FX Art Director Bill George and Model Shop Supervisor John Goodson. The two used John and Mike's sketches to transform an existing model of the *Excelsior* into the *Enterprise*-B.

▲
MODEL OF THE *ENTERPRISE*-B, CONSTRUCTED AT INDUSTRIAL LIGHT & MAGIC (ILM).

IT'S A BIRD, IT'S A PLANE, IT'S...THE *U.S.S. LAKOTA*? ACTUALLY, THIS IS/WAS THE *ENTERPRISE*-B. THE MODEL WAS REUSED AND RENAMED FOR AN EPISODE OF *DEEP SPACE NINE*.
▼

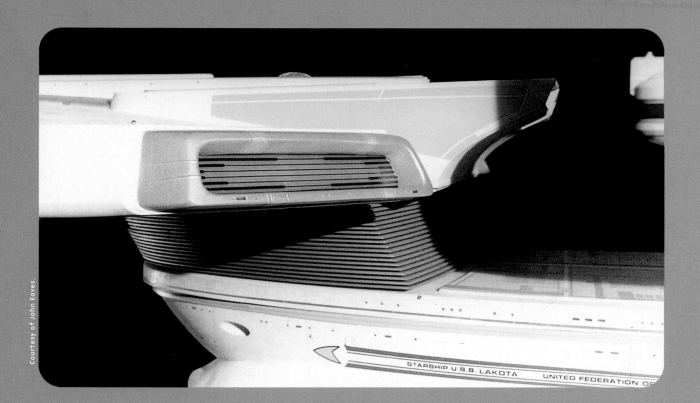

IMPULSE-ENGINE DETAIL ON THE
*LAKOTA/ENTERPRISE-*B MODEL.

MAIN BODY DETAIL. THE FAMOUS REACTOR
ROOM WHERE KIRK MET HIS FATE LIES
ABOVE THE DEFLECTOR DISH "SCOOP."

Once the "healthy" *Enterprise*-B existed, the next job was to show her with damaged and distressed details caused by the energy ribbon. The ribbon was to hit the reactor room on the front of the B, apparently dissolving it and exposing three or four decks to space. John's first drawing shows the damage, and three exposed decks; he included a lot of blackening from the ribbon's blast, extending it well beyond the damaged area.

When ILM got the drawings, they decided to place the damage lower, on the protruded area John and Mike had designed, so that when the force field was activated, the audience could see a crew member standing at the edge of the damage, looking out into space.

JOHN:

ILM's change is an example of the collaboration that's necessary among the illustrator, the model maker, and the FX supervisors. In a two-dimensional drawing, you can't always see what the best angle will be; that's why it's good that the model makers and FX supers have the freedom to change the design and say, "Hey, why don't we try putting the damage here instead of where it was drawn?" When the time comes to compose the shots, alterations are made. Because of the mutual desire to make the best shots possible, there's total collaboration among the art and model shop departments, the FX art director and FX supervisors; we all work together toward the same goal. That's what makes working on feature films so exciting: the ability to get input from a number of extremely talented, creative people on one project, and watch that one project evolve into the best it can possibly be.

AN EARLY SKETCH OF ▶
THE DAMAGE TO THE B.

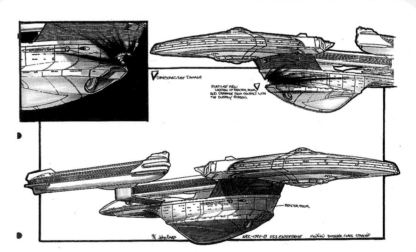

A MORE DETAILED VIEW, SHOWING
THE DAMAGE LOWER ON THE SHIP.
▼

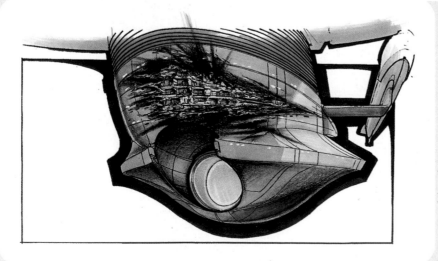

▲ THE B ENGULFED BY THE ENERGY RIBBON;

STORYBOARDS BY MARK MOORE, SHOWING:

▼ THE DAMAGE TO THE SHIP;

▼ THE EXPOSED DECKS, WITH CAPTAIN HARRIMAN, SCOTTY AND CHEKOV PEERING INTO SPACE.

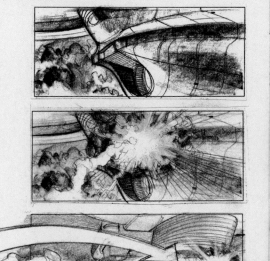

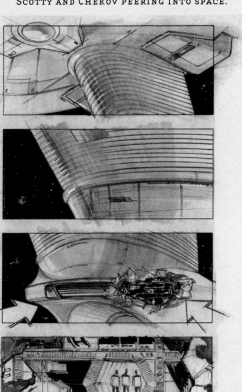

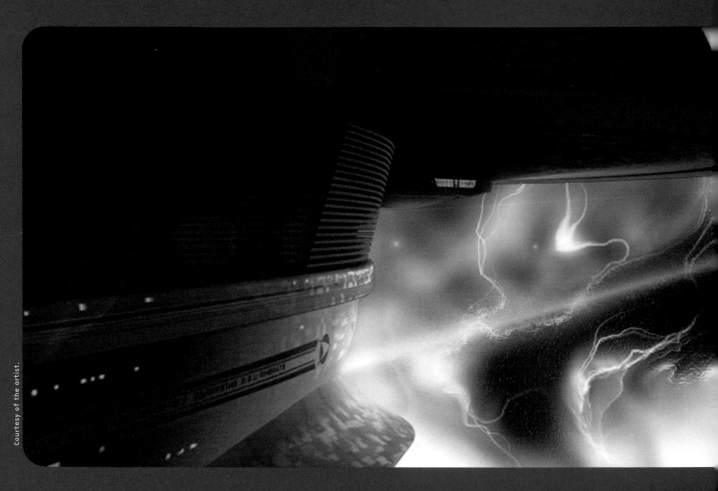

THE CGI COMPOSITE SHOT BY MARK MOORE
AND HOW IT APPEARED IN THE FILM. THE
RIBBON APPROACHES THE *ENTERPRISE*-B.

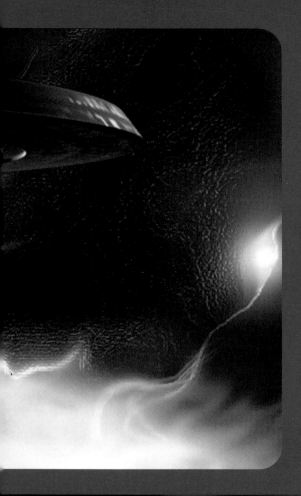

SPACEDOCK

Industrial Light & Magic's art department, under the direction of Bill George, was also hard at work on a number of design projects for *Star Trek Generations*. Illustrator Mark Moore directed his creative talents towards storyboards, and ship and energy ribbon designs. One of his first assignments was the retrofitting of the Spacedock in the film's opening *Enterprise*-B scenes—an assignment that would prove quite a challenge, especially since it required him to utilize the actual Spacedock model from the 1979 movie, *Star Trek: The Motion Picture*.

Mark and Bill trimmed the size of the dock and changed the shape of its worklights; they also added a series of living/working quarters for Starfleet personnel, as well as a docking mount atop the Spacedock that attached to the back of the *Enterprise*-B saucer.

Once the designs were approved, the drawings went to ILM model shop artists Jeff Olson and John Goodson. The original 1979 Spacedock model arrived still packed in its crate—but when Olson and Goodson opened it, they discovered the sad remains of the once-beautiful model lying in a heap, with a fragment of roof detail hanging from the top of the crate. From that maze of debris, they managed to create the handsome dock seen in *Generations*.

Courtesy of the artist.

THE *ENTERPRISE*-B IN SPACEDOCK, BY MARK MOORE, ILM. ▲   ▼ CGI OF THE SAME.

Courtesy of the artist.

The orbital skydiving props. *Early versions of the* **Generations** *script included a scene wherein Kirk landed in an open field after "orbital skydiving." The scene, which originally featured the characters Spock and McCoy (and later, the characters of Scotty and Chekov, when Leonard Nimoy and DeForest Kelley opted not to appear in the film), were cut from the film's final version. Star Trek illustrator Clark Schaffer designed the props for the scene, including:*

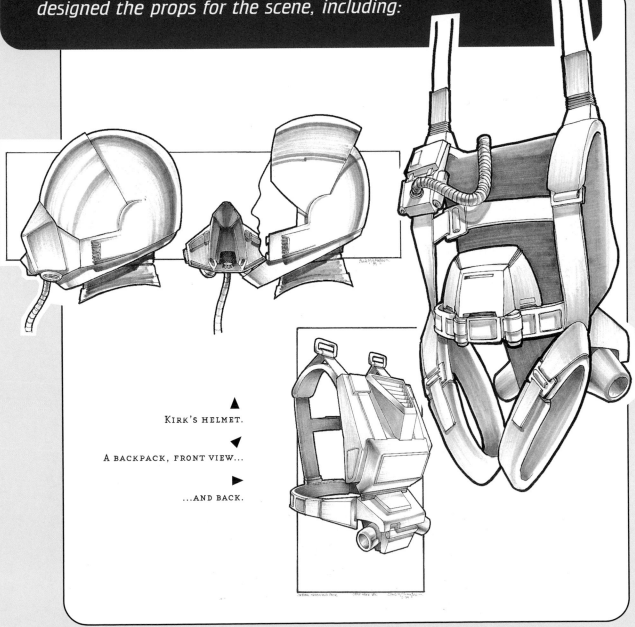

▲
KIRK'S HELMET.

◀
A BACKPACK, FRONT VIEW...

▶
...AND BACK.

the LAKUL

Mark Moore then designed the *Lakul*, the ship trapped by the energy ribbon; its passengers (including Soran and Guinan) are rescued by the *Enterprise*-B. Mark did a series of sketches of the *Lakul*, all of which are admirable; the best of all the designs was chosen for the film.

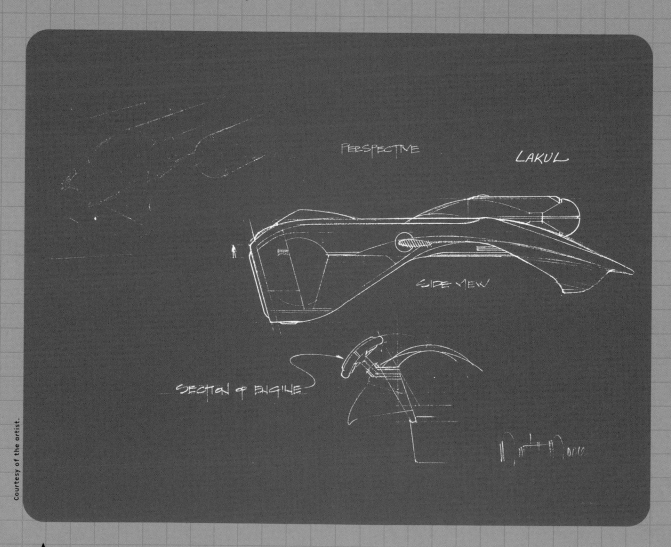

▲
AN EARLY SKETCH OF THE *LAKUL*, BY MARK MOORE.

A FULL-COLOR PAINTING OF THE SAME. ▶

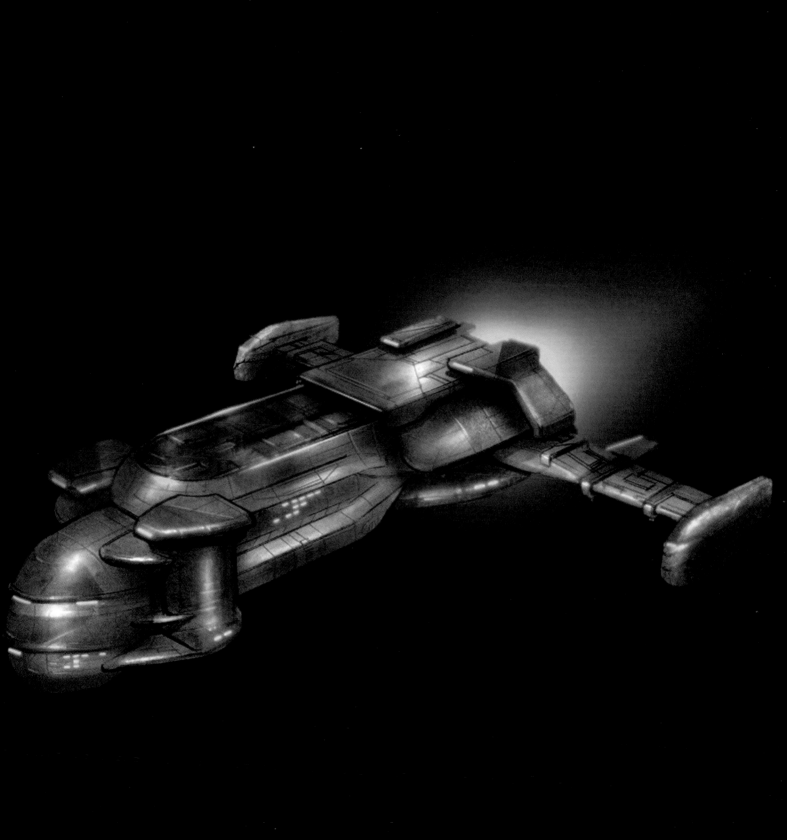

FX STORYBOARDS:

The Energy Ribbon and the Crash of the ENTERPRISE-D

Moore, Bill George, and FX Supervisor John Knoll all did a great deal of work on designs of the fiery energy ribbon and its tenebrous aftermath. Some of the most impressive of Moore's color storyboard renderings show the shock waves of the exploding Amargosa sun hitting the planet where the *Enterprise-D* has crashed. Moore also storyboarded the FX shots for the saucer-crash sequence.

JOHN:

The storyboards for the crash sequence are great examples of illustrated storytelling. Mark's an extremely talented artist and a vital asset to ILM's art department.

John Knoll then had the awesome task of deciding, based on Moore's storyboards, which shots of the ship would be CGI (computer-generated illustrations) and which would be photography of miniature models—*and* how the final composition would be rendered. (Computer fans, take note: Much of the CGI software Knoll uses is designed by Jay Roth of Electric Image.)

▲

MOORE'S STORYBOARDS, SHOWING THE *ENTERPRISE*-D SEPARATING FROM ITS SAUCER.

▲ THE VERIDIAN SUN EXPLODING NEARBY.

A CGI SHOT OF THE SAME. ▼

THE SAUCER CONTINUES ITS DESCENT. ▲ ▶

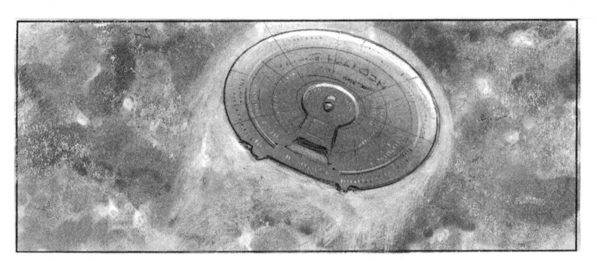

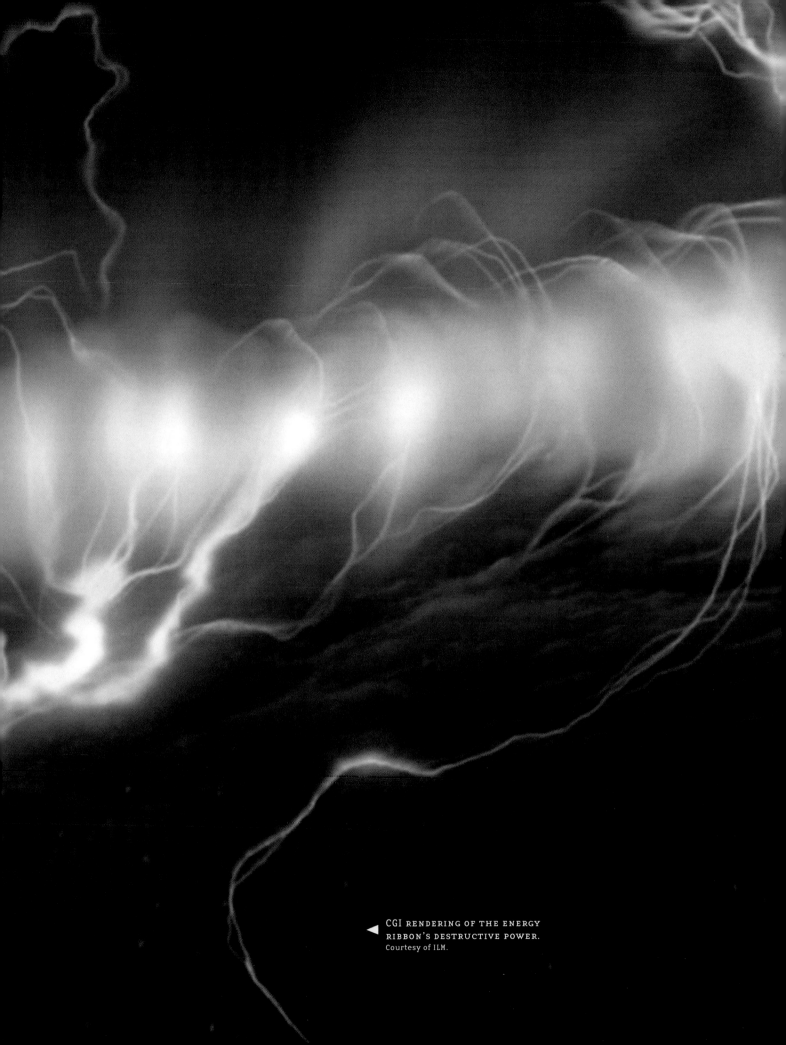

◄ CGI RENDERING OF THE ENERGY
RIBBON'S DESTRUCTIVE POWER.
Courtesy of ILM.

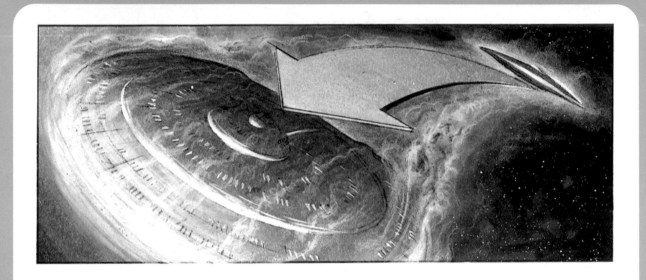

▲
ENTERING VERIDIAN III'S ATMOSPHERE...

Sean Casey. Courtesy of ILM.

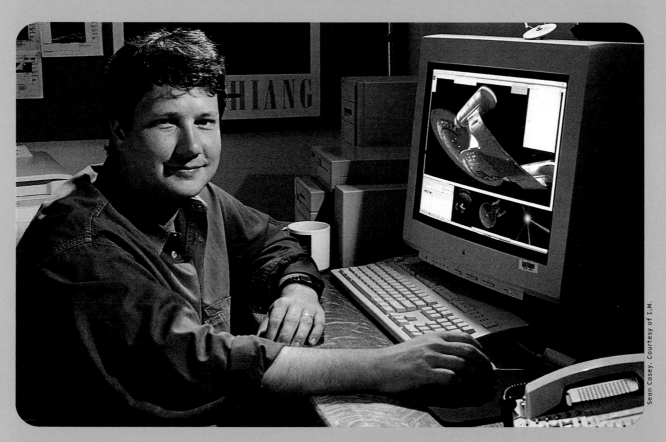

Sean Casey. Courtesy of I.M.

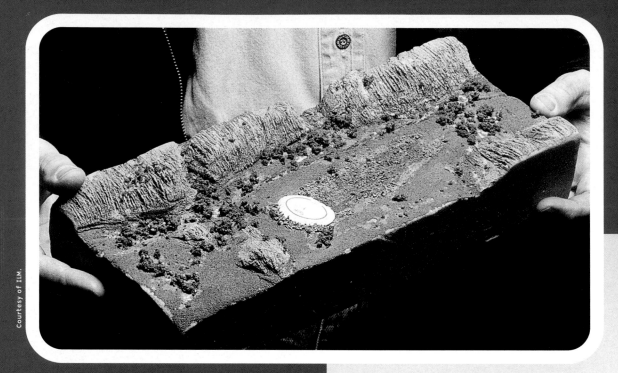

▲ GOODSON'S MINIATURE MODEL FOR THE CRASH SEQUENCE, WHICH SERVED AS PROTOTYPE FOR THE 40' X 80' SET WITH A 12' SAUCER.

THE 12' *ENTERPRISE-D* MODEL, HURTLING DOWNWARD VIA CABLES. ▶

ILM's CGI shot of the saucer
crashing on Veridian III. ▶

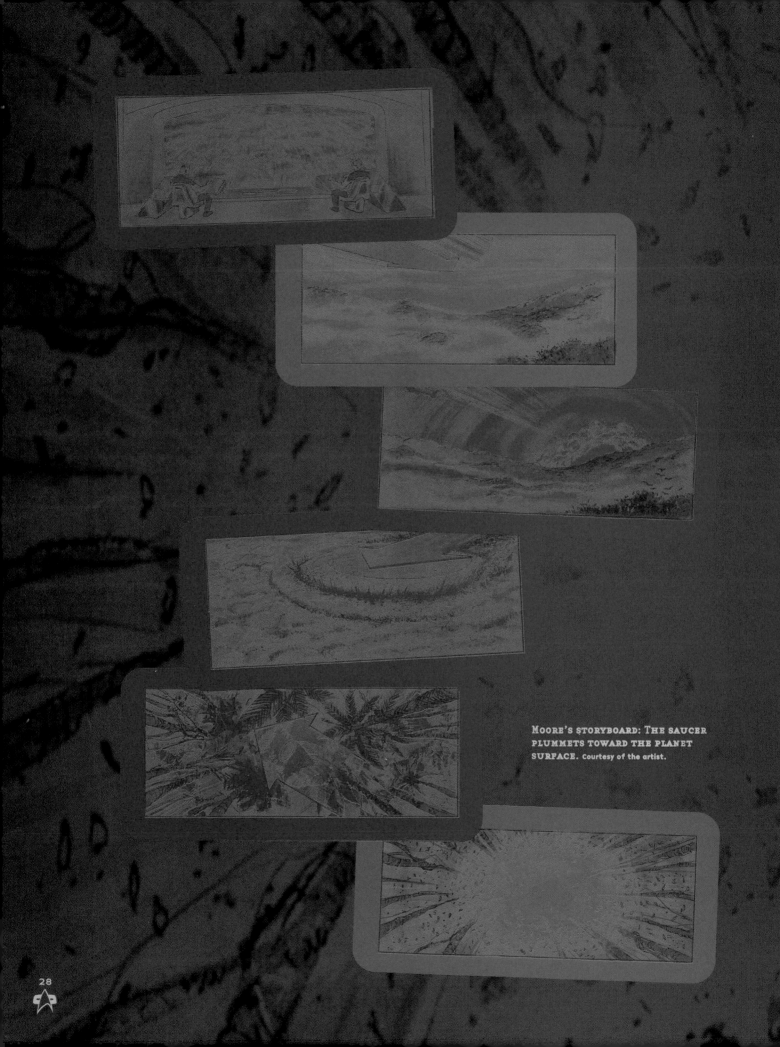

MOORE'S STORYBOARD: THE SAUCER
PLUMMETS TOWARD THE PLANET
SURFACE. Courtesy of the artist.

Sean Casey. Courtesy of ILM.

◀ ...AND ON FILM.

▲
MARK MOORE'S CGI DESIGNS
OF A PLACID VERIDIAN III...

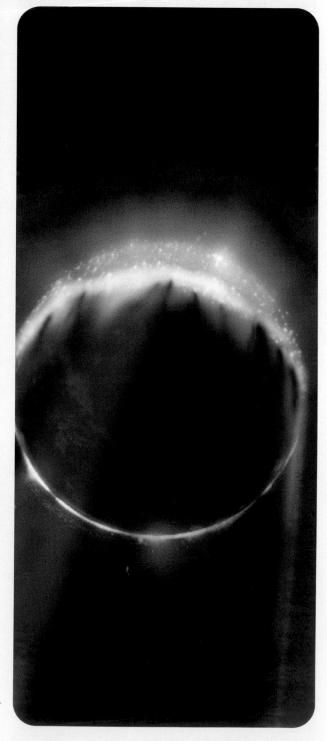

...ITS ENCOUNTER WITH ▶
SORAN'S PROBE...

▲
◀ ...AND ITS FIERY DOOM.

GENERATIONS

The next item on John Eaves's "to-do" list was a new communicator pin for the crew. The previous design had been based on the familiar Starfleet chevron with an oval behind it—but once again, the producers wanted to give the movie audience something new.

JOHN:

Okay, I confess: When I began designing the new communicator, I'd never seen an episode of *Star Trek: The Next Generation* before. Call me old-fashioned, but I was a loyal fan of the original show and figured I already knew enough about *Star Trek* to design some cool, futuristic communicators. So as my jumping-off point, I used the old flip-up communicators, and drew a bunch of sketches, which I delivered to Herman.

He was in his office talking to some other people at the time I handed him the sketches, but the minute he glanced at them, he looked up at me with a startled expression and demanded, "What in the world is *this*?"

Taken aback, I faltered, "These are your new communicators...."

"No, no, NO," Herman countered, just as the other people started laughing hysterically. "John...things have changed since you last watched *Star Trek*." And it was graciously pointed out that I might want to familiarize myself with *TNG*'s communicators before I did any more sketches. Ashamed, I slunk back to my desk and set back to work.

Welcome to the twenty-fourth century.

Fortunately, John soon came up to speed and delivered eight or nine different versions of the pendant; Rick Berman liked two of them. So it was back to the drawing board, quite literally, and after another six or seven sketches, Berman chose the pendant seen in the film (and also on *Star Trek: Deep Space Nine* and *Star Trek: Voyager*). At the same time, Eaves also designed a Klingon communicator badge—one with a "jaggedy, hard-edged, multilayered background" behind the Klingon logo. That, too, required a few passes before the final version won approval.

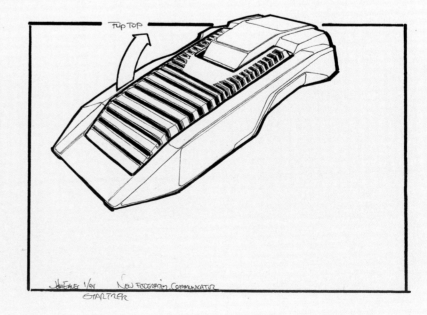

BACK TO THE FUTURE:
EAVES'S "OLD-FASHIONED"
ST:TNG FLIP-TOP COMMUNICATOR. ▶

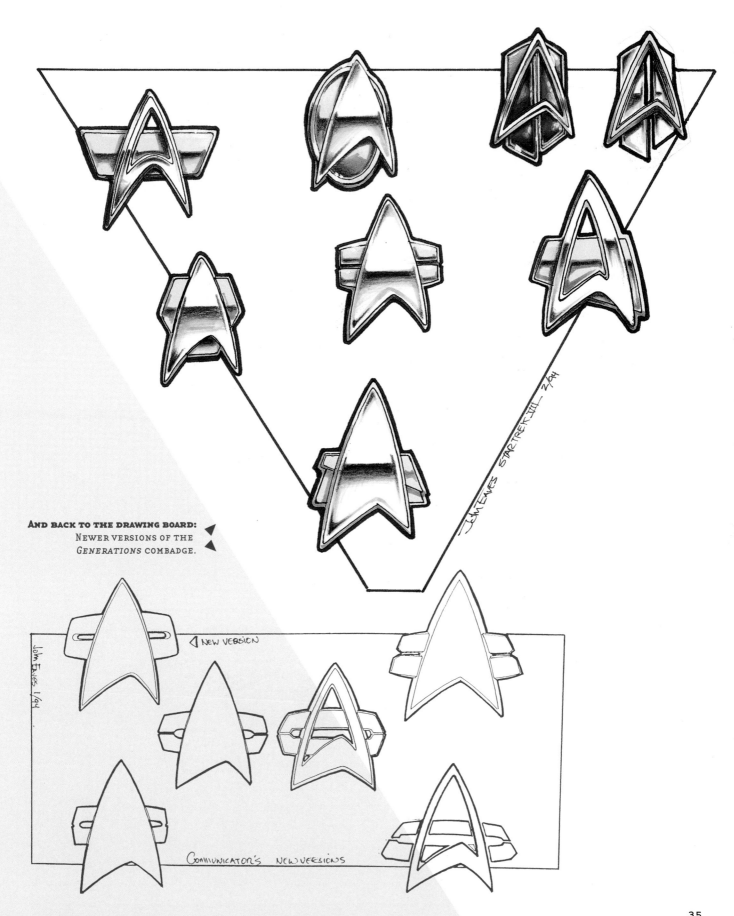

AND BACK TO THE DRAWING BOARD: NEWER VERSIONS OF THE *GENERATIONS* COMBADGE.

J.M EAVES STAR TREK VII - 2/94

JOHN EAVES 1/94.

NEW VERSION

COMMUNICATOR'S NEW VERSIONS

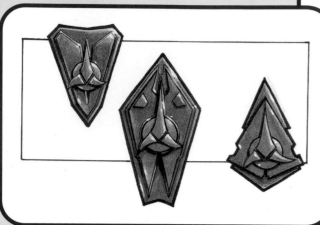

Klingon combadge possibilities. ▲

The final version. ▶

More Klingonalia, from
illustrator Clark Schaffer.
▼

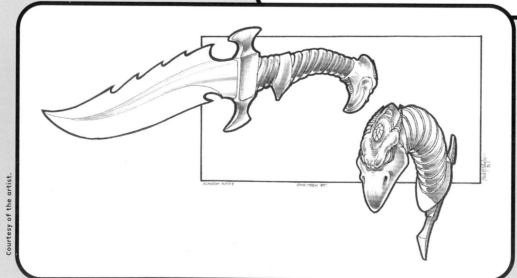

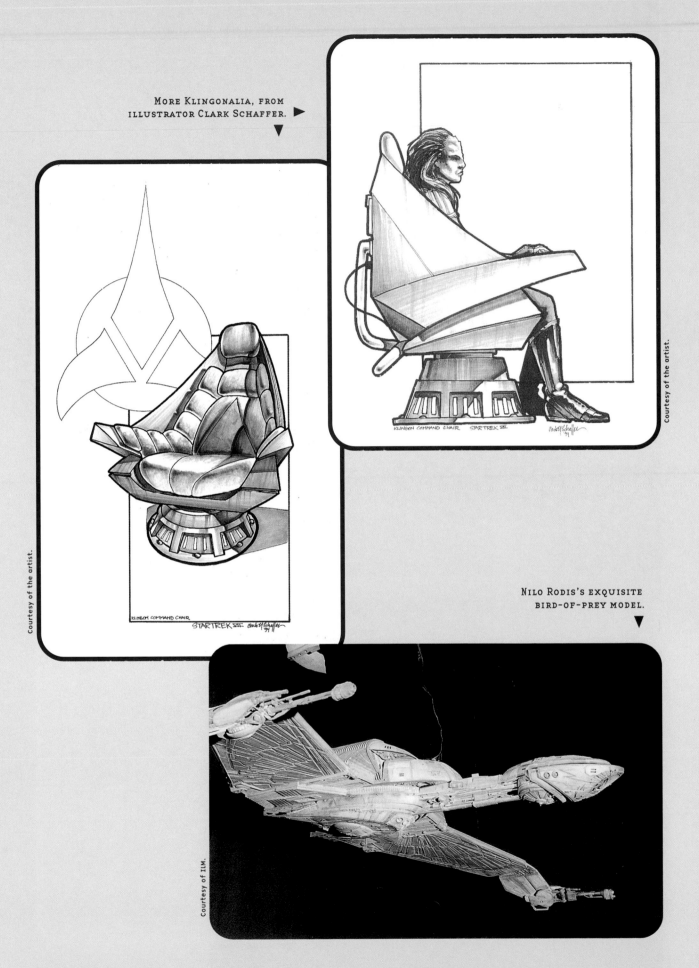

MORE KLINGONALIA, FROM
ILLUSTRATOR CLARK SCHAFFER. ►
▼

Courtesy of the artist.

Courtesy of the artist.

NILO RODIS'S EXQUISITE
BIRD-OF-PREY MODEL.
▼

Courtesy of ILM.

The U.S.S. Enterprise NCC-1701-D bridge

Why mess with the tried and true? For one thing, Production Designer Herman Zimmerman wanted to retrofit the *TNG* television series bridge in order to bring it up to the more luxurious standards befitting a feature film; for another, the film's producers were still always thinking of their audience, constantly improving existing designs and offering up new surprises. Zimmerman and Art Director Sandy Veneziano darkened the set's colors and added more tones to its palette; in addition, they chose richer textures.

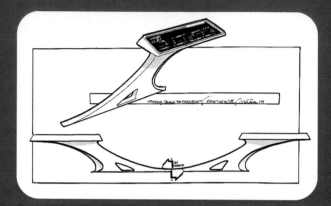

▲
THE STANDING CONSOLE.

ONE VERSION OF THE *ENTERPRISE-*D BRIDGE:
WITH STAND-UP STATIONS...
▼

JOHN:

Herman also wanted to make the bridge more functional. To accomplish that, we raised the captain's chair slightly (symbolically putting his authority higher than those sitting in the two chairs flanking him).

For functionality, we also split the ramps on either side of the command center. We still had a ramp going down, but added two elevated stations, one against either wall, where crew members could work. We also replaced an alcove filled with lockers and storage panels with a new graphics station (courtesy of Mike Okuda).

At one point, we had added some new standup stations behind the captain's chair, where Worf works. It was a nice design, but it wound up being simply *too* much of a modification, so we dropped it.

STAR TREK VII   JOHN EAVES 1/94   NEW BRIDGE - ENTERPRISE "D"

▲

...AND WITHOUT.

CONSOLE GRAPHICS BY STAR TREK
ARTIST ALAN KOBAYASHI.

▼

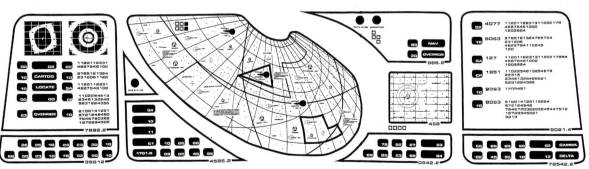

U.S.S. Enterprise (NCC-1701-B) - Navigation Console Artwork

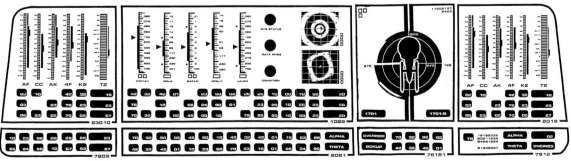

U.S.S. Enterprise (NCC-1701-B) - Helm Console Artwork

Star Trek: Generations

By Alan Kobayashi: Assistant Scenic Artist (4/94)

Hands down, the most ambitious set for *Generations* was that of Stellar Cartography, a room where members of the intrepid *Enterprise*-D crew could go and consult star maps—in a three-dimensional way, by "immersing" oneself in space.

JOHN:

Herman and I were very excited about designing this room. We had both recently visited the Laserium at Griffith Park, a laser show where you sit in chairs and look up at a beautiful domed ceiling on which different star scenes are projected. If you let yourself go, you'd swear you were floating in space, encompassed by these stars.

That's the feeling we hoped to recreate in Stellar Cartography.

Originally, the idea was to do the room spherically, but construction would have been too difficult and costly, as would the special effects. So a simpler,

more cost-effective solution was found: The room became a cylinder, a three-story structure with a platform suspended in the center. At first, the room was segmented into four pieces, with structural beams extending floor to ceiling, and the map appearing in between. But as time went on, it became clear that four beams obstructed too much of the map; the final version of the set had three beams, giving a tripod effect, and allowing for more of the starmap to be displayed. Rick Sternbach contributed a painting of the stars displayed on the major map; the painting was blown up, hung on the set, and backlit.

JOHN:

At one point, we'd come up with the notion of a "floating frame" that would roll around the room to any particular area of space you wanted to view. Inside that frame would be the visual effects, including any necessary mathematical readings. You could zoom in on planets and plot trajectory headings, for example.

But after thinking it over for a while, we decided that the above was too outdated a technology for the twenty-fourth century... therefore, we redesigned the room so that the whole wall would be your visual effect. You'd pick a star, and the whole room would zoom to that area of space, and all the information would appear on the wall. You could pull back, move forward, zoom in—do whatever you wanted,

unrestricted by this frame that moved around.

Clark Schaffer [another illustrator who worked in the art department] **had just started on the film at this time, and he helped out with the immense load of drawings that had to be done. He took a rough console design I did for the cartography platform, and did a breakdown of the way the console should be put together. Again, I have to say that one of the exceptionally nice things about working on the *Star Trek* films is that everyone is so involved and helpful with design ideas. Mike and Herman contributed a number of wonderful ideas of how this room should look, and I have to say that the final set was an impressive thing to see (not only in the finished film, but in real life).**

EAVES'S FOUR-BEAM VERSION OF THE STELLAR CARTOGRAPHY SET... ▶

REVERSE VIEW OF STELLAR CARTOGRAPHY
STELLAR CARTOGRAPHY N.T. JON EAVES 12/93
STARTREK 7

▲ ANOTHER PERSPECTIVE.

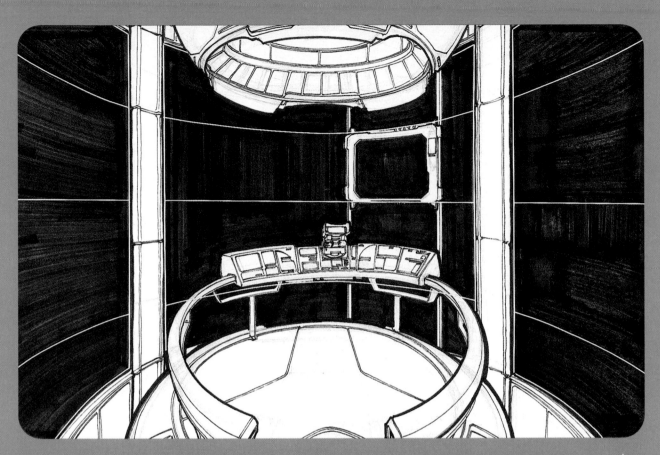

THE VIEW FROM THE STELLAR ▲
Cartography platform.

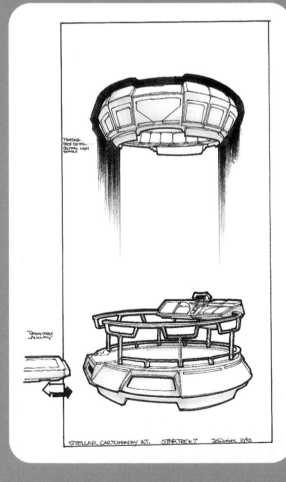

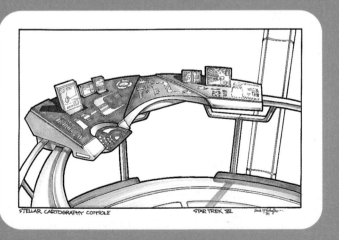

STELLAR CARTOGRAPHY CONSOLE   STAR TREK VII

▲

STELLAR CARTOGRAPHY CONSOLE
DESIGN BY CLARK SCHAFFER.

The Amargosa Observatory

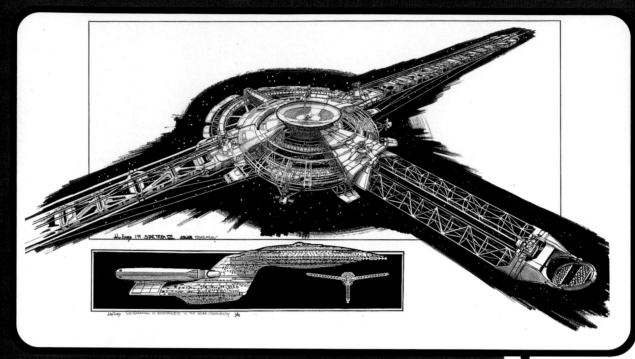

THE AMARGOSA OBSERVATORY, SKETCHES BY JOHN EAVES. ▲ ▶

TOP AND SIDE VIEW OF SOLAR OBSERVATORY

*T*his, of course, was the observatory from which the evil Doctor Soran (played with delicious malevolence by Malcolm McDowell) planned to blow up the Amargosa star, killing innocent billions. Operated by the Federation, the station functioned as a giant telescope in space.

For inspiration as to the observatory's exterior design, John turned to his memories of NASA satellites including *Voyager* (the original, folks, not the *Star Trek* version).

JOHN:

I designed a living area with a giant observation array in the center; from that, two massive, complicated framework structures feed out on either side of the station. A telescopic optical sensor extends outward from the center, and feeds back information to the communications area on the station.

In profile, the station is very thin; there's not much to see except for an intricate cable system, which keeps the framework appendages structurally sound and parallel to the station itself. The back area—the living area that contains Soran's probe room—has several windows facing out into space. So not only can you observe space from the windows, you can also observe the station and all its functions from this control area.

Eaves also provided the observatory with a few phaser cannons—making sure they were no match for the Romulan attack that was to destroy the station in the film. In addition, he kept in mind the fact that the structure would need a method for keeping its position stable in space.

JOHN:

You can see in the drawing these little ball-type thrusters extended out from the station, with some exhaust port shielding, so you can maneuver your station or stabilize its position. There's a major engine port on the bottom of the station, but it's not designed to fly on its own; it's pretty much hauled or towed to where it needs to be. The thrusters can change the observatory's position, but they're more like a trolling motor on a boat—they won't take you very far.

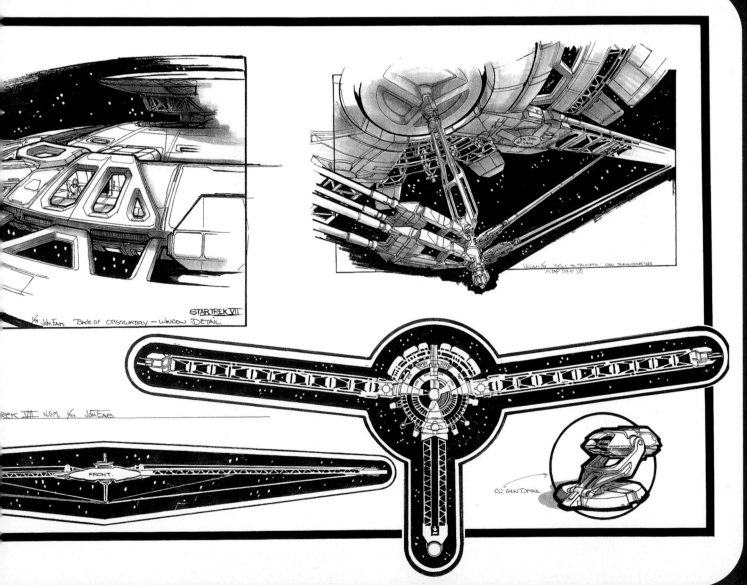

Once the drawings of Amargosa had been approved, they were sent on to model makers Jeff Olson and John Goodson at Industrial Light & Magic. At the time, Goodson was so overwhelmed by the amount of work generated by the film that he wound up creating a lot of the models in his own garage.

JOHN:

One of the sad parts of making beautiful models, as John [Goodson] **does, is having to watch them get blown up and destroyed. Not only did he have to build a station damaged by an attack, he also had to destroy it at the end of the film. It's a heartbreaking experience to spend that much time and care on a model, only to see it obliterated on the screen. One can feel proud when the destruction looks good on screen— but it's saddening as well.**

Once the ill-fated observatory's exterior was taken care of, the task of designing its interior remained. The first major set— the one seen when *Enterprise* crew members first beam aboard the station—was actually a revamp of the *Enterprise*-B bridge set, severely battle-damaged to disguise its previous incarnation. When Geordi and Data return, they find the outline of a door in the bulkhead; when they later find a way into the room, they discover Soran's trilithium probe (designed by Clark Schaffer). Eaves and Herman Zimmerman worked backwards from the Amargosa's exterior, this time imagining what they might see if they peered inside the station's windows.

JOHN:

Herman came up with the idea of a structure that was suspended from the center of the room, making it the station's ops center. The room itself is a semicircle, with frames radiating out from its center up across the ceiling, to form a much larger framework that goes from ceiling to floor. Here we created a giant torpedo launcher and an array of Mach V torpedoes, with operations centers on either wall, and a giant torpedo lift on the roof that picks up the torpedoes and drops them in the launcher.

The racks, torpedoes, and probes were designed by Eaves and Zimmerman. The "probe room's" control panel, designed by Clark Schaffer, was one of many items that served double duty in the film; it had been purloined from the *Enterprise*-B's sickbay.

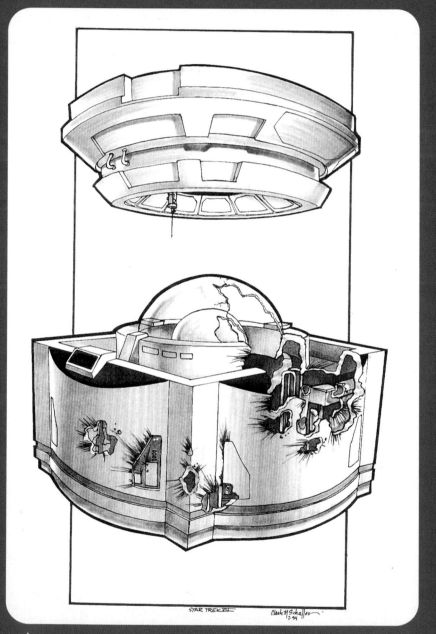

DAMAGED CONSOLE FROM THE OBSERVATORY'S INTERIOR, BY CLARK SCHAFFER.

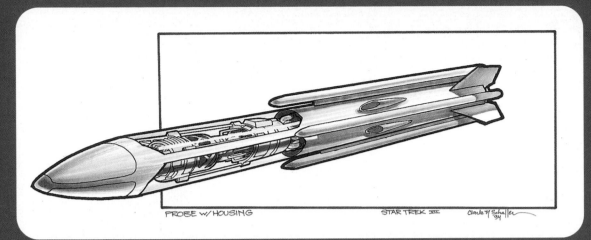

▲ PROBE WITH HOUSING...

PROBE w/ HOUSING   STAR TREK XII   Clark H Schaffer '94

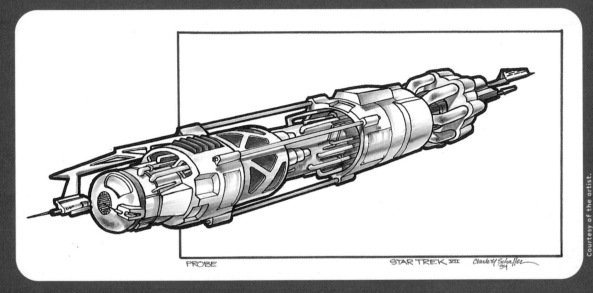

PROBE   STAR TREK XII   Clark H Schaffer '94

▲ ...AND WITHOUT. SKETCHES BY CLARK SCHAFFER.

RACKS OF PROP PROBES.
▼

Enterprise-B Sets

One of the sets most meaningful to fans was, of course, the *Enterprise*-B's deflector room—the place where James T. Kirk heroically met his fate in the form of the atom-scattering energy ribbon.

Typically, most sets begin as grand, no-holds-barred, cost-be-damned concepts—then are gradually scaled back to what the budget actually allows. This was indeed the case for the famous deflector room. Its first incarnation was as a vast, two-story room accessible via a hallway. One entered out onto a balcony that overlooked a chamber filled with components and wall relays, and a giant section of deflector dish emerging from the deck.

JOHN:

Herman and I wanted a set that would create a lot of movement and action for Kirk as he altered the deflector dish. So off the balcony, we had a service elevator parked on the bottom floor—but it had two running guides from ceiling to floor that the elevator tracked on. We were going to use those for Kirk to firepull himself down to the lower level. From there, he'd move to the forward hatch, at the base of the deflector components sticking through the floor. Then he'd open up a hatchway that uncovers a relay box; he'd jump in there and alter all the chips to trigger the antimatter discharge.

Unfortunately, the set would have required cutting through the stage floor to put in the lower room (the alternative was to put the rest of the set up on a platform, which would also have been prohibitively expensive). Eventually, the proposed set became so large and expensive that its design was radically overhauled.

The new room also had two stories, but consisted of a quarter-circle, accessible from a corridor and step-down ladder; the walls were filled with piping and circuitry.

A VERY EARLY SKETCH OF THE
DEFLECTOR ROOM SET, BY JOHN EAVES

▼

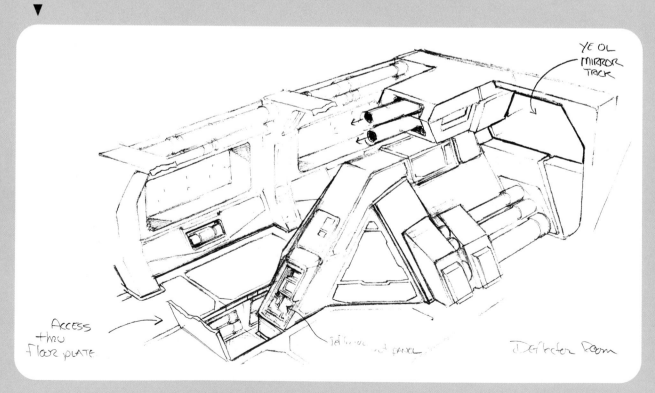

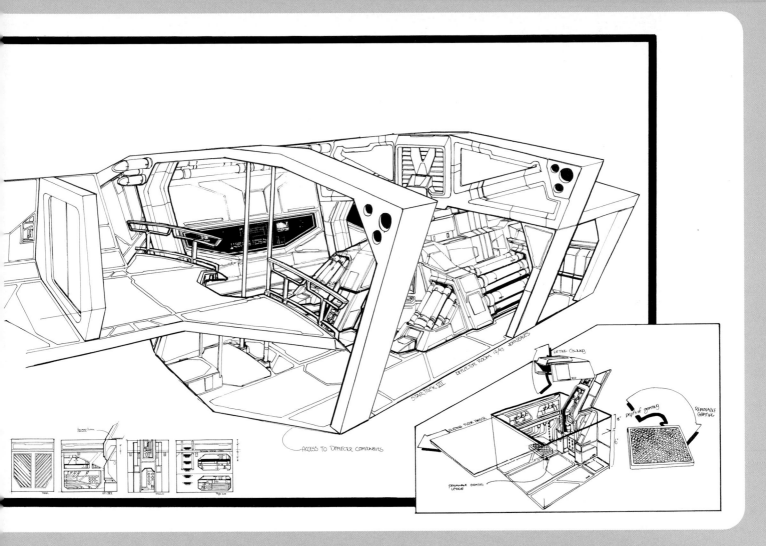

ACCESS TO DEFLECTOR COMPONENTS

THE GRAND AND GLORIOUS VERSION OF THE SET. ▲

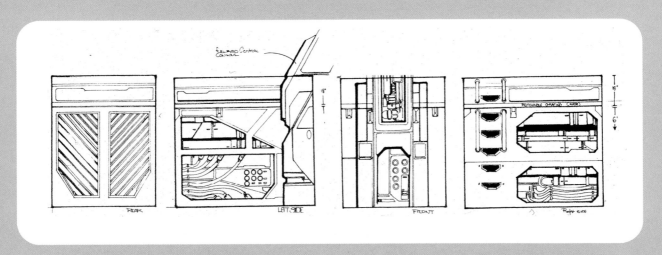

DETAILS BY EAVES. ▲

THE FINAL, MORE BUDGET-CONSCIOUS VERSION OF THE DEFLECTOR ROOM.

JOHN:

So Captain Kirk went down these stairways to a platform in the floor, which was graded so that you could see another level below that. So he'd proceed down even lower. Clark designed a giant relay wall accessed from a control panel; a huge, open-faced display of circuits and components came out. This allowed us to view Kirk and the display from either side, and allowed some really dynamic camera angles of Kirk altering the components. After the energy ribbon wipes out this part of the ship, we re-establish the massively damaged area when Captain Harriman, Scotty, and Chekov stand on the upper balcony, with only the ship's force field protecting them from the cold vacuum of space.

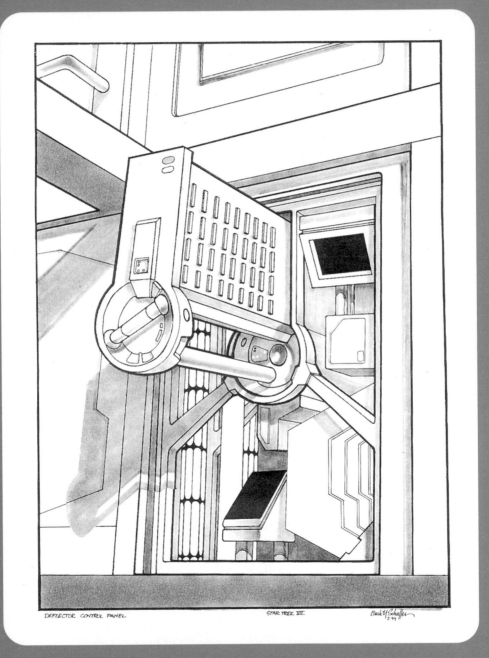

DEFLECTOR CONTROL PANEL   STAR TREK VII

▲

DEFLECTOR CONTROL PANEL, BY CLARK SCHAFFER.

▲

Revamping or redressing was not just done on the *Enterprise*-B. This is Clark Schaffer's design for Guinan's quarters, which was a redress of the quarters on the *Enterprise*-D.

▼

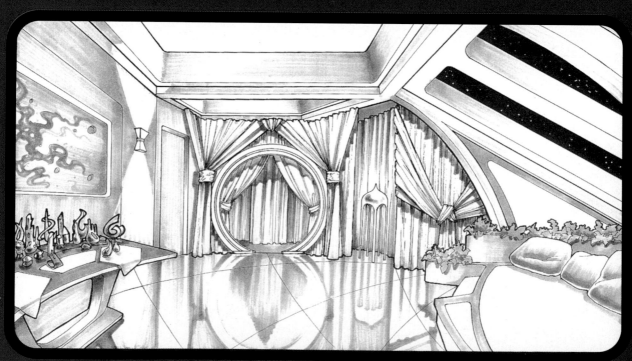

Other *Enterprise*-B sets wound up serving more than one function. For example, at the beginning of *Star Trek Generations*, one sees an observation window similar to that seen in the floating Spacedock from *Star Trek III* and *IV*. The *Generations* Spacedock, however, is an open-faced structure more closely resembling that seen in *Star Trek: The Motion Picture* (of course).

JOHN:

Mark Moore and Bill George from ILM came up with some drawings for the exteriors of living and working structures on the Spacedock framework. For the interior, we designed a lounge from which you can observe the *Enterprise*-B being christened in the opening sequence.

Courtesy of ILM.

▲
THE *ENTERPRISE*-B FROM THE
SPACEDOCK OBSERVATION LOUNGE.

A FAMILIAR LABEL WITH ▲
A VERY UNUSUAL DATE.

A GHOSTLY-LOOKING CGI
CHAMPAGNE BOTTLE. ▶

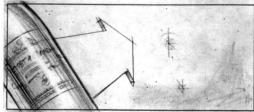

STORYBOARDS BY ILM'S MARK MOORE, EXPERIMENTING WITH DIFFERENT ANGLES FOR THE CHAMPAGNE BOTTLE'S "LAUNCH."

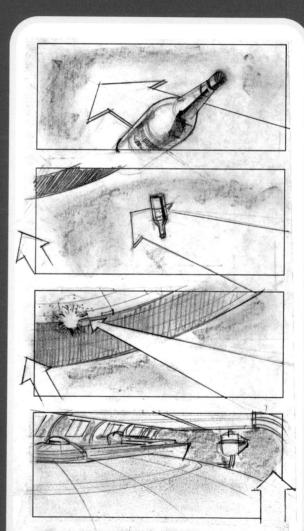

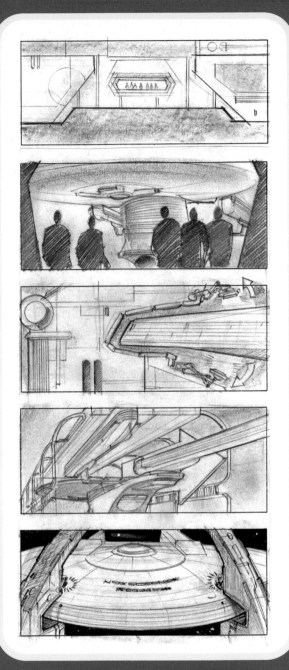

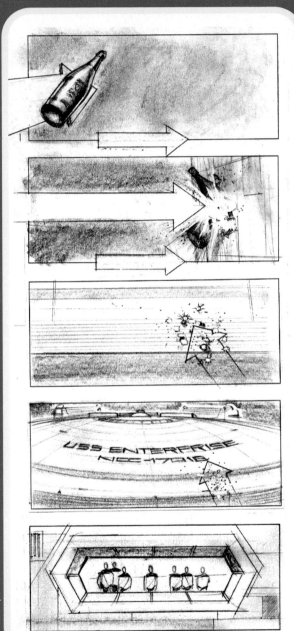

THE *ENTERPRISE*-B IN SPACEDOCK.

2 SEC FADE IN TO STARS

2 SEC AFTER THE PARAMOUNT MOUNTAIN
FULL OR LOGO FADES OUT ... A STARFIELD

CARD 1 FADES IN ... SOMETHING IS MOVING,
3.5 SEC.
(INCLUDES A TINY, FAINT, SHIMMERING OBJECT
FADE IN
& OUT)

CARD 1

2 SEC. CADENCE BETWEEN CARDS ...

THE OBJECT CONTINUES
ITS APPROACH ...

CARD 2

114 SEC.

CARD 3

CARD 4
↓
CARD 20

THE OBJECT
CONTINUES MOVING
FORWARD AND RIGHT,
BUT IT IS IMPOSSIBLE
TO DETERMINE EXACTLY WHAT IT IS ...
IT EXITS FRAME. RIGHT

CUT TO

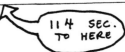

114 SEC.
TO HERE

①

10.

A RING LIKE SHAPE ENTERS

FRAME... IT TAKES ON THE

SCALE OF SOMETHING LARGER...

THE SHOT CONTINUES...

11.

10 SEC. CUT

THE SHOT CONTINUES...

Reclorision by
XLKZNX BLFSKNX

12.

CARD 21

124 SEC.
TO HERE

9.

WHATEVER IT IS STILL APPROACHES

CARD 14
↓
CARD 20

EASE INTO
SLIGHT PAN
AS SHIMMERING
THING EXITS
FRAME RIGHT

WE BEGIN TO DETECT IT MAY BE
A BOTTLE

CUT TO

10.

A RING LIKE SHAPE ENTERS

FRAME... IT TAKES ON THE

SCALE OF SOMETHING LARGER...

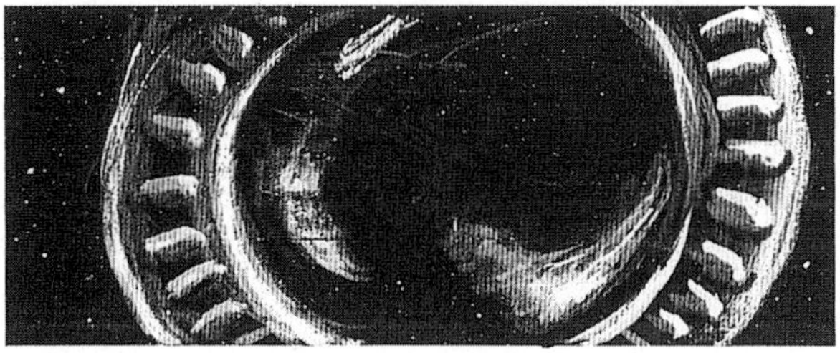

11.

THE SHOT CONTINUES...

THE SHOT CONTINUES...

CARD 21

12.

CUT TO

13.

A GLOSSY GREEN CYLINDER
SWOOPS UP INTO FRAME

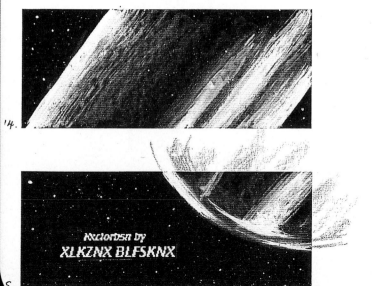

14.

Pictorized by
XLKZNX BLFSKNX

5.

CARD 22

16.

THE BOTTLE TUMBLES FORWARD
REVEALING THE DOM PÉRIGNON
LABEL AND THE DATE "2265"

CARD 23

CARD 24

17.

18.

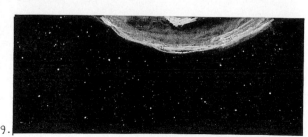

19.

ANOTHER CARD
AT TAIL?
COULD HIDE TRANSITION
TO NEXT CUT

.0.

THE FOIL WRAPPED TOP TUMBLES
UP AND AWAY FROM US

21.

Rxclorbsn by
XLKZNX BLFSKNX

CARD 25

CUT TO

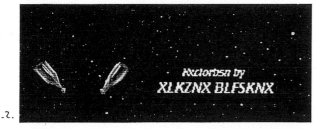

.2.

Rxclorbsn by
XLKZNX BLFSKNX

CARD 26

23.

Rxclorbsn by
XLKZNX BLFSKNX

CARD 27

CUT TO SHOT OF BOTTLE STRIKING SHIP

JOHN:

Once the scenes using the observation lounge had been shot, the windows were filled in by a wall—and voila! The lounge was suddenly converted into the *Enterprise*-B's sickbay.

Eaves designed a surgical center in one corner, where major operations would take place; this small corner set, dressed in different colors, was also seen as an ops console on Amargosa.

JOHN:

When I first started designing sickbay, I came up with a bed that had a big readout over the top of it, with all sorts of medical sensors on it, for the more severely injured patients. But design-wise, it looked too technical, so we took the big sensors down and put up smaller wall relays more reminiscent of what had been used before.

We also came up with a unique framework, separating each medical bed by using wall beams. As it happened, though, sickbay was so crowded in that scene that the audience really couldn't see it, but had to guess where they were from the actors' dialogue.

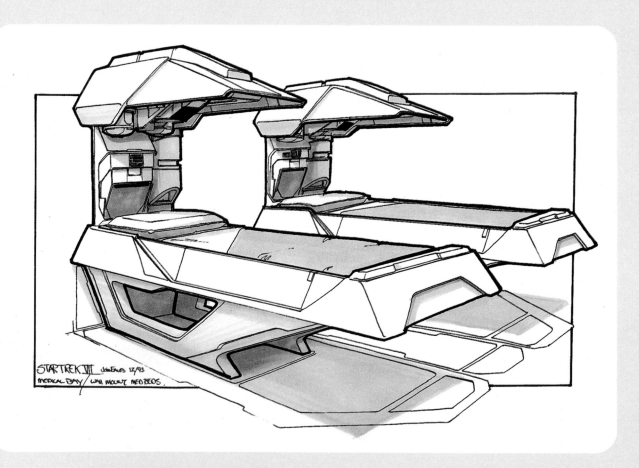

EAVES'S "TOO-TECHNICAL" SICKBAY BEDS.

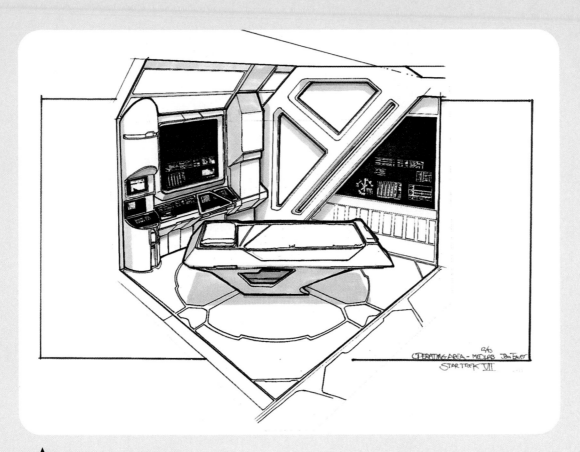

▲
THE SURGICAL AREA.

THE *ENTERPRISE*-B SICKBAY, SHOWING WALL-BEAM DIVIDERS.
▼

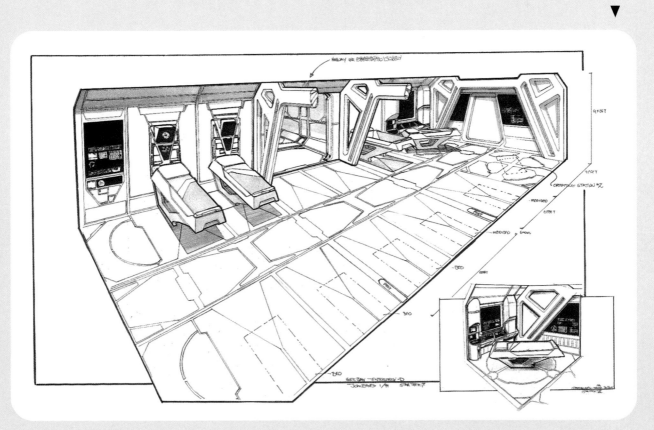

Soran's Gun

One of the more interesting aspects of working on a film set is that, often, two or more artists are given the same assignment—not to create a sense of competition, but instead to generate more interesting ideas and viewpoints, the best of which can go into creation of the finished prop or set. That's one reason why movies, more than any other form of art, truly represent the collaboration of many talented individuals.

JOHN:

One fun thing about this part of the project [i.e., prop design] was that Herman would give Clark [Schaffer] and me the exact same assignments. Since we didn't work in the same room, he figured he'd get a lot more variations this way.

When I first started to design Soran's gun, I wanted it to be completely different in feel from what we consider a "normal gun." I started with the way the weapon was held. A normal gun is held so that the barrel rests on your forefinger, and you're pointing in somewhat vertical fashion when you fire. So I went for a horizontal-type grip; you hold it crosswise in front of you, and the barrel rests on the top of your hand.

Clark's design was similar, but he was pulled off the gun assignment in order to work on other high-priority drawings.

Herman Zimmerman liked the designs, but felt they were too awkward, with the big barrel on top. He suggested Eaves keep the same shape, but rework the firing system. John redesigned the gun so that the barrel rotated ninety degrees when fired. The result added a nice effect when Soran's gun was "fired" in the film.

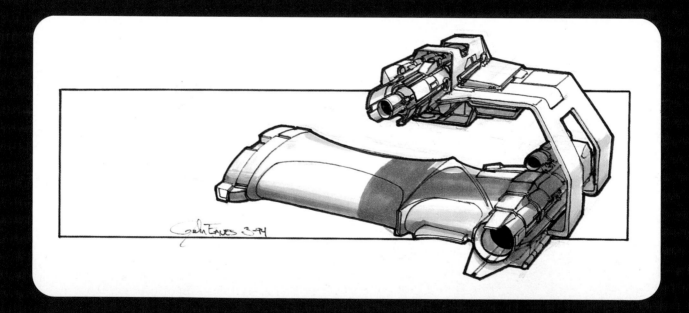

▲

AN EARLY VERSION OF SORAN'S GUN.

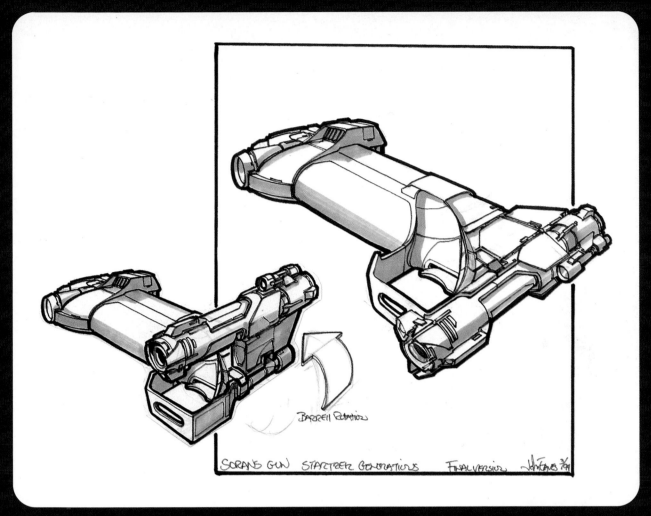

SORAN'S GUN   STARTREK GENERATIONS   FINAL VERSION   John Eaves 3/94

▲
THE FINAL DESIGN.

AND THE FINISHED PROP.
▼

Romulan Tricorders

JOHN:

For the film, we needed some Romulan tricorders. I came up with one that was rather far-fetched in its design. It had an open-faced handle on one side and a series of strangely configured buttons in its center. Herman liked the idea, but he felt a more conventional tricorder would be better, so as not to confuse the audience. We came up with a remake of the Federation tricorder, with a top that flips up; all the graphics inside are, of course, Romulan.

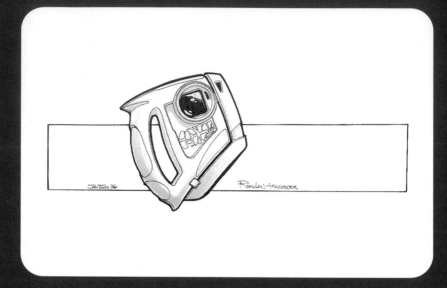

THE "OVERLY ROMULAN" TRICORDER... ▲

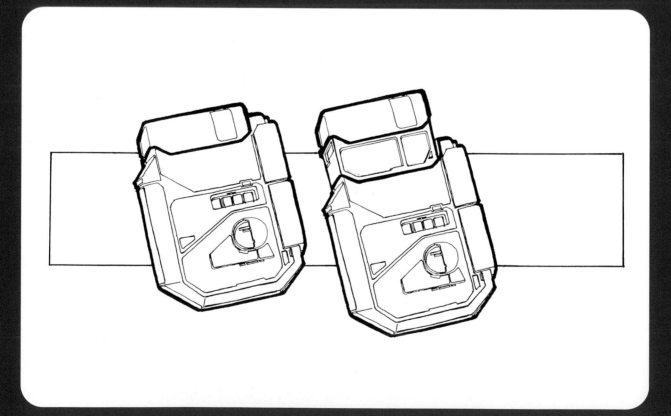

"FEDERATIONIZED" FOR YOUR PROTECTION. ▲

Camera

News

This is another example of two artists—Clark and John—working on the same assignment: Design a twenty-third century news camera for news reporters covering the maiden launch of the *Enterprise*-B.

JOHN:

I came up with a "biker helmet" version with a flip-down lens and a spotlight off to the side; the hands were kept free for better maneuvering. Clark came up with a similar version, but it was more compact and less cumbersome, and it featured a big, bright spotlight. It was a great drawing and was chosen for the film.

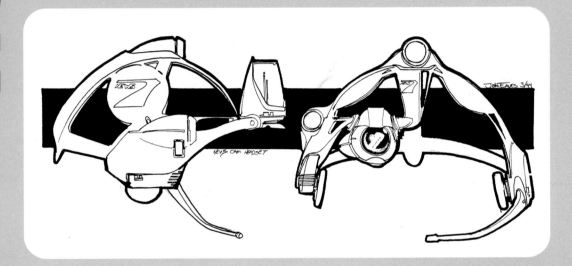

▲
EAVES'S NEWS CAMERA...

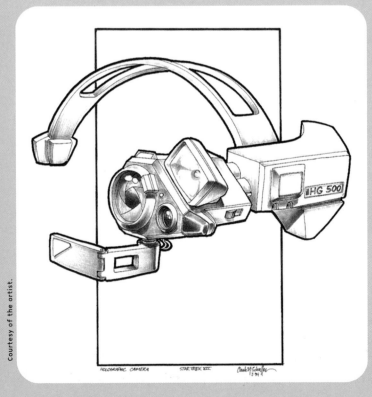

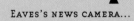

Courtesy of the artist.

◀ ...AND SCHAFFER'S VERSION.

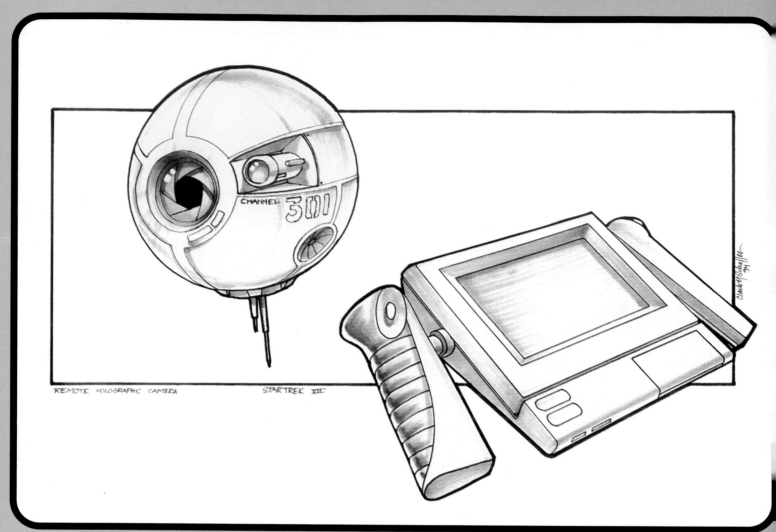

REMOTE HOLOGRAPHIC CAMERA   STARTREK VII

▲

SCHAFFER'S REMOTE CAMERA.

Sailing Ship Navigational Table

E arly in the movie, on a holograph of an eighteenth-century sailing ship, *The Next Generation* crew cheerfully prods Worf to walk the plank, while Riker and Picard stand nearby. It was decided that, in order to separate them from the rest of the crew, Riker and Picard should be standing at something; hence, the navigational table was born. It included an open-faced box, inside which rested a sighting compass; atop it stood a cast "dolphin bell."

JOHN:

The original version had only one dolphin holding the bell—but I kept remembering the Ark of the Covenant from *Raiders of the Lost Ark*, with the two cherubs facing each other. So instead of two angels, I had two dolphins facing each other. It's my little inside *Raiders* tribute to artist Ron Cobb.

▲

THE SINGLE-DOLPHIN
NAVIGATIONAL TABLE.

▶

THE *RAIDERS* TWO-
DOLPHIN TRIBUTE.
NEITHER TABLE WAS
EVER CONSTRUCTED.

The Valley of Fire Set

Originally, the set that served as backdrop for the final confrontation among Kirk, Soran, and Picard was to be built on a soundstage, and was designed so that either an optical background or a real site could be put behind it.

JOHN:

Herman and I designed this set as a multilevel crown on top of a mountain—with a bit of climb space, then a plateau where the torpedo launcher would be, then a jagged peak that separates off to one side (where Soran would run to meet the energy ribbon).

However, the producers soon decided that the scene should be shot on location, in Nevada's Valley of Fire. Scouts returned from the area with photos, which were used as backdrops for artists' renderings, made on transparencies, of platforms and scaffolding. These transparencies were placed over the photos, to show how the scaffolding would look on site. Since the terrain had a mind of its own, the drawings served only as aids; the shape of the platforms was dictated by the rock face itself.

Courtesy of ILM.

CGI SHOT OF THE VALLEY OF FIRE SET. DAVID OWEN.

THE ORIGINAL DESIGN FOR SORAN'S SOUNDSTAGE "MOUNTAIN." ▶

WHERE PLATFORM
WILL BE

Rock type
stairs

MISSILE GANTRY SITE

Kirk
-N-
PICARDS
Ascention
Point

John Eaves 94   GENERATIONS   SET IDEA SORANS MNT.

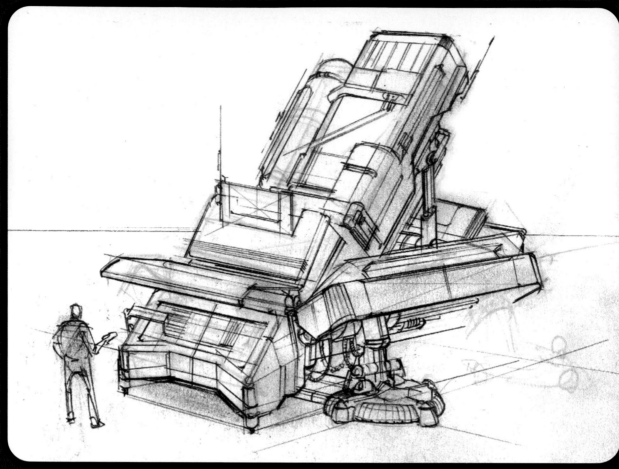

▲ A PRELIMINARY SKETCH OF SORAN'S PROBE LAUNCHER BY MARK MOORE.

...AND CLARK SCHAFFER'S SKETCH OF THE SAME. ▼

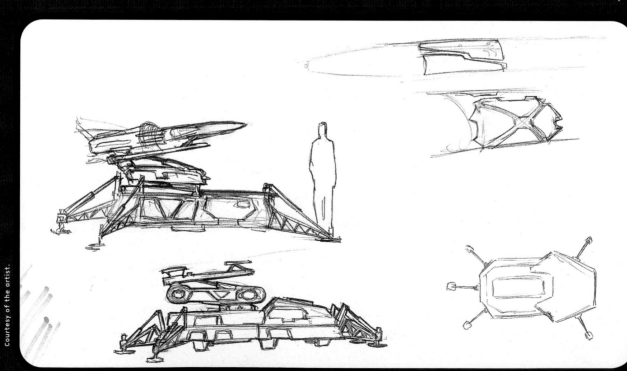

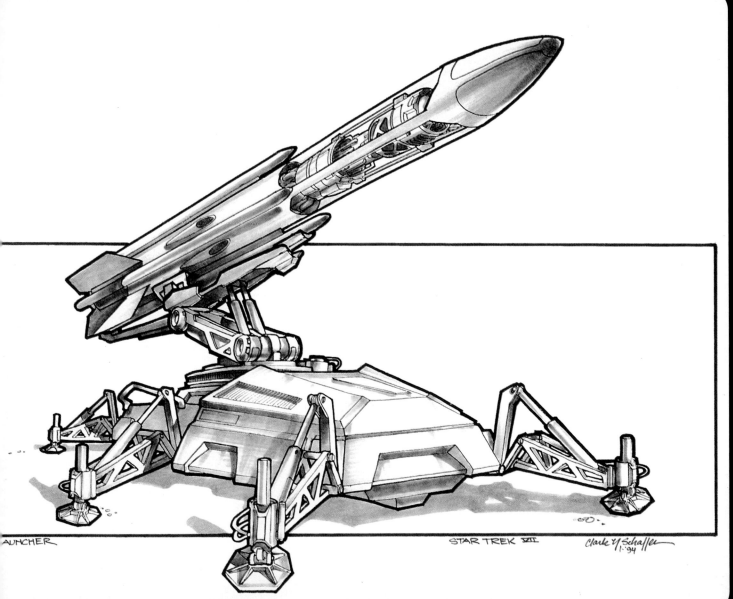

AUNCHER   STAR TREK VII   Clarke Y Schaffer
                                                                  1-94

▲

THE FINAL VERSION BY SCHAFFER.

Storyboards of the Enterprise-B

Eaves's last assignment on *Star Trek Generations* was for Director David Carson, who wanted to see some sketches of the *Enterprise*-B's departure from Spacedock. (The actual storyboards were, of course, being drawn by Mark Moore at ILM.)

JOHN:

Originally, the ship was going to back out of the Spacedock and do a quick flyby. I did four or five pages of this low angle where you're looking up at the bottom of the saucer, and we pan and move back with the ship as the *Enterprise* clears the station and moves forward with a very close flyby. This wound up changing drastically, so that the model actually flies through the station, which made a lot more sense than having it back out. The rest of the boards were drawn at ILM.

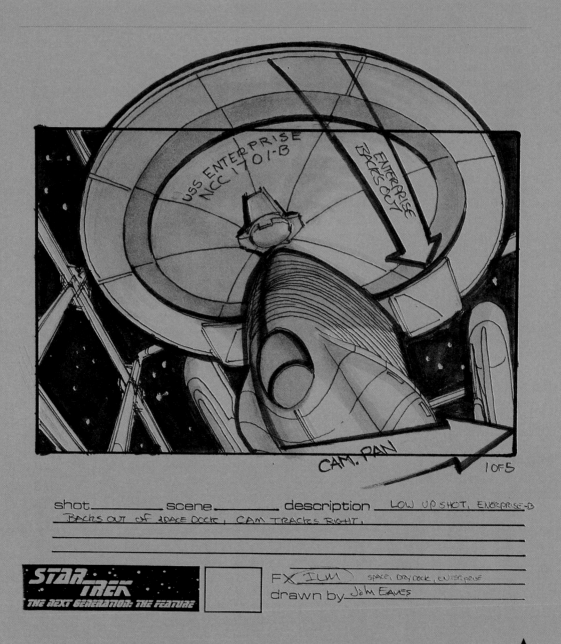

shot_____ scene_____ description ___LOW UP SHOT, ENTERPRISE-B
BACKS OUT OF SPACE DOCK, CAM TRACKS RIGHT.

FX ILM SPACE, DRYDOCK, ENTERPRISE
drawn by JOHN EAVES

EAVES'S SKETCHES OF THE *ENTERPRISE*-B'S DEPARTURE
FROM SPACEDOCK, FOR DIRECTOR DAVID CARSON

CAM CONTINUED PAN

2 OF 5

shot_____ scene_____ description <u>CONT. ENTERPRISE BACK OUT,</u>
<u>CAM CONTINUES RIGHT PANS UP TO FOLLOW SHIP</u>
_____
_____
_____

FX ILM SPACE, DRYDOCK, ENTERPRISE, EARTH
drawn by John EAVES

ENTERPRISE-B

CAM

3 OF 5

shot_____ scene_____ description _ENTERPRISE COMES_
TO A STOP AND SLOWLY PIVOTS TOWARDS THE RIGHT. CAM CONTINUES TO
TRAVEL RIGHT AND SLIGHTLY UP AND AWAY FROM SPACE DOCK
_____
_____

FX (ILM) SAME
drawn by_____John Eaves_____

CAM

ENTERPRISE
FORWARD

shot_____ scene_____ description _ENTERPRISE BANKS_
___TO THE RIGHT AND BEGINS FORWARD MOTION TOWARDS CAMERA, CAMERA-
CONTINUES ITS MOTION_____
_____
_____

FX (ILM)   SAME
drawn by_ JohN EAVES _

ENTERPRISE-B CU
FLYBY

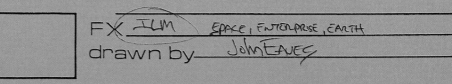

5 OF 5

shot_____ scene_____ description ENTERPRISE flys by
CAM EXTREME CLOSEUP, AFTER SHIP EXITS FRAME, SHOT IS
complete.

FX ILM   SPACE, ENTERPRISE, EARTH
drawn by   John Eaves

Then, as abruptly as it had begun, John Eaves's and Clark Schaffer's work for *Star Trek* ended.

John and Clark went back to where they started from: the model shop of famed *Star Wars* Oscar winner Grant McCune.

JOHN:

Grant gave me my first job in Hollywood, at the once-great FX house Apogee, in 1985. Not only has Grant been a great teacher and source of encouragement, he's also a good friend. I owe much of all I've achieved in my career to him.

Clark and I were originally model makers, with a lot of artwork thrown in for fun. Together, we designed and built a lot of models for Grant. After Apogee closed, Grant kept the lease on the model shop and called it Grant McCune Design. While there, Clark and I started working together on *Batman Forever*. Our assignment: to design and build Arkham Asylum, that nasty place where Jim Carrey's "Riddler" is seen at the story's end.

After I worked on *Generations*, the way I approached drawings and sketches changed. Before, I'd draw a three-quarter view, and when time for model construction came, I'd fill in details as needed. When building the model, I had in my mind all the information that wasn't on paper. Thus, if anyone else had to build a model from one of my sketches, they faced a lot of gray areas, a lot of detail that needed to be addressed. *Generations* taught me that the more sketches I make (especially plans, even rough ones), the better they assist those who had to make models from my drawings.

So when we started working on models for *Batman Forever* and I had to do the Arkham Asylum sketches, not only did I do three-quarter drawings for the producer's approval, I did plans too, which I'd never done before. The Asylum model became so large, Clark and I had a whole crew of model makers working with us—and all the plans and drawings wound up being great assets and timesavers.

A year later, Eaves got another call from Herman Zimmerman—this time, an invitation to do illustration work for a television series entitled *Star Trek: Deep Space Nine.*

JOHN:

Illustration has always been my first love, but it was a tough decision, because I also love making models for Grant. After a week of sleepless nights spent trying to decide which path to follow, I sadly said farewell to Grant.

And it was back to the ol' drawing board at Paramount....

PART 2

STAR TREK
FIRST CONTACT

THE U.S.S. ENTERPRISE

NCC-1701-E

Shortly after Eaves's arrival at *Deep Space Nine*, talk of the new feature film started surfacing. It was to be called *Resurrection*—at least, until another film dealing with space aliens announced the same title.

Production Designer Herman Zimmerman already had the story treatments, and was determined to prepare as best he could for the onslaught of work that was sure to follow. Regardless of how the story might evolve, or the title might change, he knew one thing was certain: His staff had a new *Enterprise* to design. And if they could tackle that one project and finish it before production on the film began, maybe there'd be time for all the other design work the film required.

As early as August 1995, some six or seven months before the movie received the official go-ahead, John Eaves started doing rough sketches for the *Enterprise*-E.

JOHN:

I wanted a sleek, very fast ship with favorite elements from the starships that had gone before, especially Bill George's *Excelsior*. Everyone knows the basic shape: the saucer section, the body, the two nacelles. They've been arranged so many times in so many beautiful ways, I thought: "Well, how will *I* approach this?"

I decided to start with a really sleek design. While all of the *Enterprises* were beautiful, none of them had a really streamlined, "warp speed" look. We have the "Cadillacs" of starships; I wanted to make a Porsche.

So I gave the saucer an oval shape, and designed it so that it was longer than it was wide. I really liked the older, longer nacelles, and returned to that, in order to give the ship balance. I put a lot of ships down on paper—probably twenty-five or thirty sketches—until I came up with an outline I liked.

Very early sketches of the Enterprise-E, *by John Eaves.* ▶

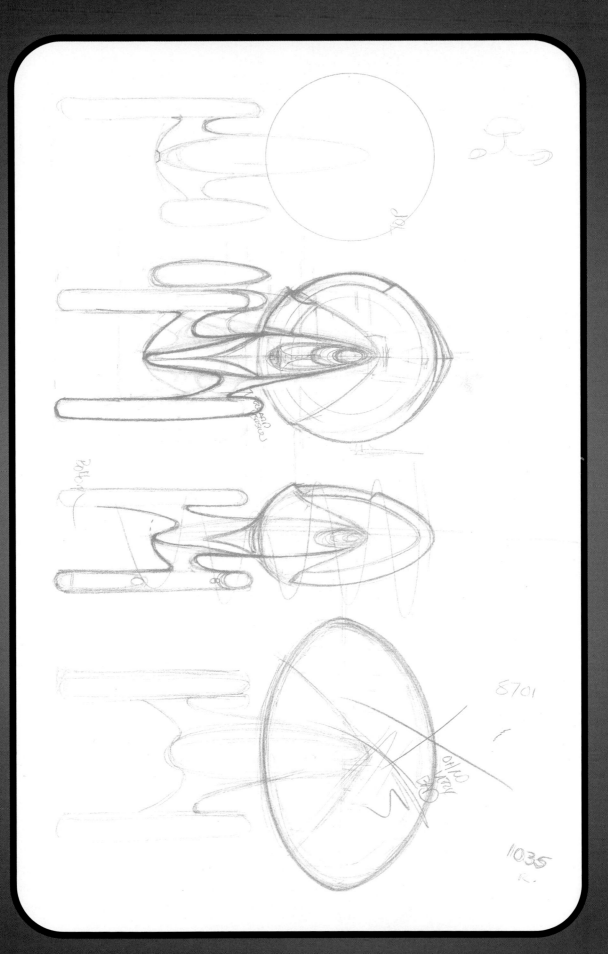

83

11.11.96

Hi John,

Thought You might be interested in these additional drawings I came across while cleaning my office. When Bill George, John Knoll, and I first heard of the introduction of the Enterprise 'E', we sat down and brainstormed for a couple of hours, and this is the result. We all thumbnailed forms and proportions we'd always wanted to see on the Enterprise (plus a few that reflected elements in the script), and I consolidated and sketched them out here.

        Enjoy.

        Mark Moore

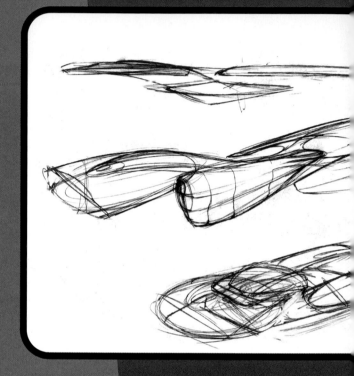

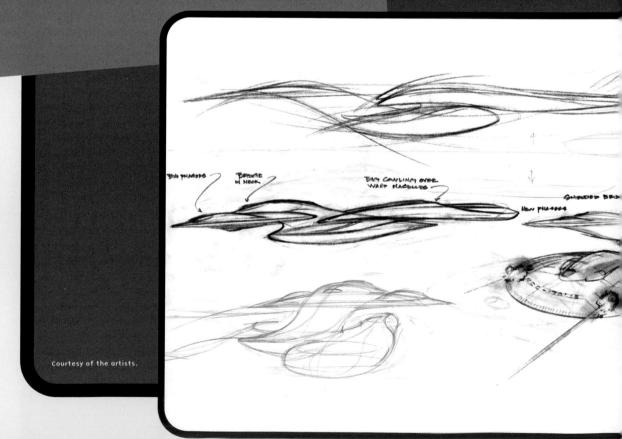

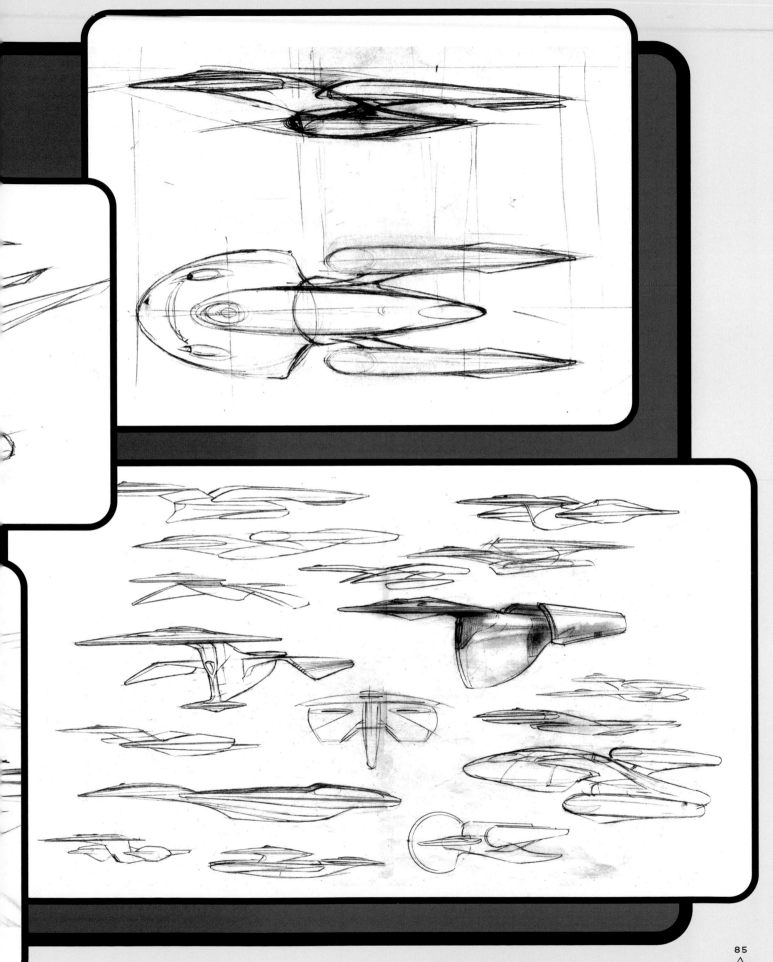

Once that finally happened, Eaves started putting in details. About the same time, he paid a visit to artist Rick Sternbach, who had recently designed the *Starship Voyager* for the new television series. As Eaves had never seen the ship or show, he wanted to see Sternbach's design, and also prepare himself for the process of getting the new starship approved.
JOHN:

It was really funny to see how similar the two ships were, in the rough sketches. We thought, "Wow, this is a nice direction to go—the new Federation design, from *Voyager* to the *Enterprise*-E."

I finally asked Rick, "What does it take to get one of these ships approved? What are the steps? I know design has a lot to do with it, but what other particulars do I need to know?"

Well, Rick reached into his desk, pulled out a huge file, and threw it atop his desk. It was about two hundred drawings thick! "*This*," he said, "is what it took to get the *Voyager* approved." And he opened up the file and showed me sketch after beautiful sketch, each with subtle changes, so that I could see how the shape began, then evolved into the final product. On top of it all, he'd made a little

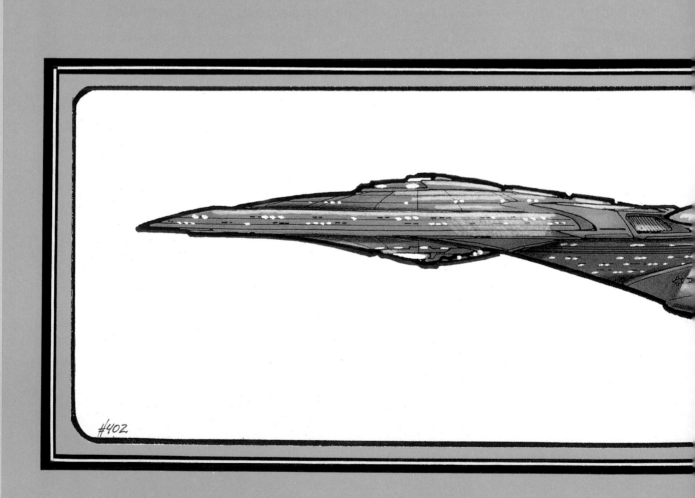

#402

▲
An early full-color rendition of
the *Enterprise*-E, by John Eaves.

booklet that included the breakdown: all the decks, what the ship could do, how it did what it did. He even had a scale chart comparing the *Voyager*'s size to the sizes of the other Federation starships.

Thanks to Rick's help, I made myself a similar packet for the *Enterprise*-E.

While the shape still needed some refinement, the time finally came to show the Powers That Be some design possibilities. Herman Zimmerman went over John's sketches, and sent those he liked best to Executive Producer Rick Berman for comment. Berman sent them back, saying, "I like this aspect,

but not this one," and Eaves went back to work.

JOHN:

I wanted to carry some of the *Enterprise*-D lines into the E—not with the saucer or body, but where the nacelles connected. At this point, the nacelles were almost a third longer than in the finished product. But I had the struts holding the nacelles up; they branched off the body and returned forward, making a little horseshoe, the way the D does. But instead of having them angled back, I had them angled forward.

STAR TREK
U.S.S. ENTERPRISE
NCC-1701·E

It was a really nice design; Herman liked it, and we presented it to Rick [Berman]. He liked it, too, and started making some changes.

Halfway through our designs on that version, Fritz Zimmerman looked at the ship from the top and said, "Hey! It looks like a chicken!" And from the moment he said that, the design was cursed. Every time I looked at it, I saw not a starship, but a chicken in a pan. Sadly, Herman saw it, too, so we had to (pardon the pun) scratch that one.

Thanks are due Fritz, for his words of wisdom. Sometimes you get so close to your own work, you need an objective party to warn you when it starts looking like a chicken.

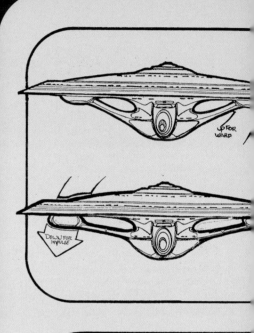

IF CHICKENS WERE STARSHIPS: FRITZ'S INFAMOUS CHICKEN. ▶

STAR TREK
U.S.S. ENTERPRISE
NCC-1701·E

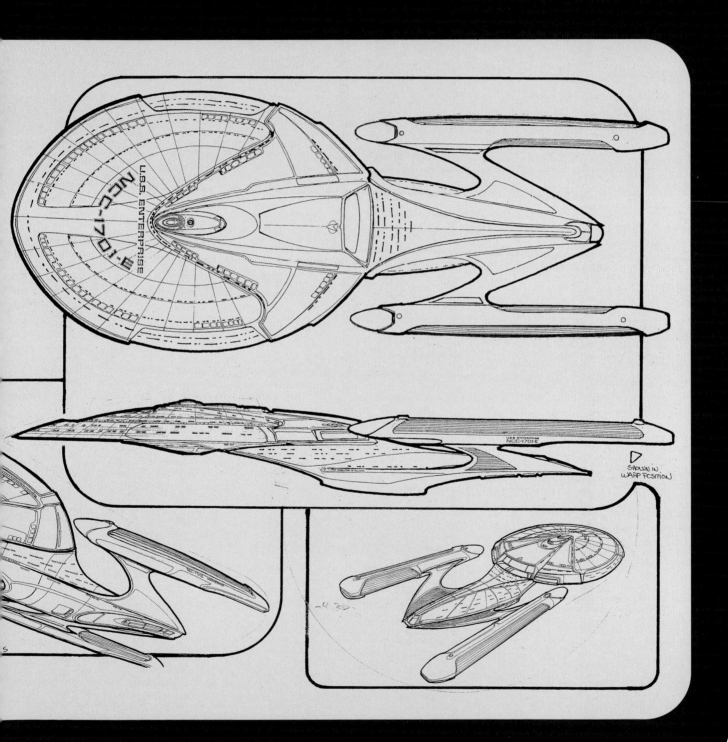

U.S.S. ENTERPRISE NCC-1701-E

U.S.S. ENTERPRISE NCC-1701-E

SHOWN IN WARP POSITION

One of the key elements of the *Enterprise*-E is its lack of a "neck" connecting the body to the saucer. Eaves chose to have the deflector dish cavity sweep far forward and merge with the saucer's bottom, which would in turn scoop down into the body. Eliminating the neck and compacting the ship gave it a more structurally sound body and made it look faster. At 2248 feet long, the E is much longer than its predecessor—but it is actually a much smaller ship when it comes down to girth and mass.

One design element, however, had little to do with structure or logic, and everything to do with nostalgia.

JOHN:

I remembered that the original *Enterprise* had these two little triangles on the forward end of the saucer. So when I was laying out the bottom of the E's saucer, I put those two little triangles up at the forward end of mine. I have no clue what they're for; they're just a neat shape, and I wanted to include something from the old ship as a "thank you" to Matt Jefferies. I also wanted to give fans of the original series something they could spot and say: "Ah, there's something carried from the past into the present."

Eaves also added something new (notches at either side of the saucer dish), as well as design elements from the *Enterprise*-B (an extension of impulse engines).

JOHN:

Also, I added a raised arrowhead shape on top of the saucer, which exaggerates the direction of the ship; on top of that, I put in a couple of other levels on the bridge, and as you go toward the back of the saucer, you find the shuttlebay. To add to the ship's function, I put a control tower atop this shuttlebay. I remembered that on the original *Star Trek* series, they had these observation windows inside the shuttlebay, so that you could look at the shuttles from another deck. I decided the deck on the E could also serve this double purpose—that once you're inside the shuttlebay, the roof concaves up so that you can have windows looking inside and outside the ship as well.

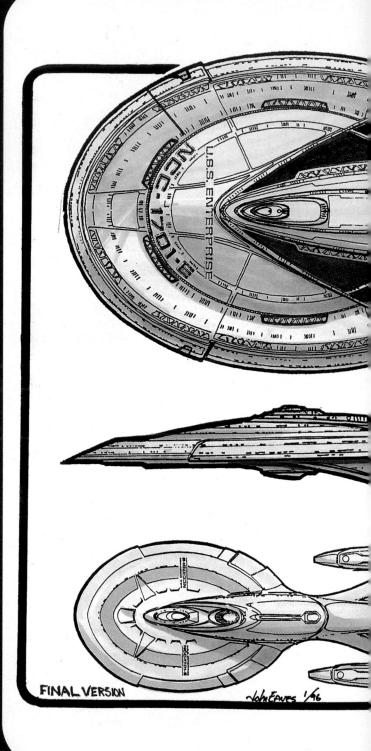

FINAL VERSION

John Eaves 1/96

▲

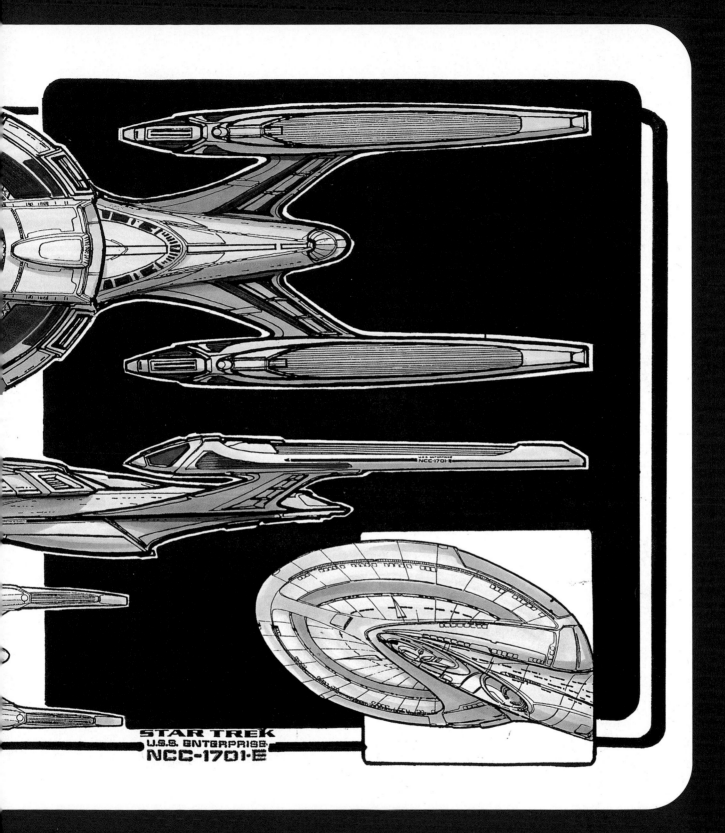

STAR TREK
U.S.S. ENTERPRISE
NCC-1701-E

Once the *Enterprise*-E's shape was complete, John drew plan views of the ship: top, side, front, and back views. At one point, Herman Zimmerman suggested lowering the nacelles, à la *Voyager*. Some sketches were drawn, but the idea was eventually dropped.

Finally, the drawings were sent to Rick Sternbach, so that he could commence work on the blueprints for ILM model makers. Using the 2248-foot length of the ship. Sternbach scaled the vessel down to determine the number of decks: twenty-four.

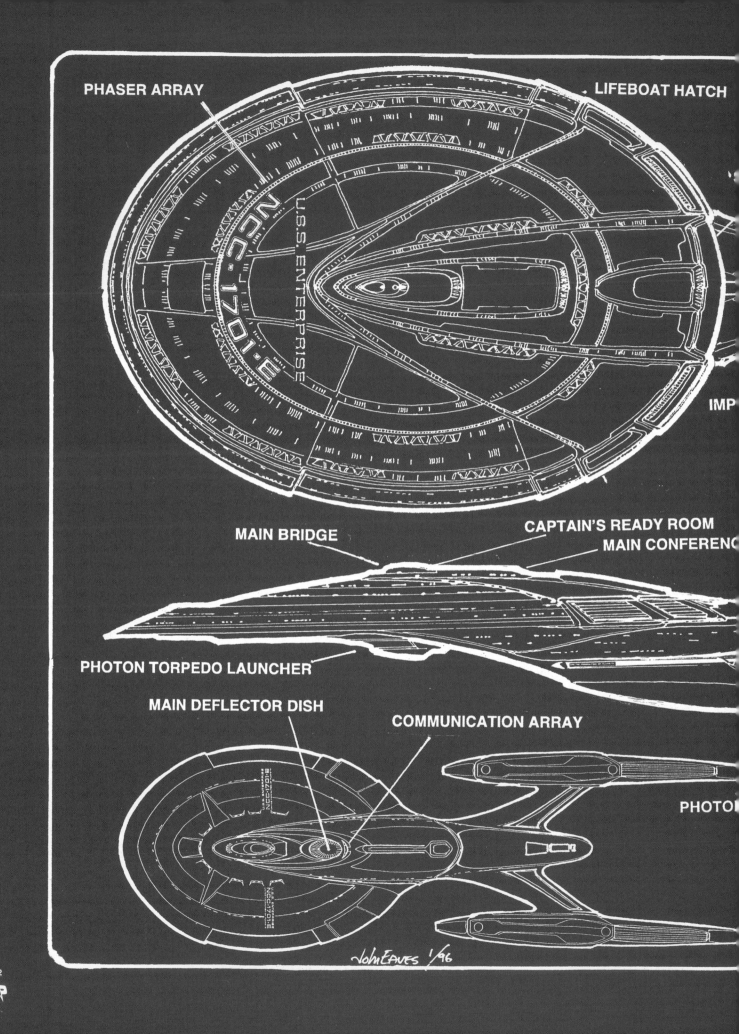

PHASER ARRAY

LIFEBOAT HATCH

U.S.S. ENTERPRISE NCC-1701-E

IMP

MAIN BRIDGE

CAPTAIN'S READY ROOM
MAIN CONFEREN

PHOTON TORPEDO LAUNCHER

MAIN DEFLECTOR DISH

COMMUNICATION ARRAY

PHOTO

John Eaves 1/96

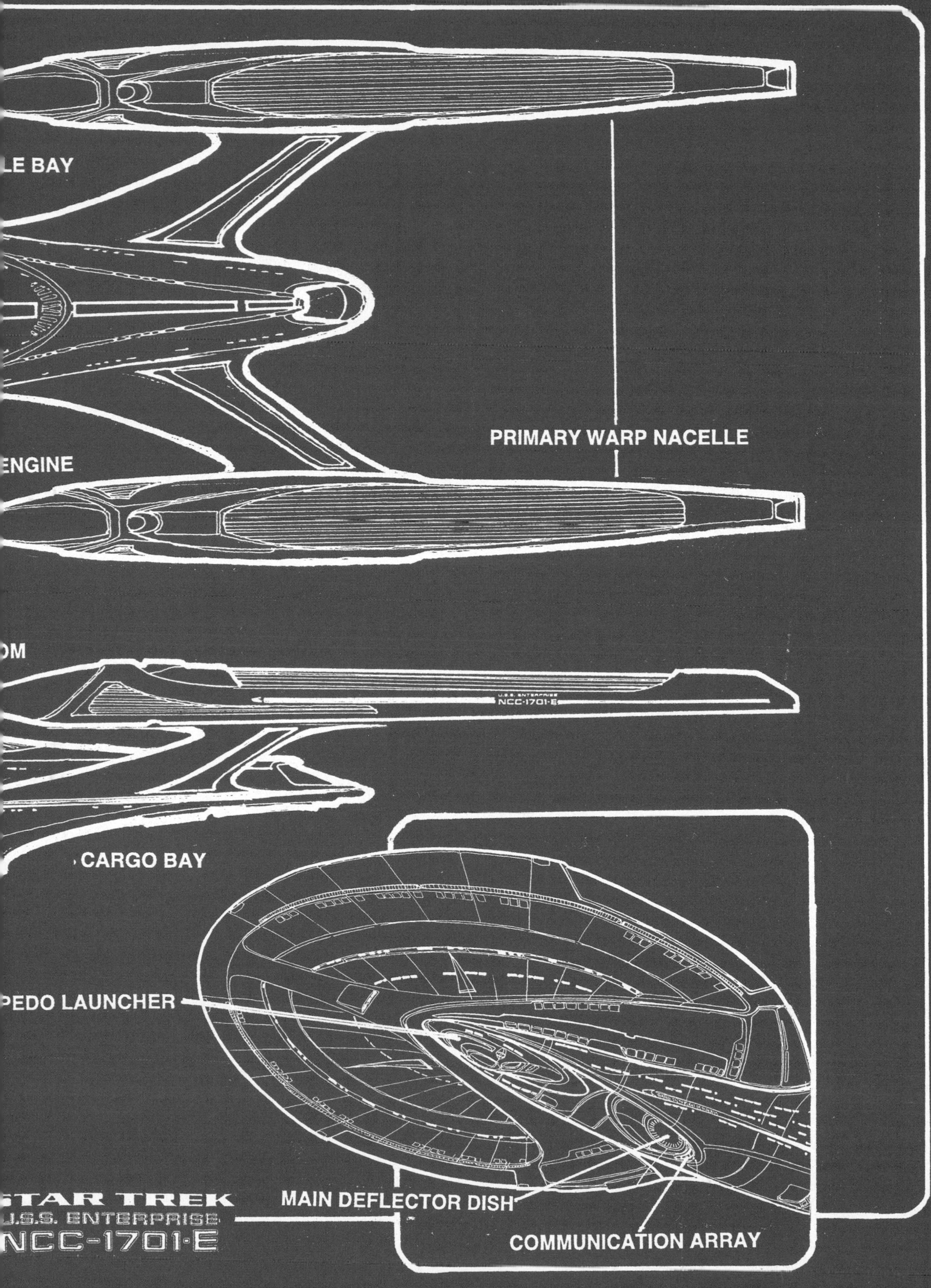

LE BAY

ENGINE

PRIMARY WARP NACELLE

OM

U.S.S. ENTERPRISE
NCC-1701-E

CARGO BAY

PEDO LAUNCHER

STAR TREK
U.S.S. ENTERPRISE
NCC-1701-E

MAIN DEFLECTOR DISH

COMMUNICATION ARRAY

We love the way it handles, but finding a big enough parking space is a bear: The E superimposed over the Paramount lot, by *Star Trek* artist Doug Drexler.

▼

A size comparison of starships, also by Drexler. ▶

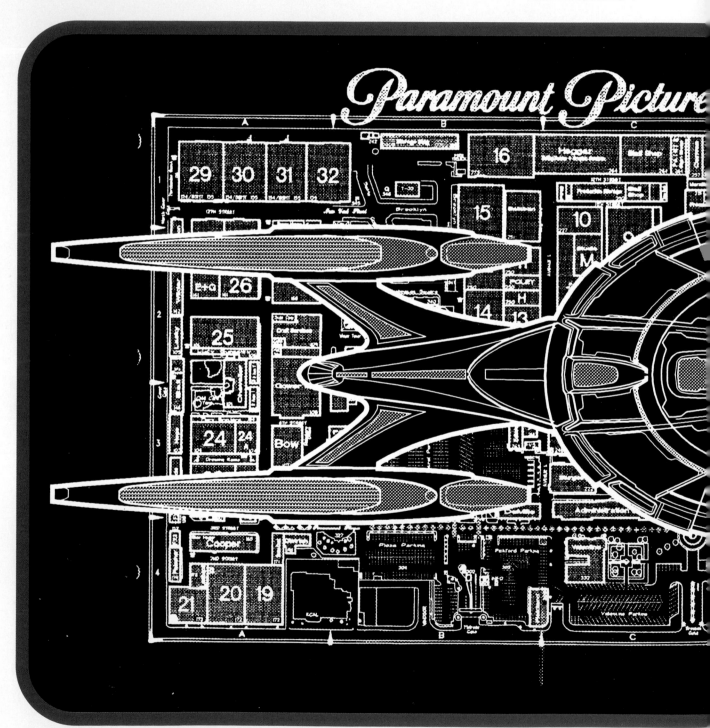

Paramount Picture

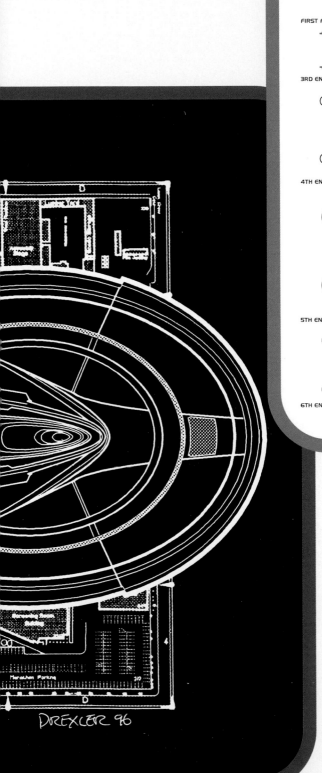

DREXLER 96

ORIGINAL ENTERPRISE NCC-1701

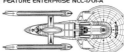

FIRST FEATURE ENTERPRISE NCC-1701-A

3RD ENTERPRISE - LAUNCHED IN "GENERATIONS" NCC-1701-B

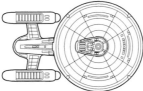

PARAMOUNT BACKLOT
APPROX 2000'

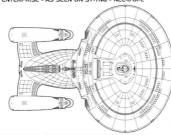

ACTUAL COMPARATIVE SIZE TO STARSHIPS

ENTERPRISE ORBITER SHUTTLE 101

4TH ENTERPRISE - AS SEEN ON ST-TNG - NCC-1701-C

ACTUAL COMPARATIVE SIZE TO STARSHIPS

AIRCRAFT CARRIER U.S.S. ENTERPRISE CVAN-65

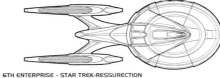

5TH ENTERPRISE - FLAGSHIP OF ST-TNG - NCC-1701-D

6TH ENTERPRISE - STAR TREK-RESSURECTION

DOUG DREXLER 96

Courtesy of the artist.

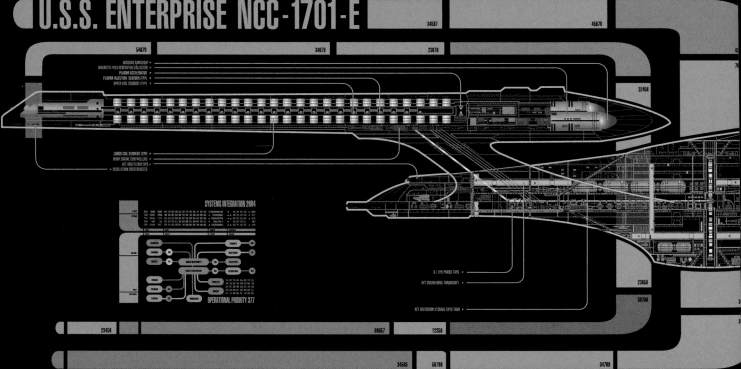

U.S.S. ENTERPRISE NCC-1701-E

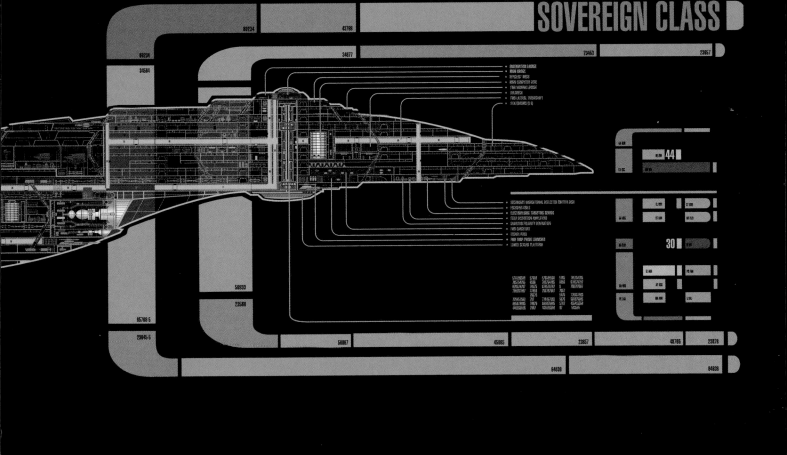

SOVEREIGN CLASS

A 2.5' X 4' PAINTING BY EAVES, COMPLETED IN ONLY EIGHT HOURS. INTENDED FOR PICARD'S READY ROOM, THE PAINTING WAS DITCHED IN THE LAST FEW MINUTES BEFORE FILMING.

AND NOW FOR SOMETHING ▶
COMPLETELY DIFFERENT:
CGI "ALTERNATE E"
BY DOUG DREXLER.

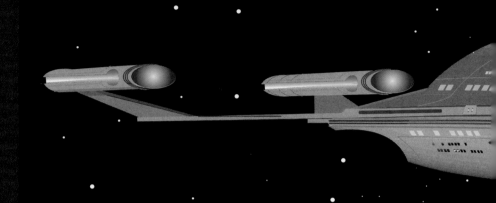

JOHN:

So now it's January 1996, and we're just officially starting on the feature. Things were extremely hectic, as I was splitting my time between *Deep Space Nine* and the movie. Herman and I started presenting the last of the *Enterprise*-E drawings to Mr. Berman, and he loved all our efforts. This gave Rick [Sternbach] the time he needed to do his blueprints. Just when I thought I was finished with the E, Mr. Berman told Herman, "You know, I love the shape we've got right now—but let's make sure. Let's do some more passes on the E, some different variations."

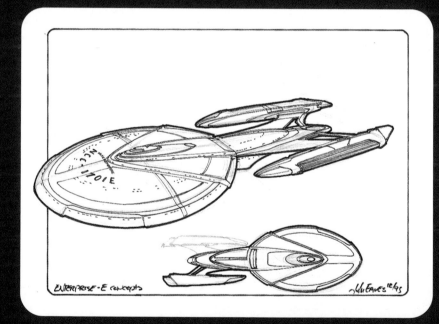

ENTERPRISE-E concepts

MORE ALTERNATE VERSIONS FROM EAVES. ▲ ▶ ▼

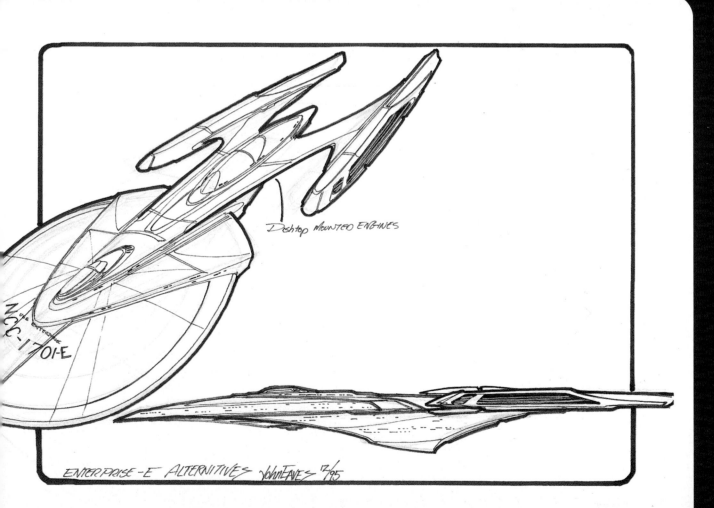

Doug Drexler

Deshtop Mounted ENGINES

NCC-1701-E

ENTERPRISE-E ALTERNITIVES John Eaves 12/95

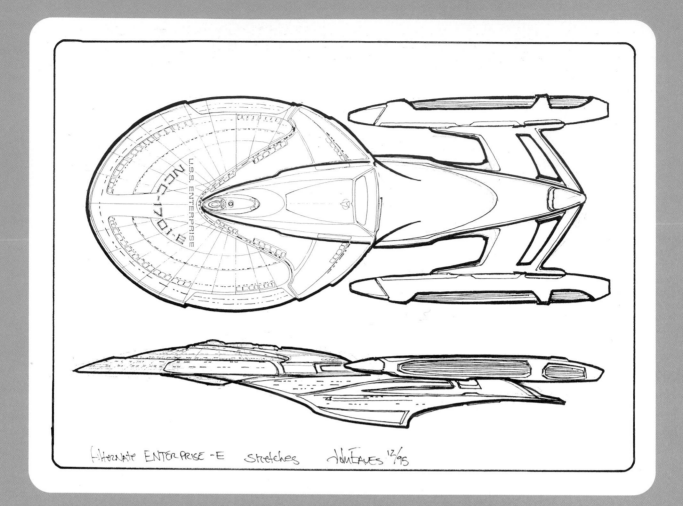

Alternate ENTERPRISE-E Stretches   John Eaves 12/95

JOHN:

I spent three or four more days drawing different ships; I confess, I was very grudging and didn't *want* to try a whole new direction. But I understood Mr. Berman and Herman's reasoning—that sometimes you need to be pushed to try something new and not become complacent. I managed to come up with five or six new designs, all of which they liked; but I was relieved and pleased when they decided to keep the original approved version.

STAR TREK
FIRST CONTACT

STAR TREK
FIRST CONTACT

EX ASTRIS, SCIENTIA

DOUG DREXLER 96

CAST AND CREW · SUMMER 96
"The human adventure is just beginning."

▲

THE LOGO FOR THE *STAR TREK:
FIRST CONTACT* CREW JACKET
(THE CREW ON THE PARAMOUNT
LOT, THAT IS, NOT THE ONE ON THE
STARSHIP), JOINTLY DESIGNED BY
DOUG DREXLER AND JOHN EAVES.

◄

THE CREW T-SHIRT
LOGO BY DREXLER.

MIKE OKUDA'S GRAPHICS FOR THE SHIP.

▼

**U.S.S. ENTERPRISE
NCC-1701-E**
UNITED FEDERATION OF PLANETS

**U.S.S. ENTERPRISE
NCC·1701·E**
UNITED FEDERATION OF PLANETS

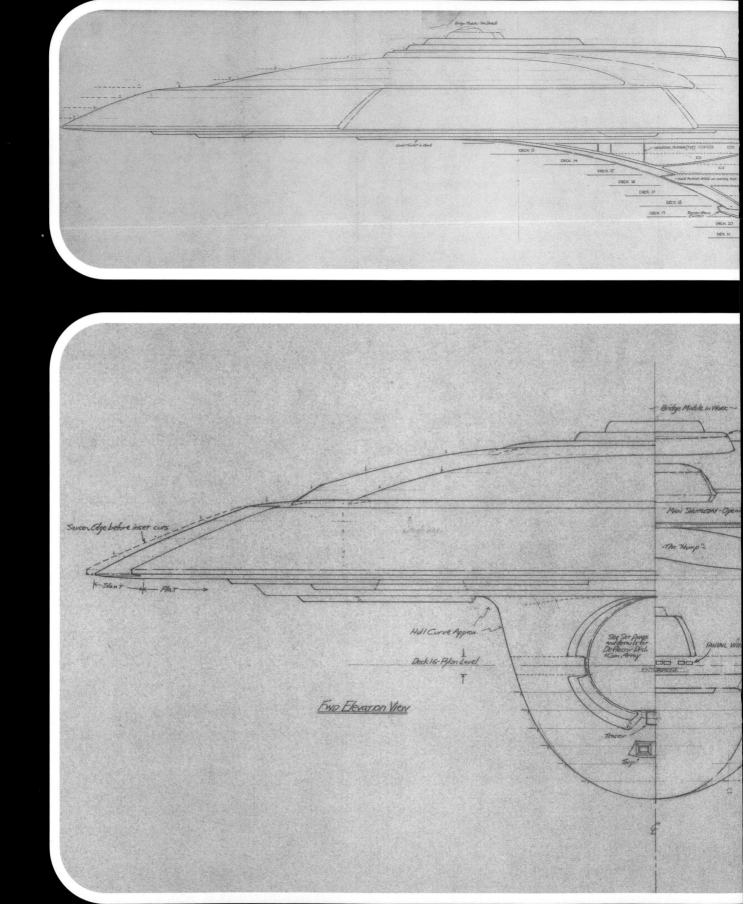

Bridge Module - For Details

DECK 13
DECK 14
DECK 15
DECK 16
DECK 17
DECK 18
DECK 19
DECK 20
DECK 21

Bridge Module in Work ~

Saucer Edge before inset cuts

Main SHUTTLEBAY - Open

-The "Hump"-

|← Slant →|← Flat →|

Hull Curve Approx.

Sdg Ser Dwgs
and demr'ls for
Deflector Dish
& Com. Array

FANTAIL WIN

Deck 16 - Pylon Level

ENTERPRISE

Fwd Elevation View

Tractor

Torp'

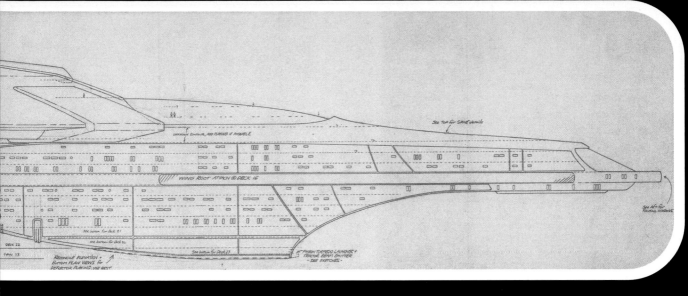

See Top for Same details

Unknown Contour, and plating if possible

See Aft for Fruital Windows

WING ROOT ATTACH @ DECK 16

See bottom for Deck 21

See bottom for Deck 22

See bottom for Deck 23

DECK 22

TYP. 23

RECNCLE ELEVATION +
BOTTOM PLAN VIEWS for
DEFLECTOR PLATING, use BEST

PHSSN TORPEDO LAUNCHER +
TRACTOR BEAM EMITTER
- SEE SKETCHES -

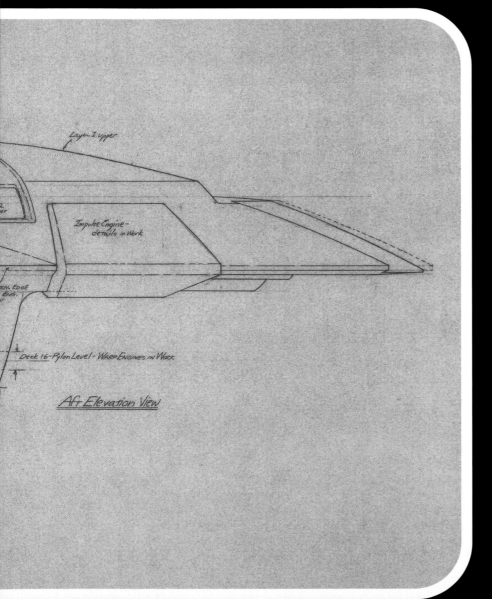

Layer 2 upper

Impulse Engine -
details in Work

Deck 16 - Pylon Level - Warp Engines in Work

Aft Elevation View

With the new ship finally approved, Sternbach went to work on the plans, while Eaves went on to the ship's details, starting with three-quarter drawings and close-up details of the bridge, then moving onto the deflector dish, the nacelles, the body, phasers, torpedo launchers—and on the list goes. A lot of the detail sketches are rather vague, in order to allow ILM model makers more creativity.

▲
◄ RICK STERNBACH'S
ENTERPRISE-E BLUEPRINTS.
▼

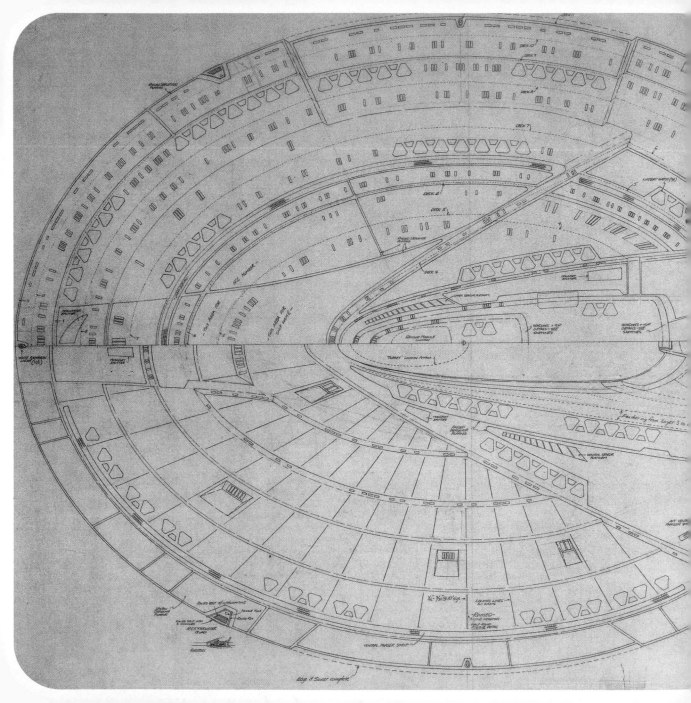

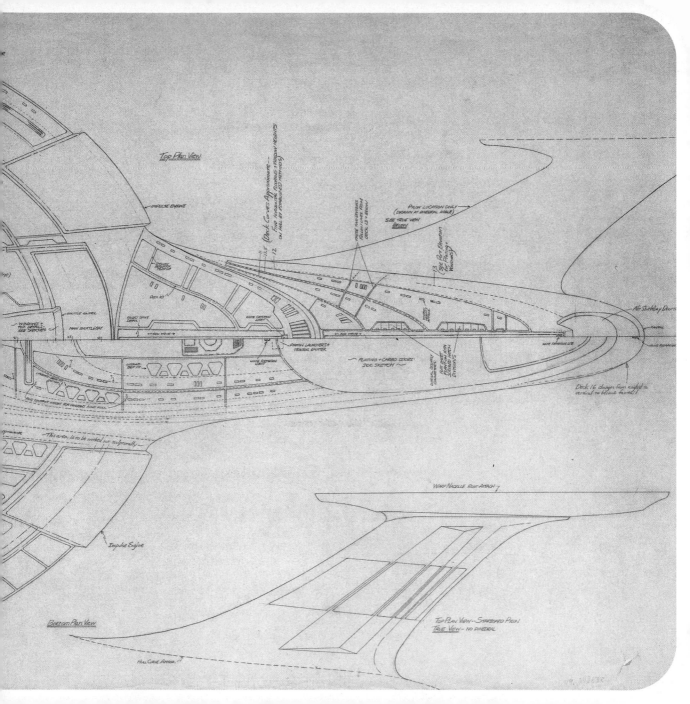

Top Plan View

IMPULSE ENGINE

Deck 10

WINDOWS + TOP DETAILS— SEE SKETCHES

MAIN SHUTTLEBAY

PHASER LAUNCHERS + TRACTOR EMITTER

PLATING + CARGO DOORS SEE SKETCH

PILON LOCATION ONLY (DRAWN AT DIHEDRAL ANGLE)

SEE TRUE VIEW BELOW

Aft Shuttlebay Doors

Deck 16 changes from angled to vertical to become pointed !

This area is to be worked out sculpturally

Bottom Plan View

Impulse Engine

WARP NACELLE Root Attach

Top Plan View—Starboard Pilon
True View—No Dihedral

Hull Curve Approx

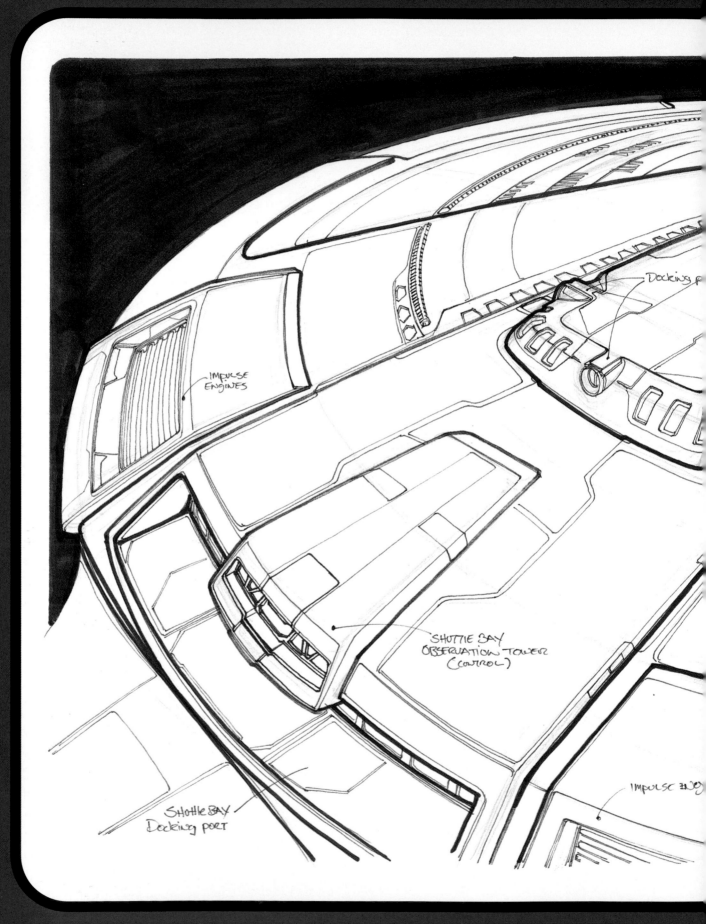

IMPULSE ENGINES

Docking p

SHUTTLE BAY OBSERVATION TOWER (CONTROL)

SHUTTLE BAY Docking PORT

IMPULSE ENG

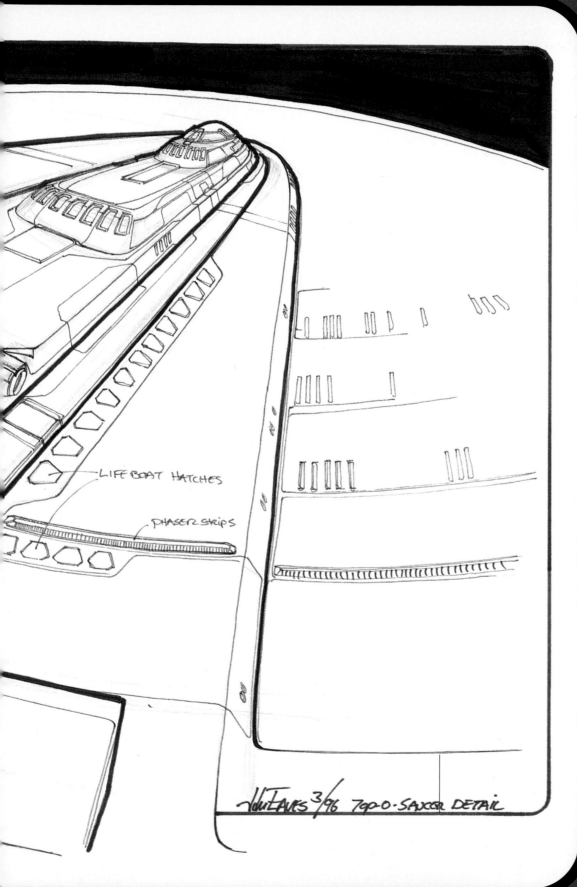

LIFEBOAT HATCHES

PHASER STRIPS

John EAVES 3/96 TOP-O-SAUCER DETAIL

JOHN:

When I'm doing sketches for something that will be built, I try to keep the model makers in mind. I want them to be creative and artistic when their work begins, so I leave areas open for their interpretation. If all the lines are rendered on paper, it takes away from their chance to be artists.

As far as the *Enterprise*-E is concerned, it was definitely a group project, a collaboration that included Rick Sternbach, Bill George, John Goodson, Herman Zimmerman, Rick Berman, Mike Okuda, Doug Drexler, and me. Everyone has contributed something to that ship, and has a right to be proud of their accomplishment. It was an honor to be able to work with such a vast group of talented artists and craftsmen.

As you can see, the model in the ILM photos is outstanding; as always, their production team went above and beyond the call of duty. Jeff Olson and the ILM team worked with Herman to come up with a unique color scheme for the outside of the E. Herman had come up with such rich colors for the interior, he wanted to carry a bit of that to the ship's exterior.

THE FINISHED RESULT. ▶

One last design involving the *Enterprise*-E's exterior had to do with the escape pods. On past starships, the hatches were somewhat rounded squares; for the new ship, they became beveled triangles. *Star Trek: First Contact* became the first film where the audience has the chance to see the pods ejected into space.

JOHN:

I worked on several escape pod sketches, and came up with a shape that reflected the triangular hatches. Please note, by the way, the serial number on the hatch and shuttle: 227. It's my dad's Arizona Highway Patrol badge number. I always use it when I need an insignificant number; it's my way of saying to him: "Hi, I'm thinking of you."

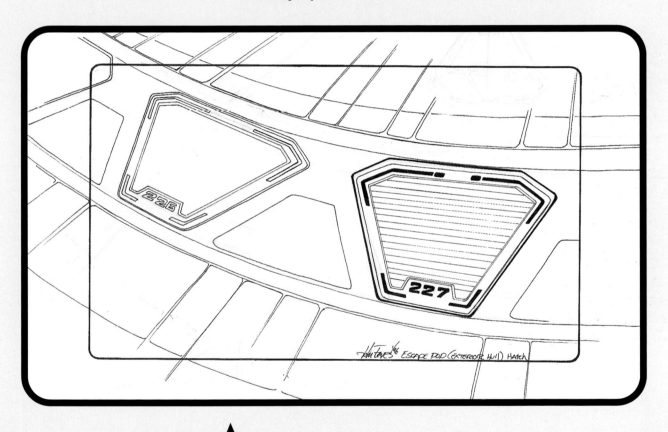

▲
Hi, Dad: Eaves's sketch of
the escape-pod hatches,
still nestled inside the ship.

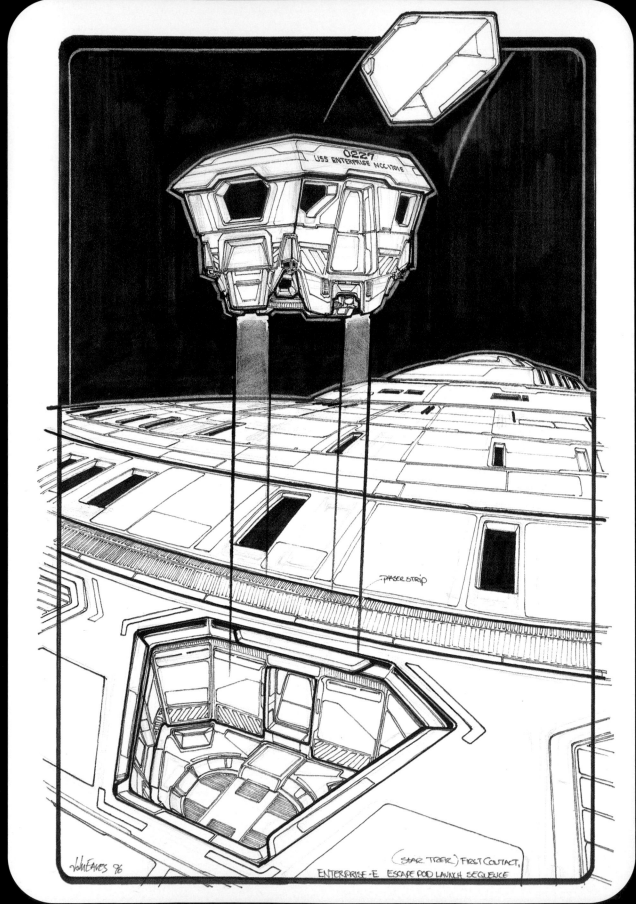

0227
USS ENTERPRISE NCC-1701E

-PHASER STRIP

JohnEAVES 96

(STAR TREK) FIRST CONTACT,
ENTERPRISE-E ESCAPE POD LAUNCH SEQUENCE

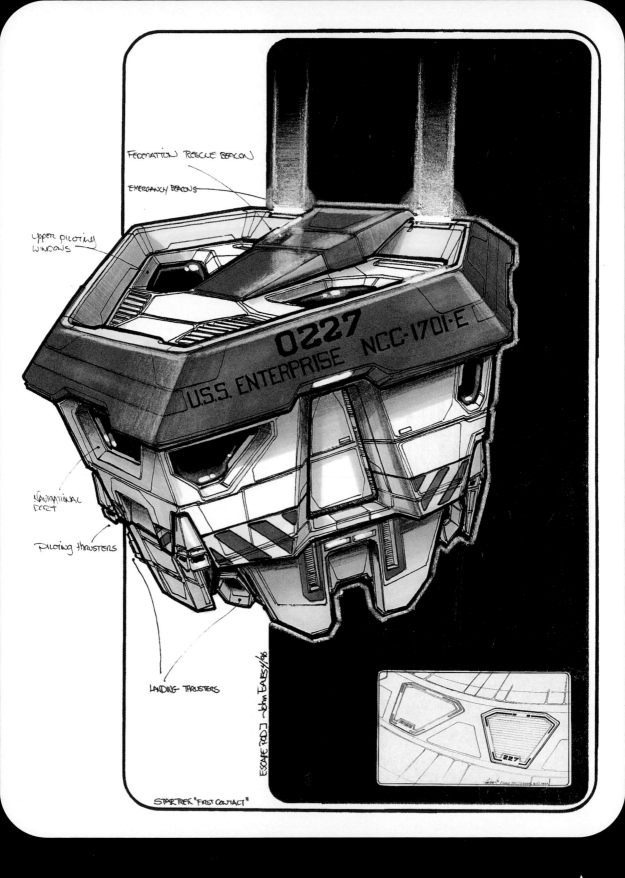

FEDERATION RESCUE BEACON

EMERGENCY BEACONS

UPPER PILOTING WINDOWS

0227
U.S.S. ENTERPRISE NCC-1701-E

NAVIGATIONAL PORT

PILOTING THRUSTERS

LANDING-THRUSTERS

ESCAPE POD John Eaves 1/96

STAR TREK "FIRST CONTACT"

227

Alex Jaeger, who served as ILM's art director on *First Contact*, had also set to work designing the escape pods. When Eaves took a look at Jaeger's drawings...
JOHN: I pushed my sketches aside.

I liked the beauty and simplicity of Alex's creations, and how he utilized the top of the pod as a heat shield for planetary re-entry. Ironically, our designs were extremely similar. Alex is an

incredibly talented artist; I wish I could have worked more closely with him. He came up with some wonderful designs, including all of the starships for the Borg battle scene.

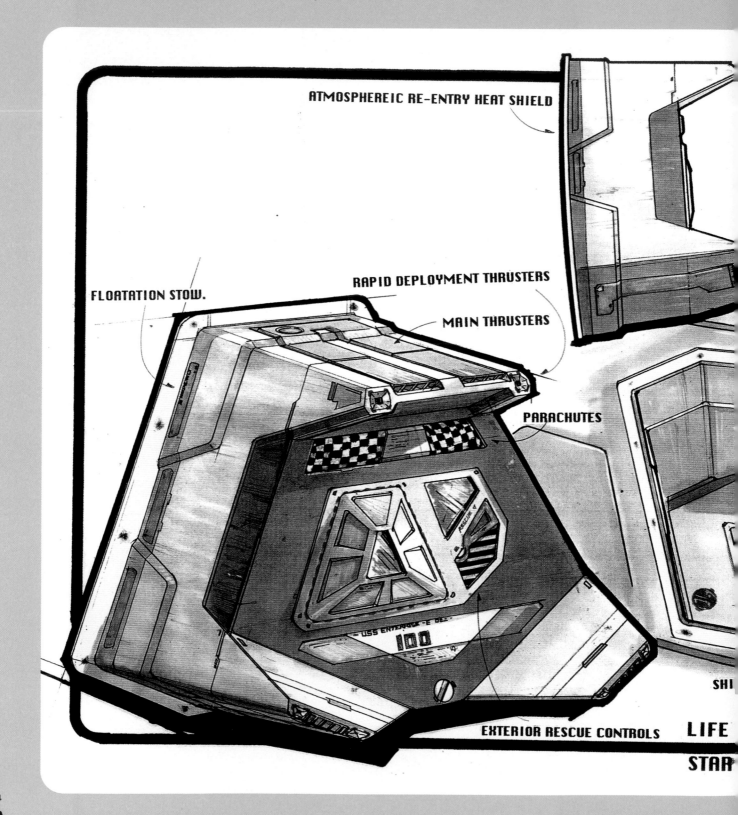

ATMOSPHEREIC RE-ENTRY HEAT SHIELD

FLOATATION STOW.

RAPID DEPLOYMENT THRUSTERS

MAIN THRUSTERS

PARACHUTES

USS ENTERPRISE-E 001
100

EXTERIOR RESCUE CONTROLS

SHI

LIFE

STAR

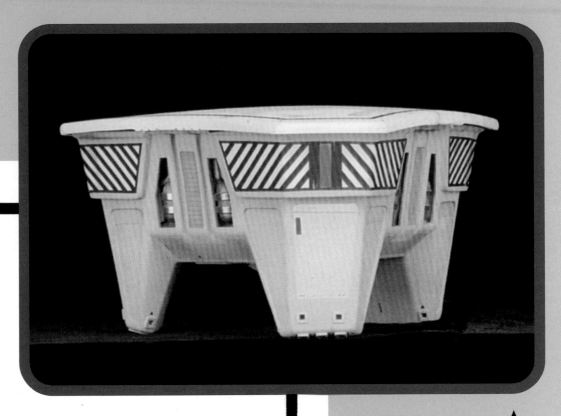

▲

THE ILM MODEL OF
THE ESCAPE POD.

U.S.S. ENTERPRISE -E

GEN. 2   Alex Jaeger 4/18/96

ALEX JAEGER'S
◄ LIFEBOAT SKETCH.

▲
CGI SHOTS OF THE ESCAPE PODS LAUNCHING...

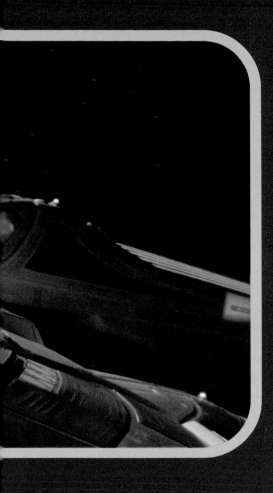

...AND HEADING TOWARDS EARTH, BY ALEX JAEGER.

▼

▼

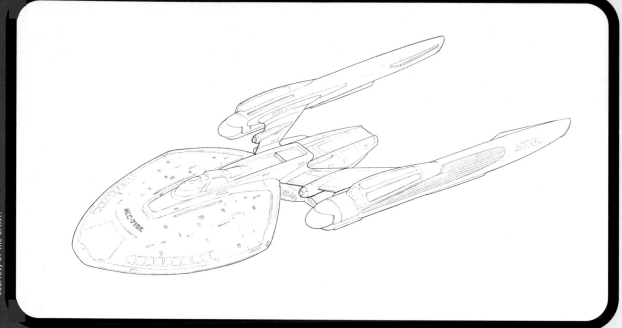

SHIPS FOR THE "BATTLE OF THE BORG"

Once again, the folks at
ILM put their imaginative
heads together to come
up with various designs
for Federation vessels—
most of which were
destroyed during the
battle with the Borg cube.

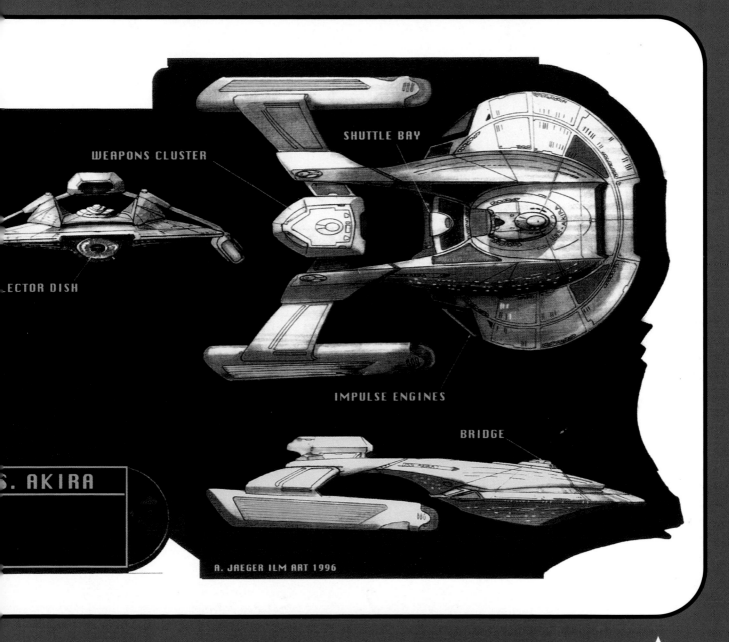

WEAPONS CLUSTER

SHUTTLE BAY

...ECTOR DISH

IMPULSE ENGINES

BRIDGE

S. AKIRA

A. JAEGER ILM ART 1996

PAINTINGS BY ALEX JAEGER...

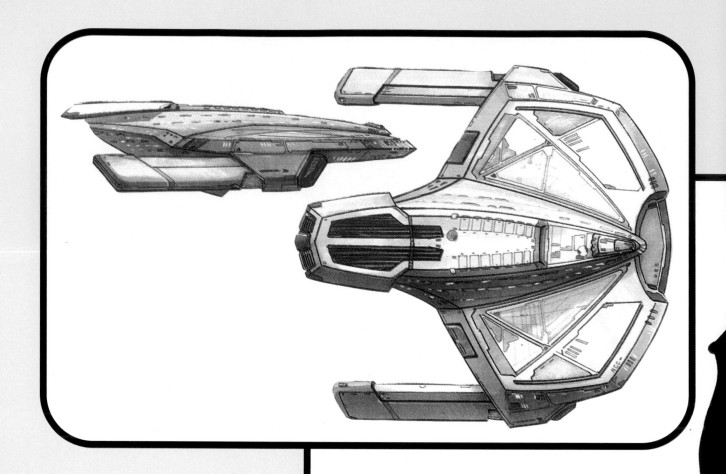

U.S.S STREAMRUNNER REVAMP

4/4/96

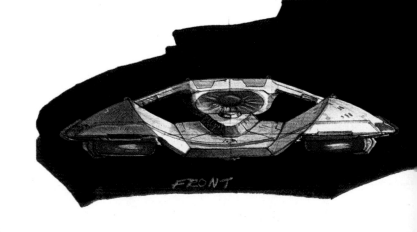

FRONT

Two new Federation Starships, also by Alex Jaeger...

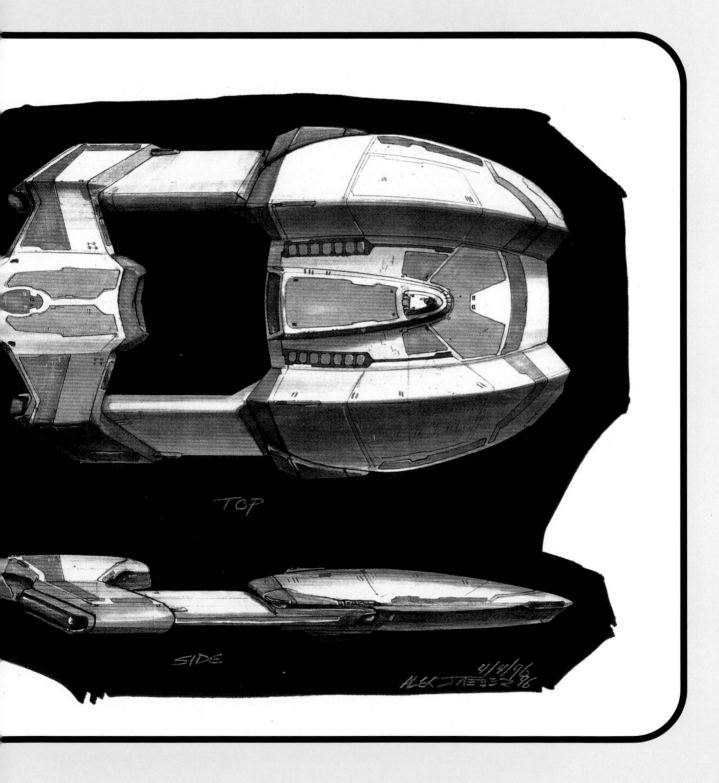

TOP

SIDE

4/4/96
ALEX JAEGER 96

Courtesy of the artist.

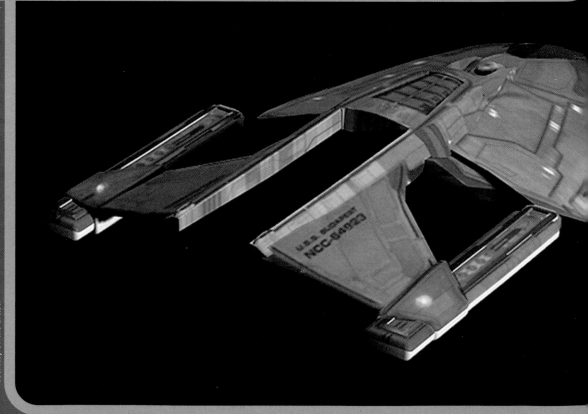

Courtesy of the artist.

▲

THE MODEL OF THE *DEFIANT*, SHOWING
DAMAGE INCURRED DURING THE BATTLE. THE
"DAMAGE" WAS ALL CGI. BY ALEX JAEGER.

STAR TREK FIRST CONTACT

ALEX JAEGER

SPACE B

TLE CONCEPT

About this time—January, February of '96—Eaves started speaking at some *Star Trek* conventions in Florida. His purpose in appearing was to speak about his work as illustrator for *Deep Space Nine*, but word spreads with remarkable swiftness in *Star Trek* fandom. Convention goers were already savvy about his *other* job on the Paramount lot, and pelted him with questions about the newest incarnation of the *Enterprise*.

JOHN:

Of course, I couldn't say anything about it, but it was exciting to see everyone's enthusiasm about the new ship.

Not long after, *Starlog* published an interview with Rick Berman, with a photo featuring an itty-bitty image of one of my *Enterprise*-E sketches. Amazingly, people with Internet access almost immediately began displaying their interpretations of the sketch. Mike Okuda pulled a few of those images off the Net, and we couldn't believe all the variations and wire frame models that people had produced on their home computers.

Fortunately, the *Starlog* photo was obscured enough that no Net surfers had been able to come up with the ship's true design.

Once the *Enterprise*-E design was truly finished (luckily, right around the time full-time production began on the film), Eaves received a list of all the space-craft designs that Co-Producer and special FX overseer Peter Lauritson needed. Prop master Dean Wilson also had a list of items he needed drawn—not to mention Herman Zimmerman, who had an equally urgent list of sets that required Eaves's attention.

JOHN:

Knowing I had to work for three people at once, I went to each and asked what projects were needed first, in order of importance. (Of course, everything was important and needed right away—but they broke the lists down and attached specific dates to each item.)

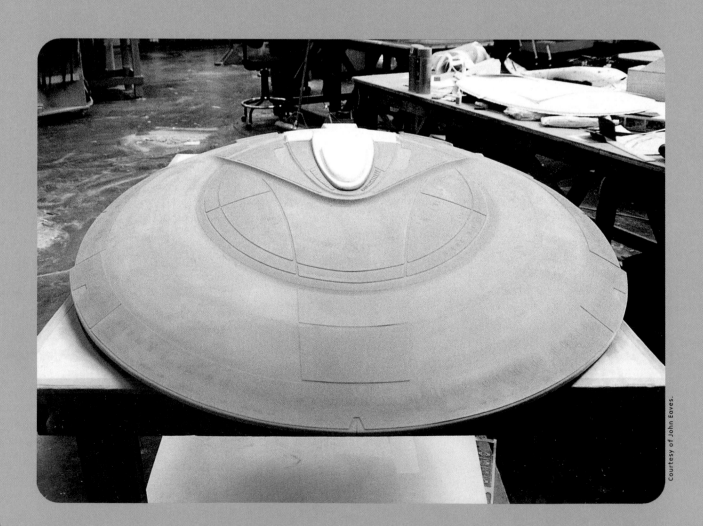

Courtesy of John Eaves.

▲
◄ THE EVOLUTION OF A STARSHIP: ►
THE ILM MODEL OF THE *ENTERPRISE-E*
SLOWLY TAKES SHAPE.
▼

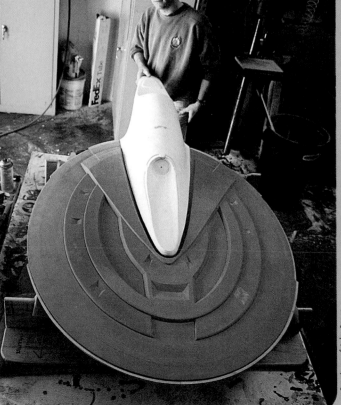

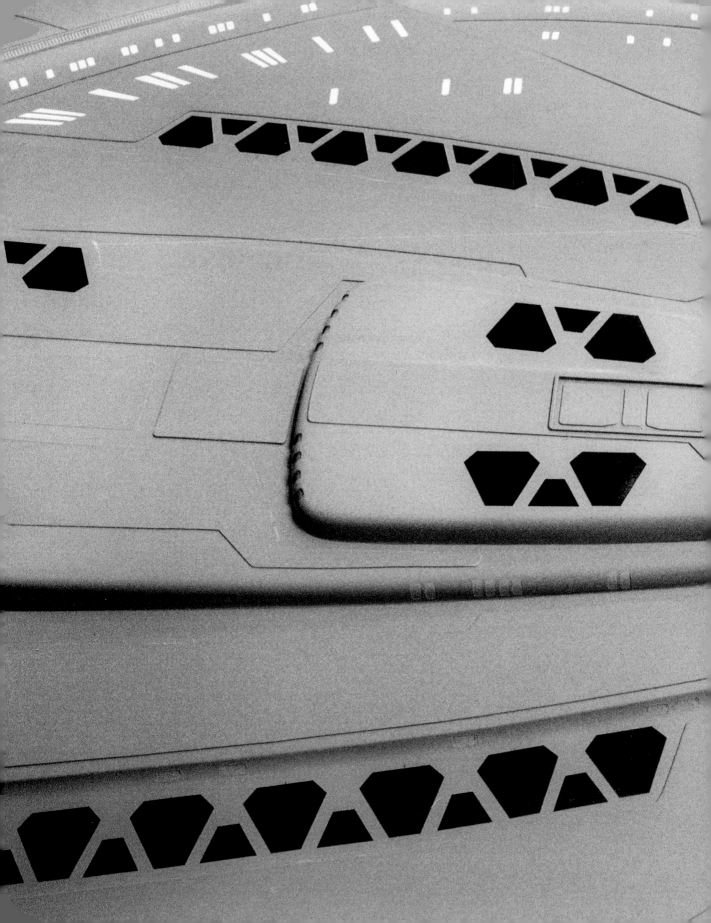

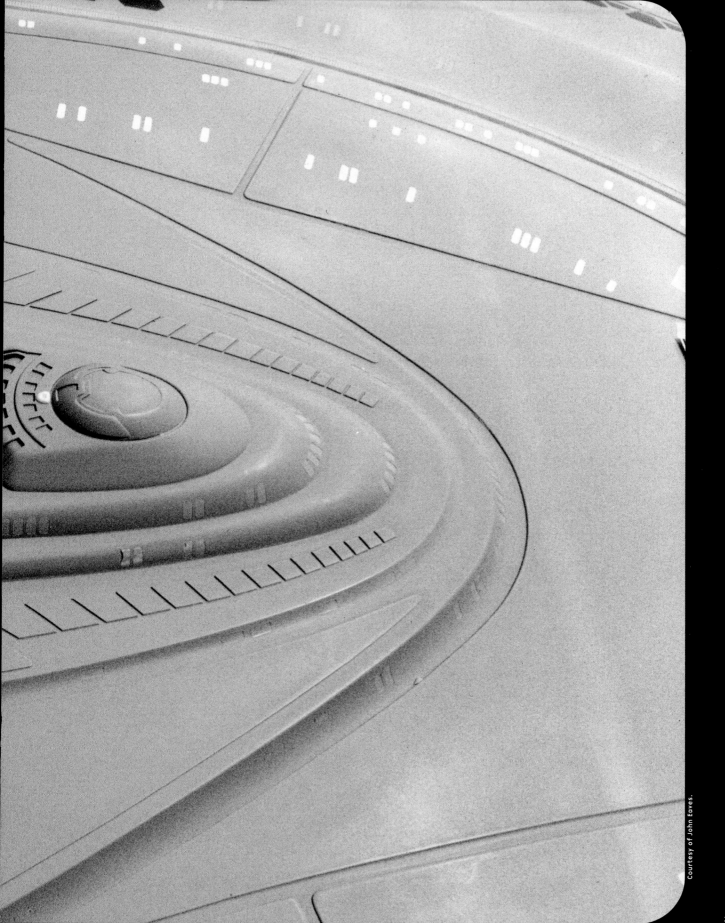

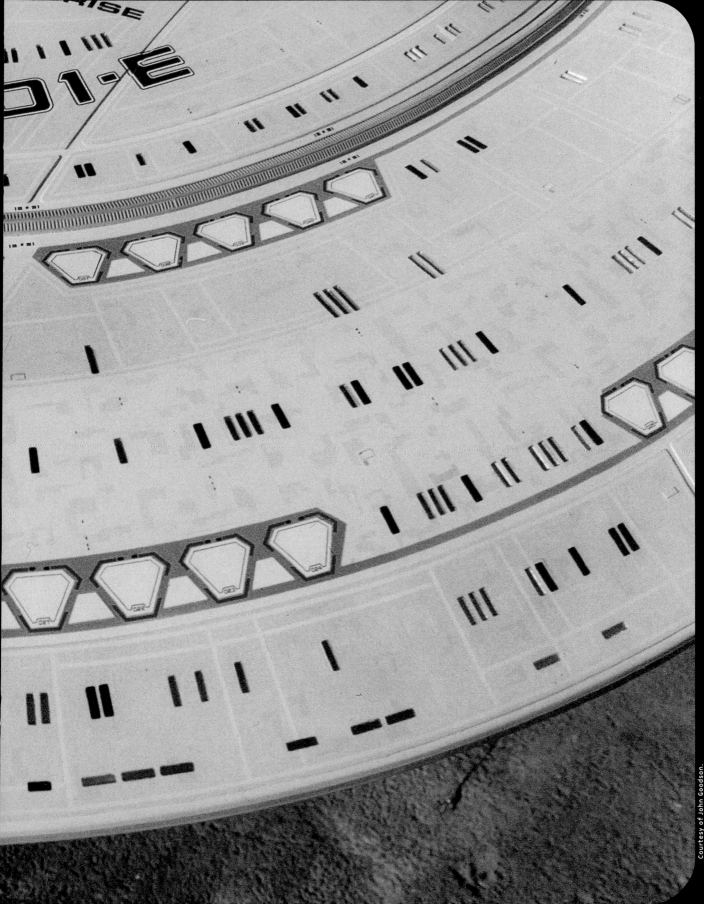

STARSHIP U.S.S. ENTERPRISE –

The **Enterprise-E**
Bridge

With the new ship's exterior design settled on, the most pressing set on Herman's list was the new bridge. The D's bridge had consisted of a circular room enclosed by walls, with a prominent wood arch; on the E, the walls were replaced by an open framework with gently sloping ramps and multiple levels.

▲

VERY EARLY SKETCH OF THE *ENTERPRISE-E* BRIDGE SET, BY JOHN EAVES.

MORE TENTATIVE BEGINNINGS... ▶

JOHN:

We left the framework but removed the walls, so that you could see other stations beyond those [former] walls. The major players are in the main bridge, and off in the alcoves you have secondary crew members working, which adds a lot of scope and function to the bridge.

We also built a main console in the back, with doorways on either side that lead to the right and left sides of the observation lounge. So if you were at the front of the ship looking back and those doors were open, you could see all the way through into the observation room, then out into space.

Immediately adjacent to those doors were the turbolifts. Moving forward to either side of the screen, one finds a door leading to the ready room, and another leading to the airlock. Zimmerman took Eaves's sketches and began drawing up construction plans. When all was finished and the set was built, it wound up being much larger than the *Enterprise*-D's bridge.

JOHN:

We thought it would be a bad thing, because we'd decided the E's bridge should be sleeker and therefore smaller. But it wound up being a great thing; it was a beautiful set, with warmth and depth, and the colors Herman chose gave the bridge a sense of ballistic beauty and great function.

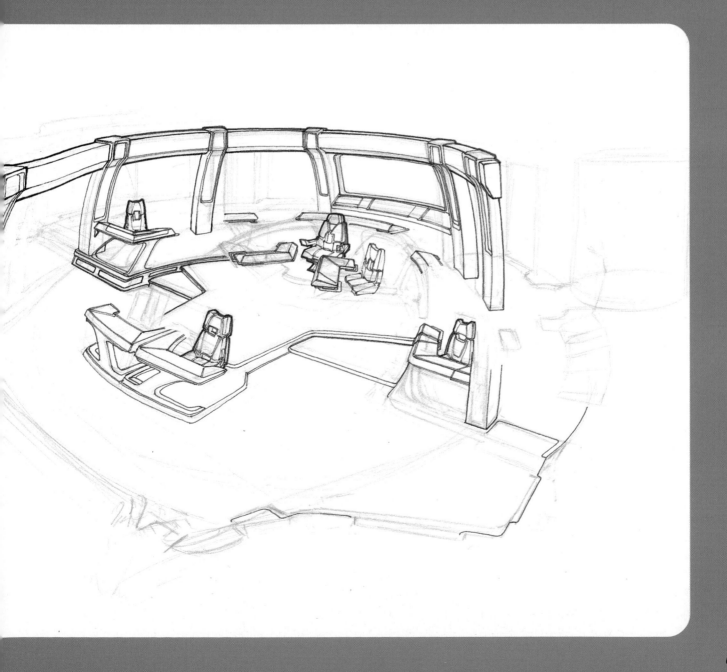

...AND EAVES'S OFFICIAL "FIRST PASS" AT THE BRIDGE...

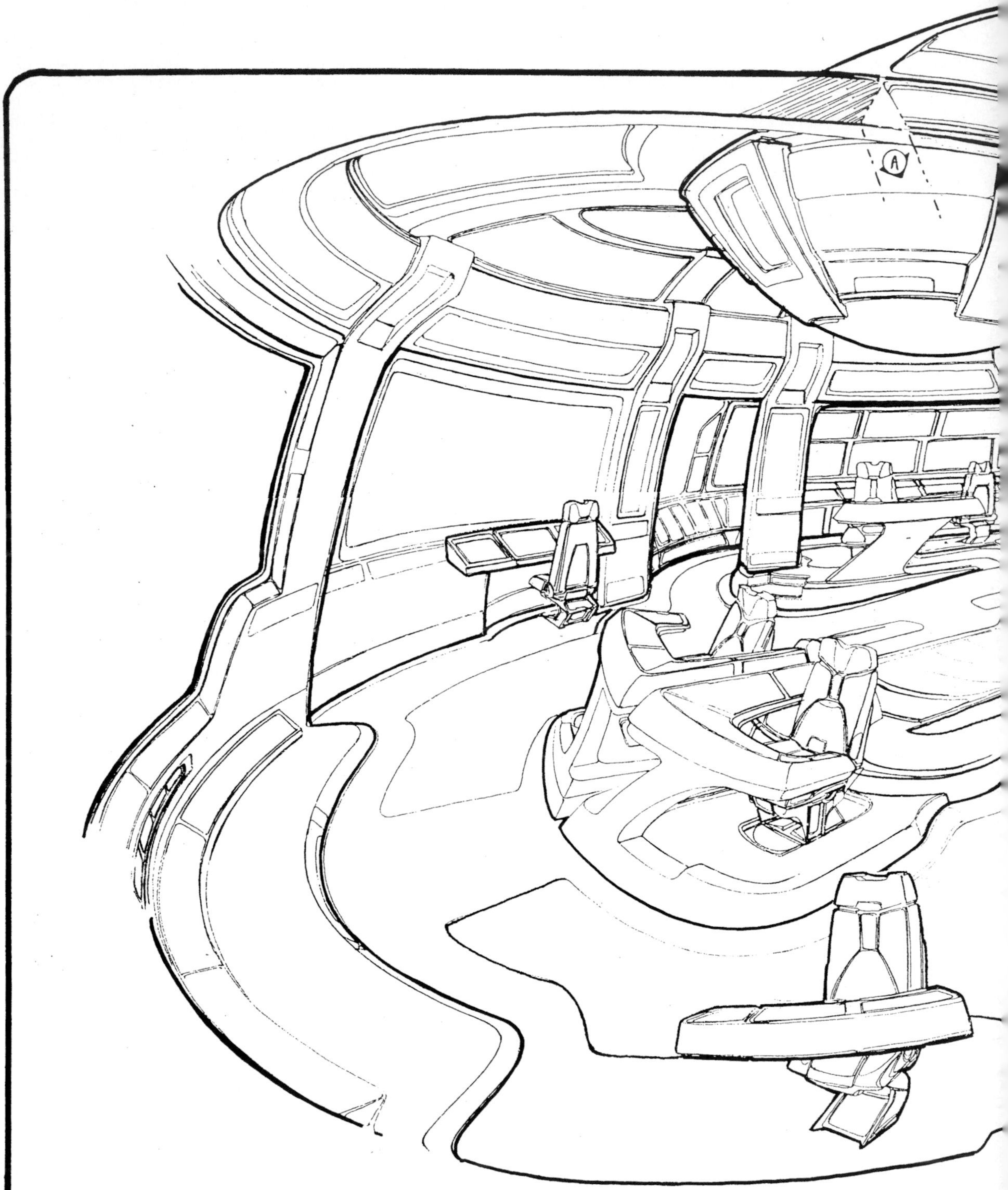

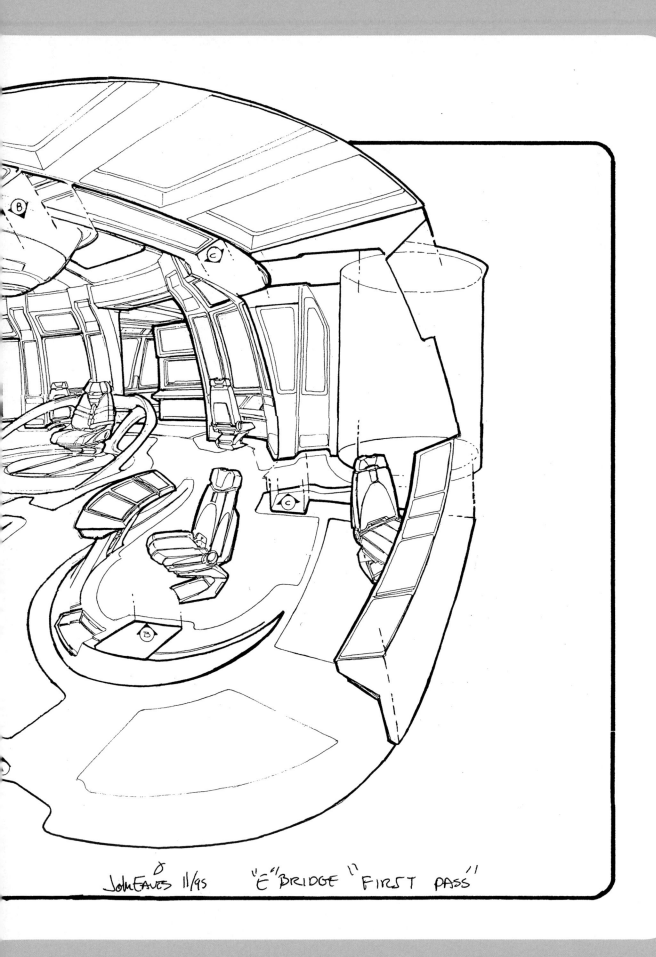

JohnEaves 11/95   "E" BRIDGE "FIRST PASS"

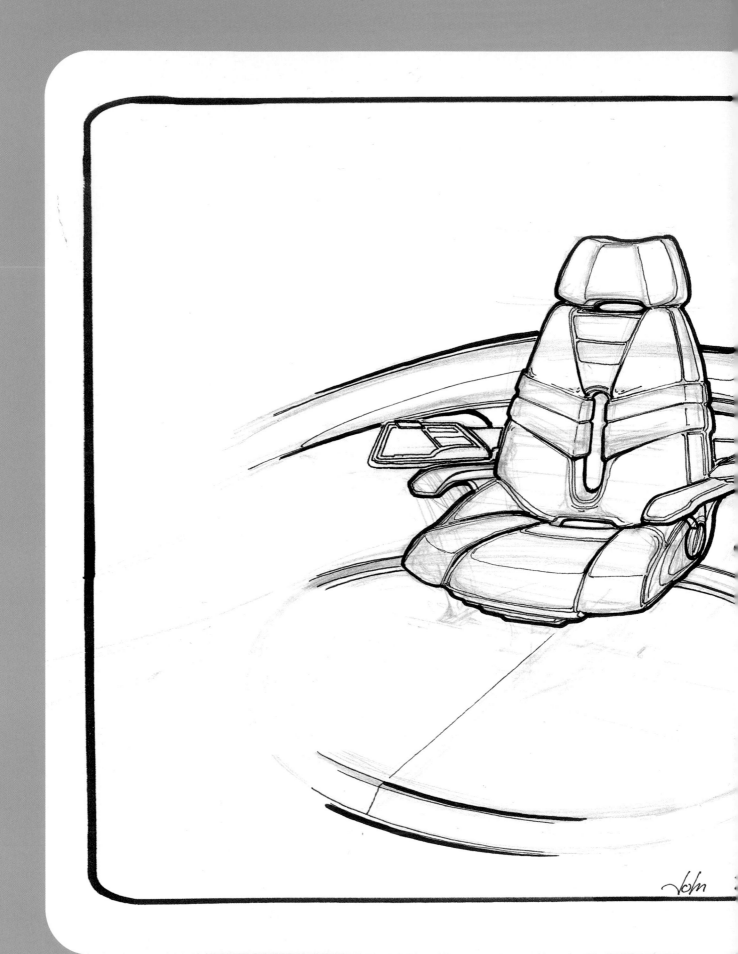

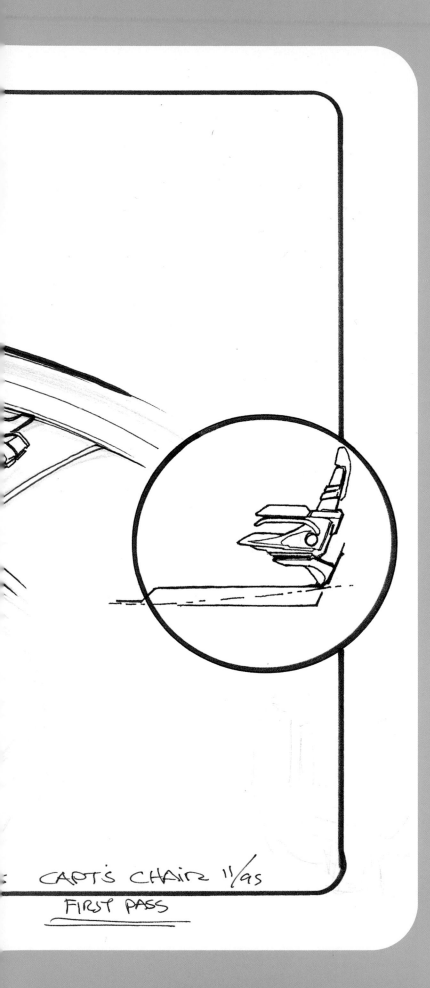

Another change to the bridge had to do with the platforms on which the characters' stations rested. On the *Enterprise*-D bridge, the three characters—Troi, Picard, and Riker—were all on the same level. On the new bridge, the captain's chair is slightly raised above the others, permitting him to oversee everyone. The chair itself is new, too, and bears more similarities to that from the *Defiant* than the one from the D. The lumbar area has been opened, and controls are set on either end of the seat.

◀ …AND THE CAPTAIN'S CHAIR.

Of course, there were other potential design changes that *didn't* work and were dismissed.

JOHN:

According to the script, all the stations were supposed to be facing the captain's chair, but when we did a rough pass on that, it just didn't look right.

Also, at one point, Troi's and Riker's stations are at something of a diagonal to the captain's chair, so that Picard can read the displays on the backs of their consoles. But those were eventually eliminated, since they wound up being too enclosing on the characters.

As for the captain, his console had a raised surface around the perimeter, which was covered with instructional diagrams, then an inset in the middle for main operations.

Mike Okuda, who along with his wife, Denise, was already enormously busy doing graphics work for *Deep Space Nine* and *Star Trek: Voyager*, provided graphics for the consoles and other equipment on the bridge. In fact, the Okudas collaborated with Shawn Baden, John Josselyn, Doug Drexler, Jim Van Over, and Anthony Fredrickson to put the finishing touches on the new bridge.

THE FINAL VERSION. ▶

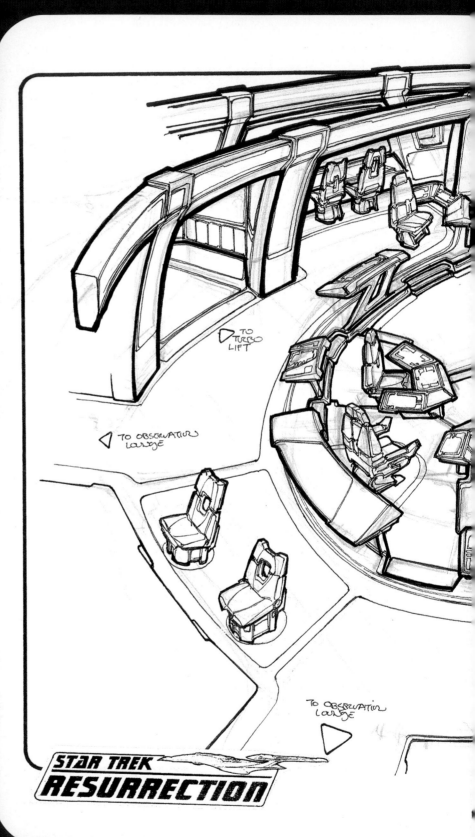

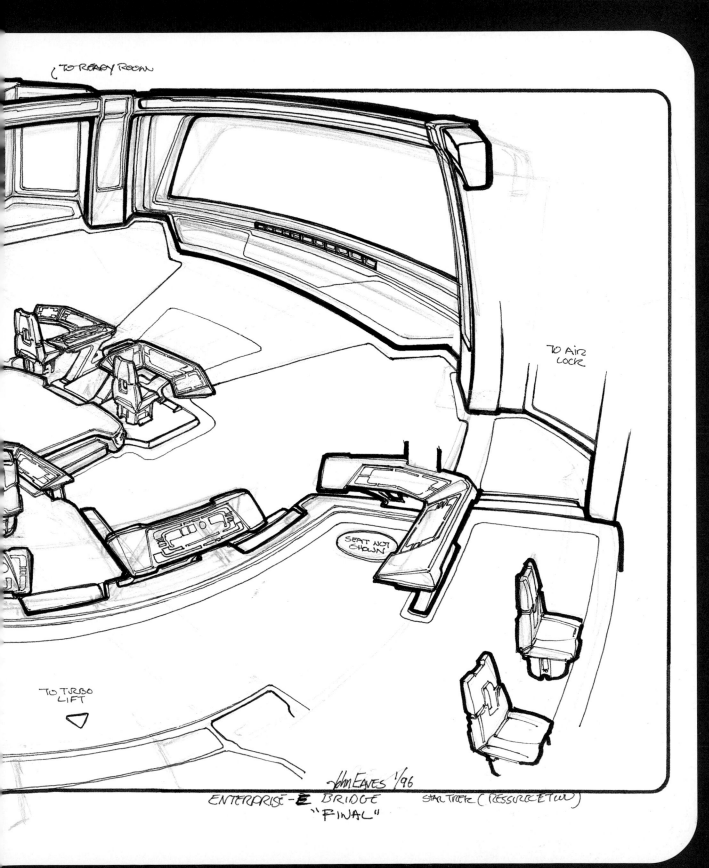

(TO READY ROOM

TO AIR
LOCK

SEAT NOT
SHOWN

TO TURBO
LIFT

John EAVES 1/96

ENTERPRISE-E BRIDGE   STAR TREK (RESSURECTION)
"FINAL"

STAR TREK

CAPTS, CHAIR, (BRIDGE) ENTERPRISE-E
"FINAL"

JohnEaves 1/96

▲

THE SEAT.

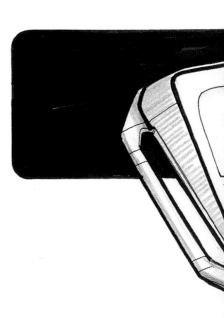

STAR TREK
RESURRECTION

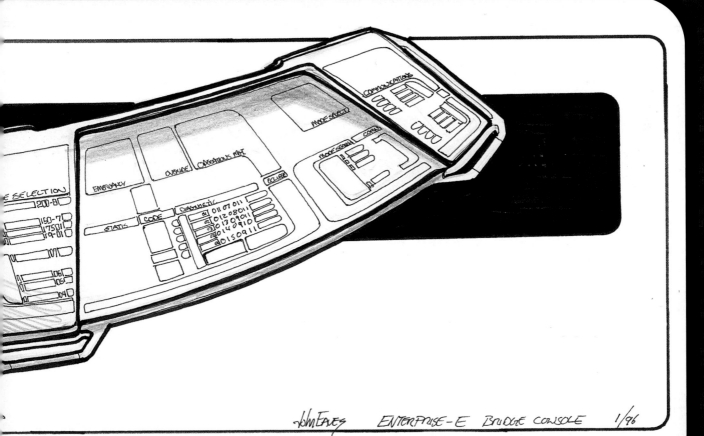

John Eaves   ENTERPRISE-E BRIDGE CONSOLE   1/96

UNDER CONSTRUCTION:
A BIRD'S-EYE VIEW OF THE
ENTERPRISE-E BRIDGE SET.

▲
CEILING DETAIL. ▶

A LITTLE PAINT, A LITTLE
CARPETING, A LITTLE LIGHTING...
AND YOU'VE GOT YOURSELF A BRIDGE.
Courtesy of John Eaves.

Even though the bridge was given a new, updated look, certain traditions—such as the viewscreen blinkies—remained.

JOHN:

Doug Drexler, who is quite the *Star Trek* expert, took a look at one of my sketches for the bridge and said, "Hey, you've *got* to have a row of blinkies—blinking running lights—under the view-screen. It's a tradition on every *Enterprise*. Those lights simply MUST be there."

Full compliance was swift. As time went on, however, Herman Zimmerman decided that the E should have a new type of viewscreen; rather than having a projection-type screen, he wanted an image to form in midair. In response, the hardy *Trek* art team designed a "screen" that was a light image projected from the floor and ceiling, rather like a two-dimensional holograph.

However, there remained the crucial issue of the traditional blinkies.

JOHN:

We wound up designing a detailed area on the floor that acted like a holographic projector array—and we attached the blinking lights to that. So when the viewscreen came on, the lights on the back of the bridge would go down, and an image would appear on our new viewscreen—with, of course, Doug's running blinkies.

To further tie the "past" to the future, these same "blinkies" were included on the tiny screen in Cochrane's *Phoenix* capsule.

SOME OF THE DAZZLING GRAPHICS,
COURTESY OF OKUDA AND COMPANY.

The Phoenix

At the same time that Eaves was working on the *Enterprise-E* bridge, he was also designing a very different sort of ship for Peter Lauritson: Zefram Cochrane's *Phoenix*, the ship that would make *Star Trek* "history" as the first faster-than-light vessel. The script called for it to be made from an old Titan missile, so this time John had measurements and specs to work from.

JOHN:

But it was still difficult, in the sense that I was trying to design a space vessel that was in our future—yet at the same time, in *Star Trek*'s "past." It's a tricky concept.

By this time, the *First Contact* art department had grown so large that it moved out of the main art department in *Deep Space Nine*'s office building, into a trailer closer to the sound stages where filming took place. The official headcount for the department consisted of Production Designer Herman Zimmerman; Art Director Ron Wilkinson; Set Designers Les Gobruegge, Bill Hawkins, Linda King, and Nancy Mickelberry; Scenic Artist Mike Okuda; Set Decorators John Dwyer and Bill Dolan (and crew); Art Department Assistants Penny Juday and Tony Bro and Todd Bushmiller; Costume Designers Deborah Everton and Gina Flanagan; and Concept Illustrators Joe Musso and John Eaves.

JOHN:

Now, when it comes to NASA and the rockets of the world, Mike Okuda has every book ever printed. So when it was time to design

DIANE CARR'S COOK SHACK
BIRTHPLACE OF THE PHEONIX CAPSULE

the *Phoenix*, Mike hauled about three or four books over to our trailer. There was one that showed all the dimensions of a Titan missilehead. The sets were to be constructed in Tucson, Arizona, in a place called Green Valley. The actual missile had been stripped down because of the Cold War treaty; it was in its silo, but was hollow—the main thrusters had been removed from the bottom, and there were holes in the center of the body so you could look inside and verify that it had been dismantled.

We knew we had to build and design a capsule that fit over the existing rocket warhead—after all, the ship was supposedly constructed after a major war had taken place. I started out by drawing a standard space capsule cone; I figured they had used whatever pre-existing technology they could find, then added to it whatever was needed.

I elongated the cone and gave it an outward curve, plus four riblets that have their widest base at the bottom, then tether together at the nose. I wanted something that had a double window on the front and two side windows—bubbled, so that you could

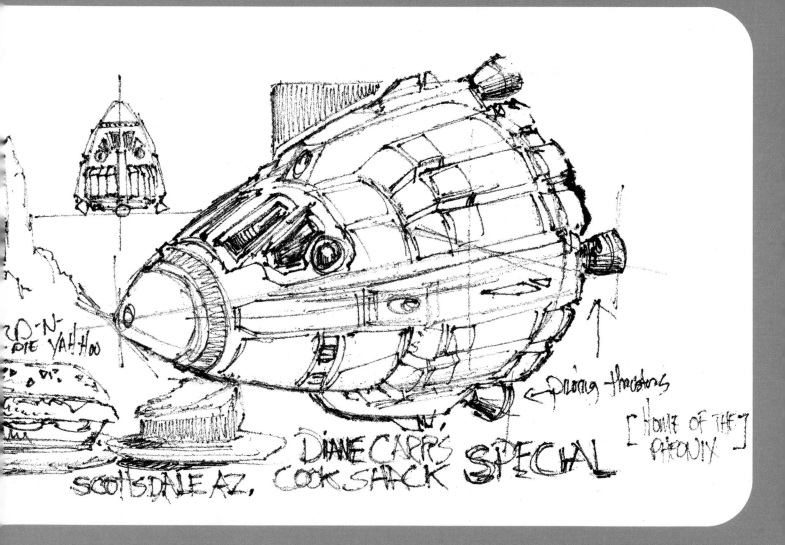

 EAVES'S *FIRST* "FIRST PASS" AT THE CAPSULE DESIGN, RECORDED ON A DINNER NAPKIN.

◄ **THE "BIRTHPLACE" OF THE *PHOENIX* CAPSULE:** WELL, OKAY, MAYBE JUST THE BIRTHPLACE OF THE FIRST SKETCH.

look out and around. However, construction-wise, a flat window was easiest, so that's what we did.

Once the nose-cone design was approved, it went to Clete Cetrone in construction. Without any plans, he built it from the above sketches (one three-quarter view, plus a top and side). He measured the actual nose cone on that missile and built it, according to the missile specs, adding his own artistic touches: facets here, surface details there.

When it came time to design the body of the *Phoenix*, however, Eaves was aware that Mike and Denise Okuda's *Star Trek Chronology* already had an illustration of Cochrane's famous first warp-drive ship. Eaves took a picture from the book over to Peter Lauritson, who said, "This is a nice ship, but we need a new ship that will fit inside that Titan missile."

JOHN:

So when I started drawing it, I tried to keep in mind what Mike and Greg [Jein, the model maker] had designed for *Chronology*. Doug Drexler, meantime, had done some computer designs based on Greg's rocket—how it would fit into a rocket body, how it would lift, separate, and break apart into a warp ship. The *Chronology*'s *Phoenix* simply didn't fit inside a Titan missile. So the design had to be based on a long body that would fit inside the Titan, with nacelles that folded out of the ship's center.

Since the specs on the Titan missile called for a width of only ten feet, there wasn't much room to work with; the nacelles were, by necessity, very narrow.

JOHN:

I made them as big as I could while still fitting them side-by-side, and having room for an apparatus to open up inside that ten-foot space.

I came up with a sleek, open-frame design with big thrusters on the bottom. Herman liked its direction, but decided it looked overdesigned, rather than being a collection of salvaged parts patched together onto a ship.

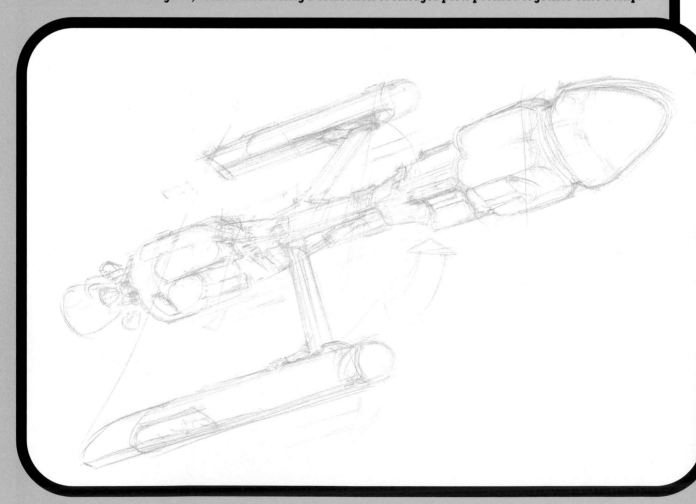

So it was back to the drawing board. This time, Eaves elected to work on two versions of the *Phoenix*'s body at once—one longer, one shorter, knowing that the Titan body would peel away to reveal the nacelles and the more detailed panels inside. The length of the *Phoenix* would determine the length of the solid fuel booster. When the time came to design the engine section with its fledgling warp drive, he wanted to come up with something special.

JOHN:

I didn't feel a section of typical NASA-type thruster engines would work, so I came up with a launch pattern on the bottom cone that consisted of segmented controls encompassing the engines. I had a main cone and four smaller cones coming off its sides for directional control.

Long ago, I saw a film on how they made the trigger for an atomic bomb. It had a large circumference of elements that had to all key off and fire at the same time in order to trigger the detonators. If the elements didn't fire simultaneously, the bomb wouldn't go off. I carried that same type of technology to the *Phoenix*. At the warp ship's base, above the thrusters, there are a ring of warp triggers that have to sequentially fire in order to thrust the ship forward for the nacelles to take over. Thus light-speed is achieved.

In keeping with the notion of "future past," Eaves gave the nacelles a look similar to that of the original *Enterprise*—or, at least, a look befitting the *Enterprise*'s ancestor: chunkier, with more details, and even a circular ball inset in the bud of the nacelle.

Eaves turned in both long and short versions of that basic design. Herman Zimmerman leaned toward the long version, but Rick Berman preferred the shorter. Berman also wanted the nacelle deployment struts lowered as far as they could go. Upon final approval, the sketches went to ILM so that Jeff Olson, John Goodson, and crew could start making the model that would be filmed. Meantime, Alex Jaeger started coming up with color schemes for the *Phoenix*.

JOHN:

John [Goodson] **and Bill George, all those guys up at ILM, they all worked so hard; I've never seen a drawing translate so accurately into a finished model. They came up with a beautiful color scheme for it—a gold capsule with a lot of silver framework on the rocket, with silver, white, and black graphics.**

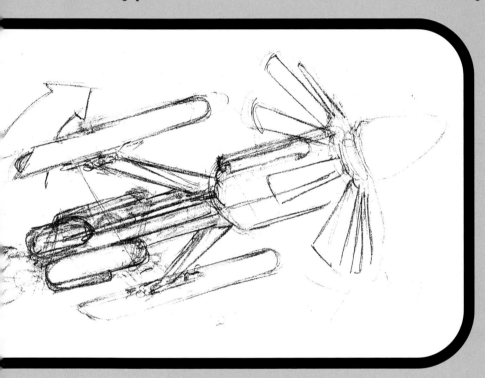

▲
◄ EARLY ROUGHS OF THE *PHOENIX*.

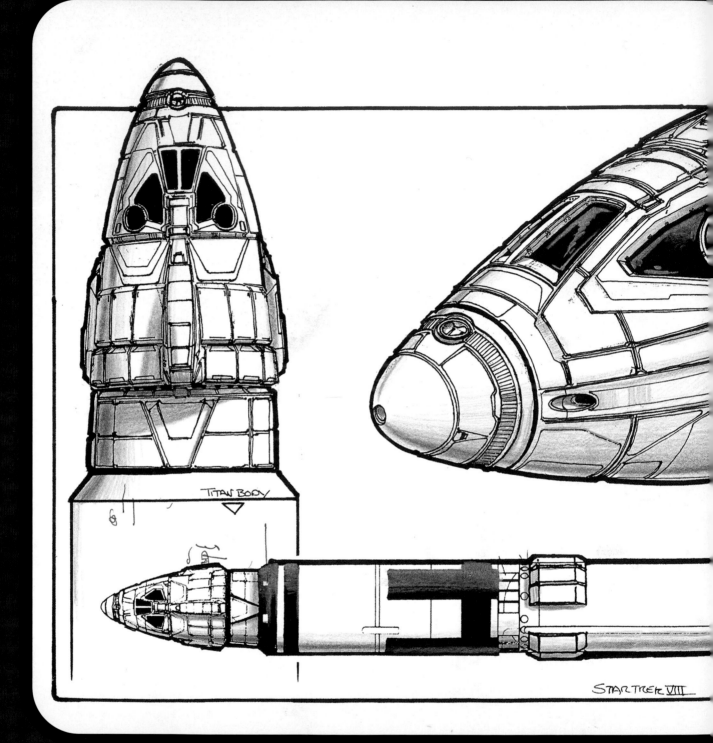

Titan Body

Star Trek VIII

▲ THE "OFFICIAL" FIRST PASS ON THE *PHOENIX* CAPSULE,
BY JOHN EAVES. NOTE BLUE INK SQUIGGLES—MADE BY
RICK BERMAN DURING A DISCUSSION WITH EAVES.

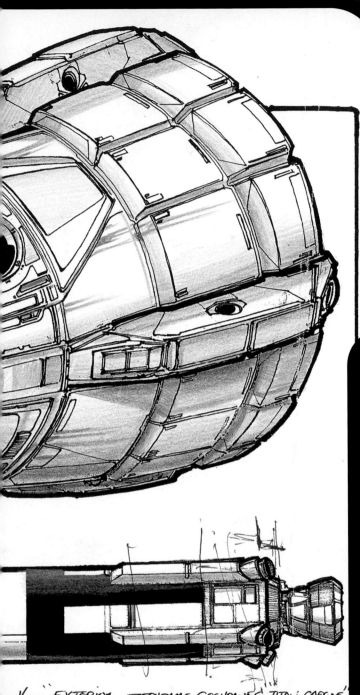

s/96 "EXTERIOR ZEPHRAME COCHRANES "TITAN CAPSULE"

EARLY DRAWINGS OF THE *PHOENIX*... ▶

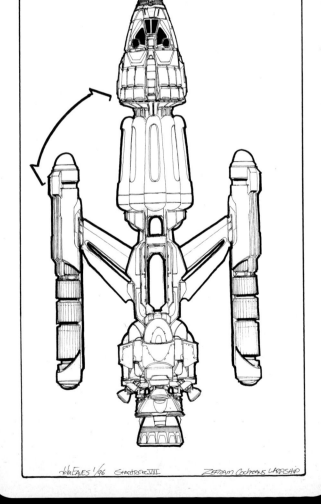

John Eaves 1/96   STARTREK VIII   ZEFRAM COCHRANES WARSHIP

▼

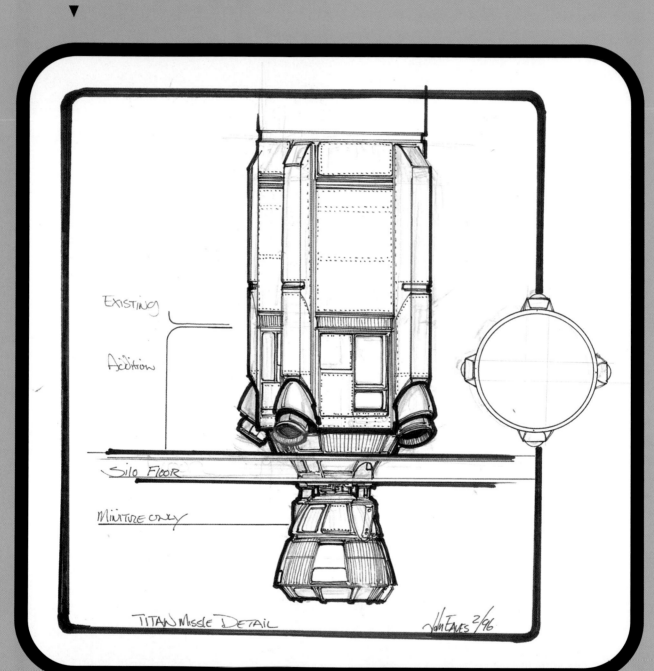

EXISTING

Addition

Silo Floor

Miniture only

TITAN Missle Detail

John Eaves 2/96

THE *PHOENIX* IN HER SILO, BY JOHN EAVES. ▶

PHOENIX IN SILO   "STAR TREK/BORG"   JohnEaves 3

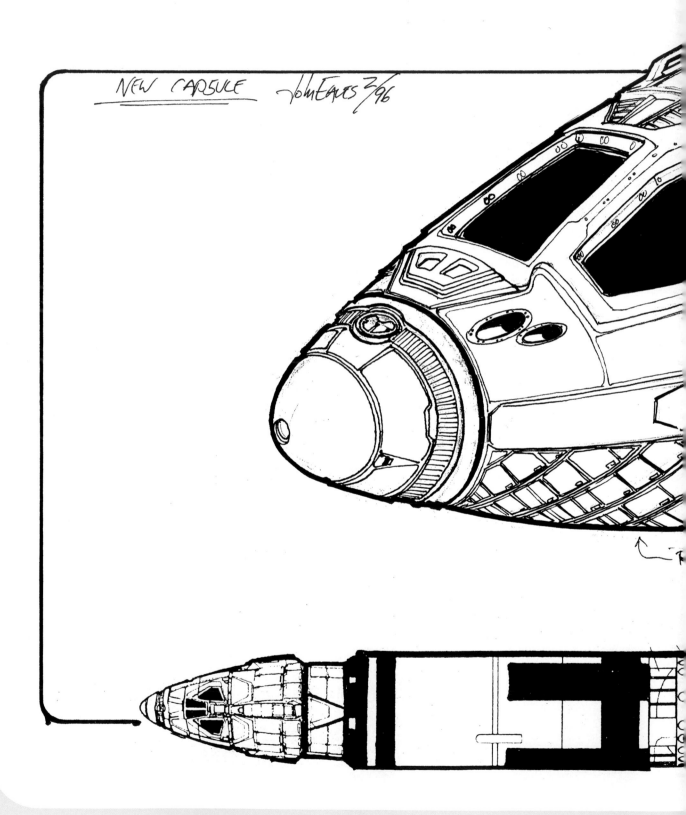

NEW CAPSULE   John Eaves 3/96

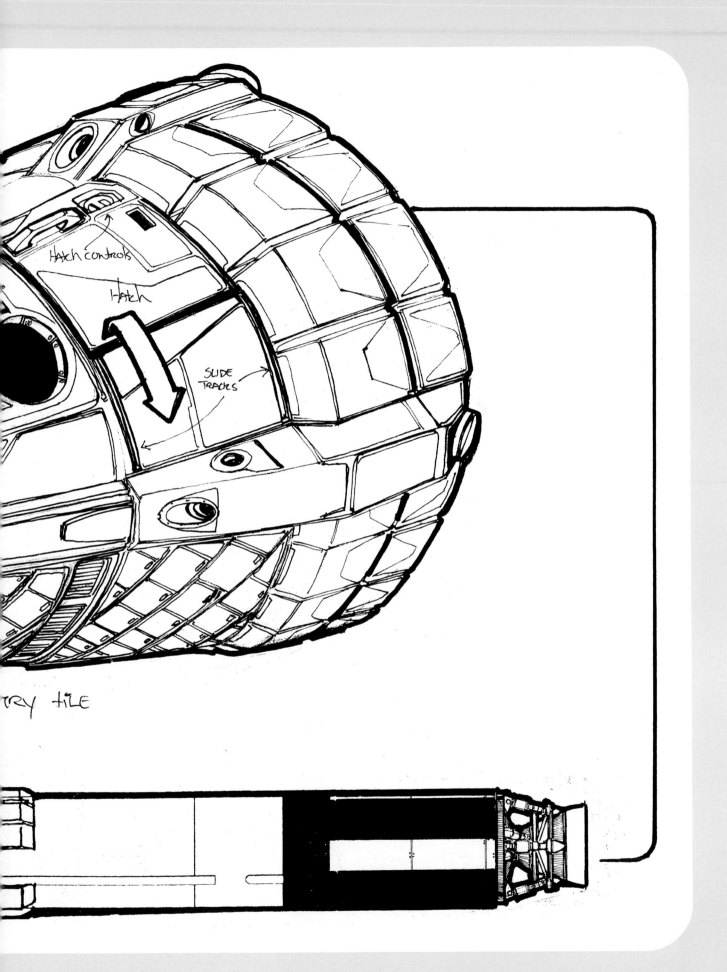

Hatch controls

Hatch

SLIDE TRACKS

...TRY tiLE

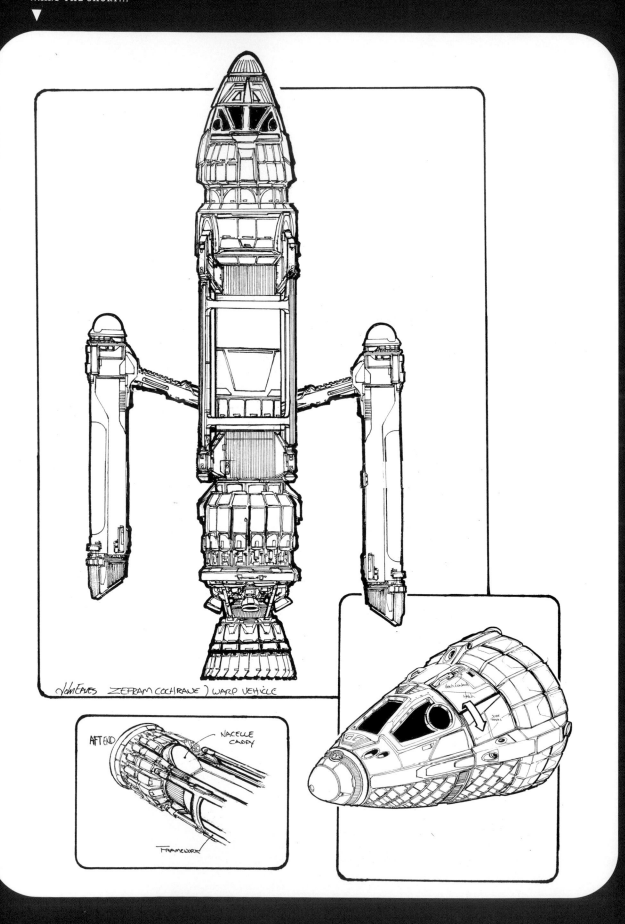

John Eaves ZEFRAM COCHRANE) WARP VEHICLE

AFT END

NACELLE CADDY

FRAMEWORK

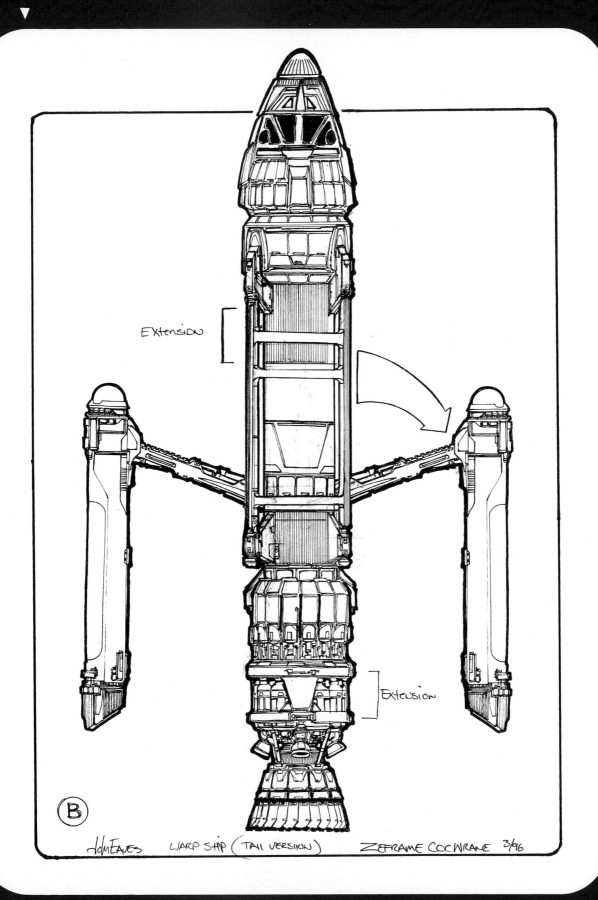

EXTENSION

Extension

B

John Eaves   WARP SHIP (TAIL VERSION)   ZEFRAME COCHRANE 3/96

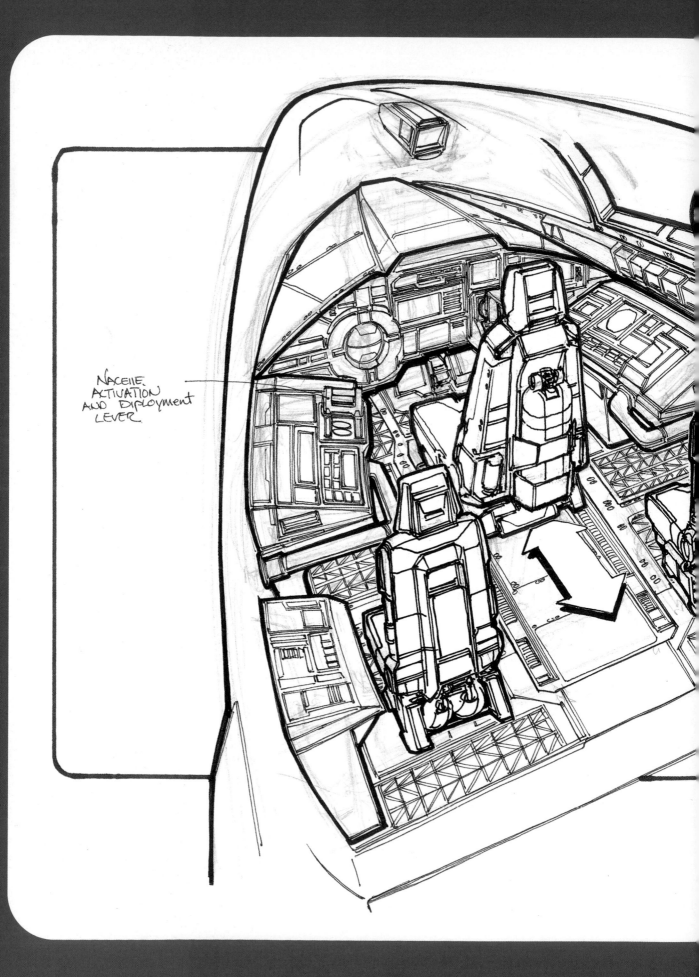

NACELLE.
ACTUATION
AND DEPLOYMENT
LEVER.

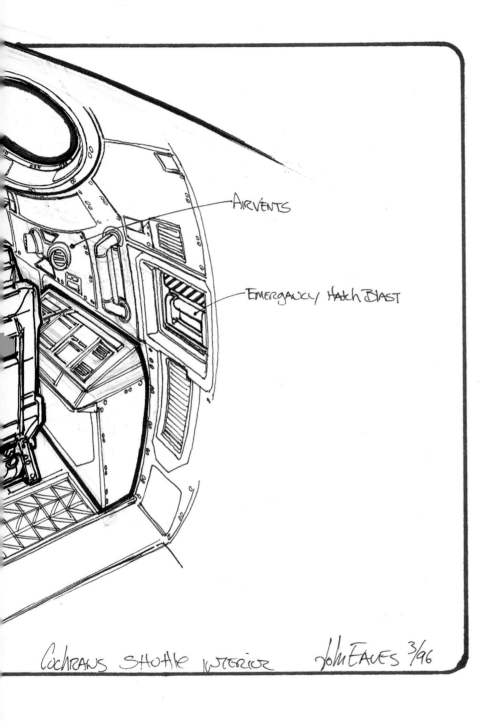

AIRVENTS

EMERGANCY Hatch Blast

Cochrans Shuttle interior   John Eaves 3/96

◄ THE UNAPPROVED DESIGN
FOR THE *PHOENIX* COCKPIT.

CLETE CETRONE'S AMAZING HANDIWORK:
THE LIFE-SIZED *PHOENIX* CAPSULE.
▼

ITS "SISTER SHIP," THE
MINIATURE OF THE CAPSULE. ▶

Courtesy of John Eaves.

Courtesy of John Eaves.

IT STILL REQUIRES
SOME ASSEMBLY. BUT...

...VOILA! A FULL-SIZE WARP SHIP
IN THE ARIZONA SILO SET.

▲
THE SMALLER MODEL, UNDER
CONSTRUCTION AT ILM.

But work on Cochrane's ship was far from done. One of the most important sequences in the film was the launch of the Titan missile, which would break apart in stages to finally reveal the warp rocket inside. At ILM, John Knoll and Alex Jaeger came up with the look of the launch sequence, all the way from the silo in Montana to deep in Earth orbit.

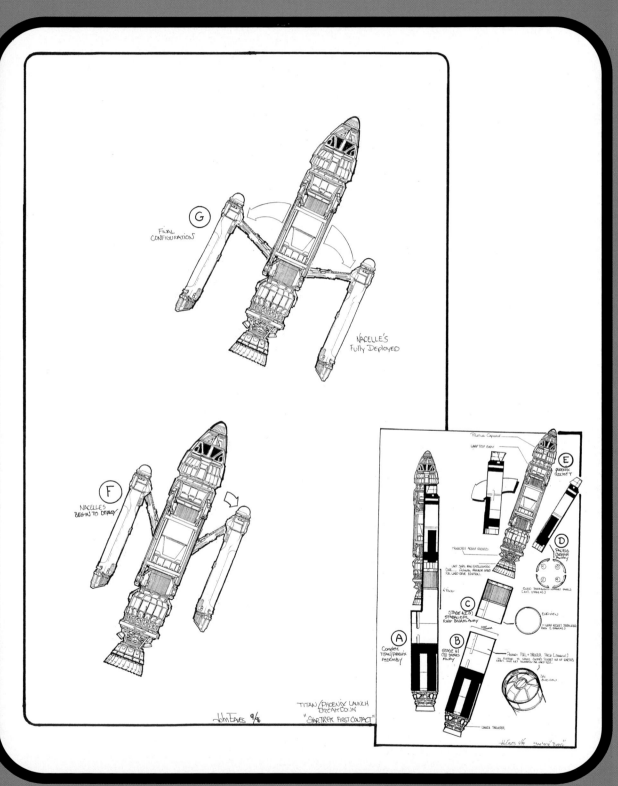

THE *PHOENIX* LAUNCH
SEQUENCE, EAVES SKETCH.

JOHN:

The next step was to design the stages of the missile, so we took an outline of the Titan from one of Mike Okuda's books, and we scaled down the drawing of the *Phoenix* to see how it fit inside the missile body. Then we segmented the rocket, so that its bottom half contains the main fuel and thruster, thus to achieve orbit. What remains above the solid-fuel stage is the siding that conceals the *Phoenix*. These panels break off into four individual panels; when those drop away, you're left with the warp rocket. I remembered the Apollo series, when they would show the camera view from behind the rocket as the stages broke free. I wanted that same type of look and feeling.

John Goodson at ILM decided at one point that three break-off panels would be better, so drawings were done with three panels; ultimately, however, it was decided to go ahead with four panels. Goodson and company also came up with an entire series of detail for the inside of the Titan. When the bottom half of the missile breaks free in the film, one can see the fuel tank exposed on the top; when the panels break off, one can also see a great deal of detailing on their interior. The finish on Goodson's model was metal foil that was burnished onto the surface, adding a look of authenticity to the final product: Bill George also had much to do with the look and texture used on the models.

CGI BY MIKE OKUDA AND DOUG DREXLER, OF THE *PHOENIX* IN HER SILO... ▼

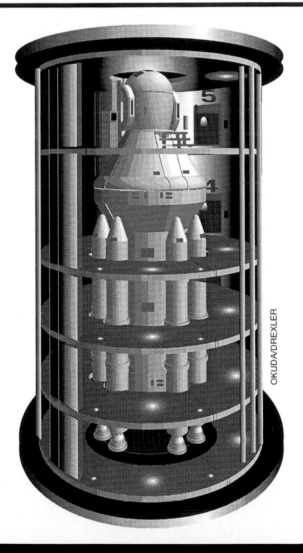

ASCENT VEHICLE/SILO

OKUDA/DREXLER

...AND HER STAGES OF ASCENT. ▶

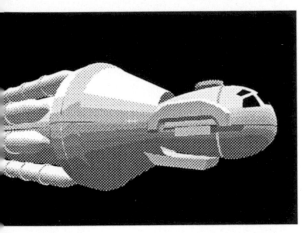

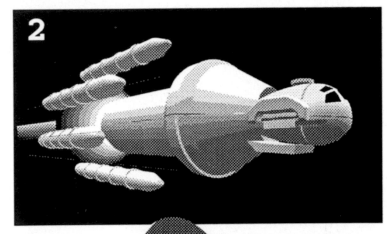

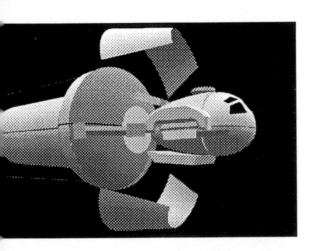

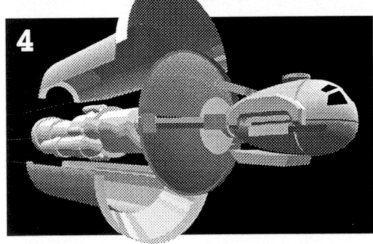

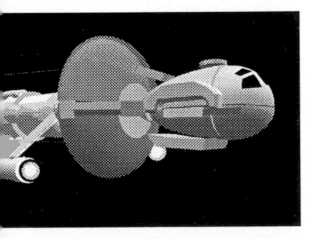

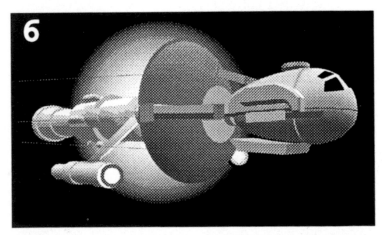

OKUDA/DREXLER

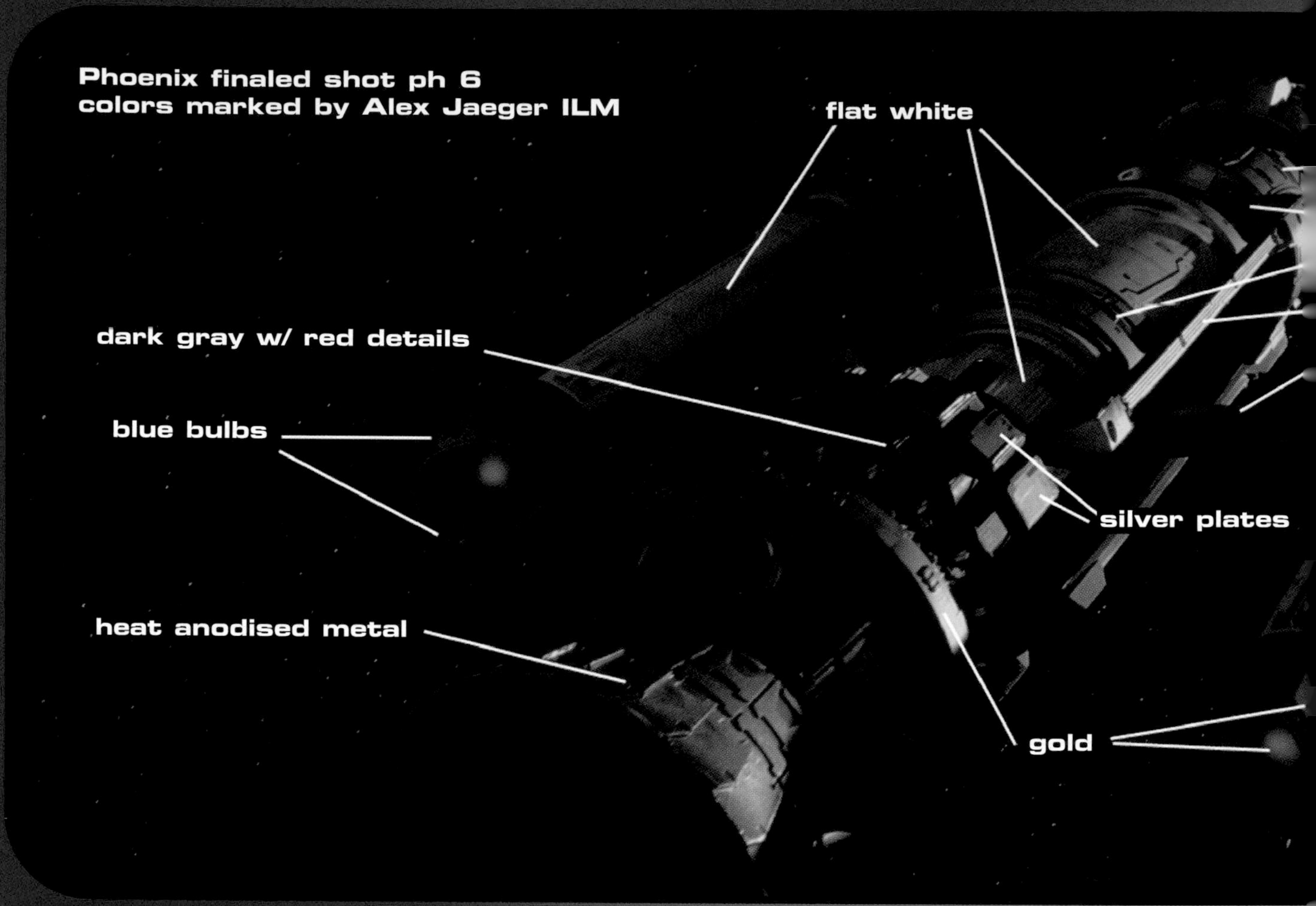

Phoenix finaled shot ph 6
colors marked by Alex Jaeger ILM

flat white

dark gray w/ red details

blue bulbs _____

heat anodised metal

silver plates

gold

capsule, gold (according to set piece)

copper plates with red decals

gold

red\orange bubble

gold

blue glowing engine side

dark gray

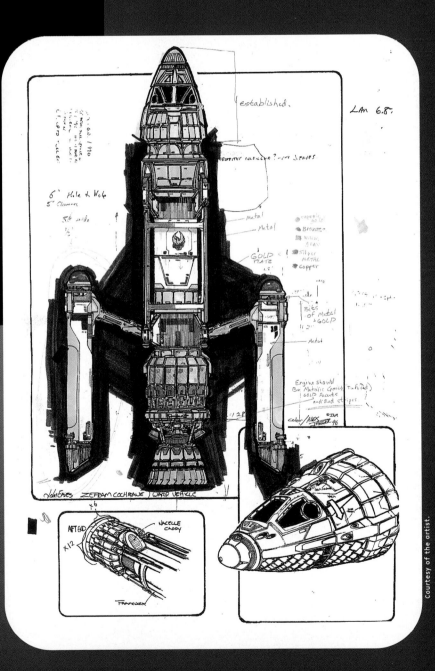

JAEGER'S COLOR SCHEME FOR THE *PHOENIX*.

CONCEPT SKETCHES FOR THE
PHOENIX LAUNCH, BY ALEX JAEGER.

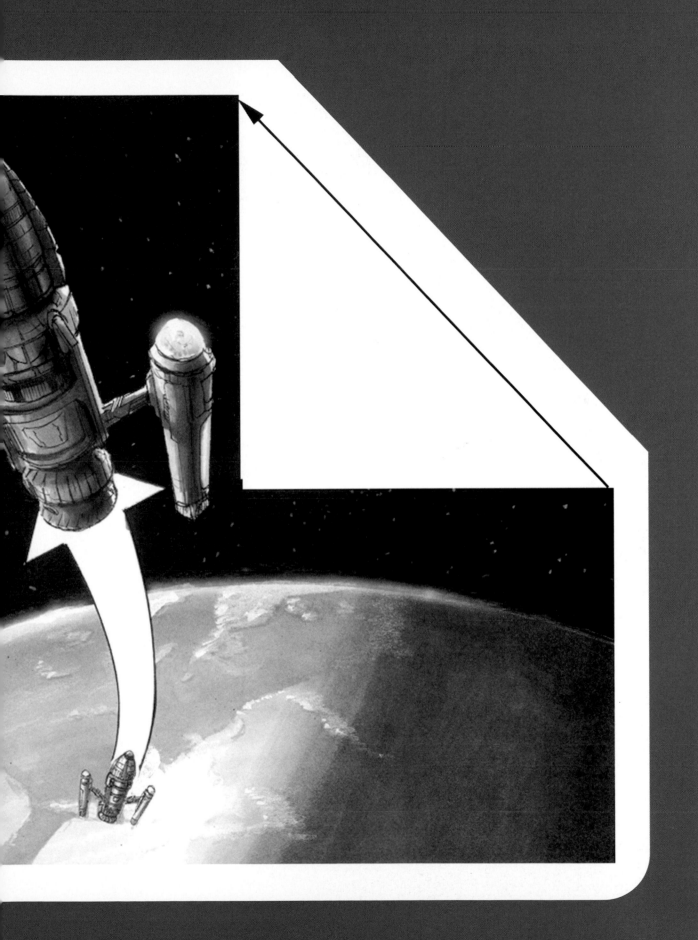

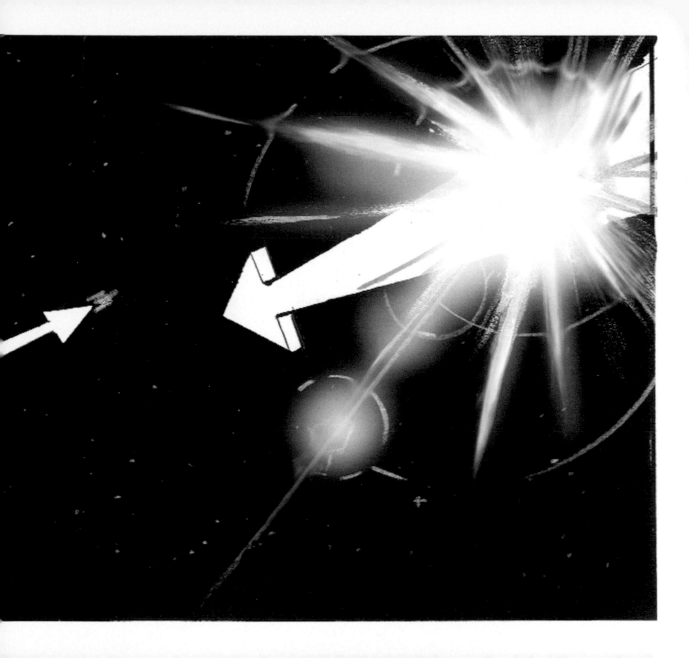

 CGI OF THE LAUNCH BY JAEGER.

THE FINAL RESULT:
THE *PHOENIX* SLIPS HER EARTHLY BONDS...

191

...AND SOARS INTO SPACE.

Think work was finished on Cochrane's rocket? Think again. The excitement was only beginning....

JOHN:

One beautiful morning, Herman ran into my office and said, "Stop what you're doing! We need a logo for the *Phoenix*, and we need it approved by eleven o'clock. This morning!"

The first thing I did was look at the clock; it was 9:45.

I'm from Phoenix originally, and immediately my mind was filled with images of phoenix birds. I especially remembered this one beautiful large abstract sculpture of a phoenix outside the Town and Country Mall, right in the heart of the city. Of course, I hadn't seen that image in about ten years, so for the life of me, I couldn't remember exactly what that thing looked like. I just knew I had to get a copy of it. And *fast*.

So I called every single gift shop I could think of in Phoenix and neighboring Scottsdale that might have a picture of the phoenix statue on a postcard or something. I finally came across a place called Apache Trading Company; a gentleman named Bud McClara answered the phone and patiently went through an entire rack of postcards looking for that particular statue. He remembered it, too, but couldn't find a photo of it. He did, however, find a card with some phoenix-bird graphics on it—and though he didn't have a fax machine there at the store, he very kindly walked down to another store and faxed this drawing to me.

In the meantime, I was drawing furiously as best as I could from memory, and came close to what the statue looked like. I didn't want to copy the image exactly, just use it as reference, since the posture of the wings was outstanding. The postcard pretty much confirmed the direction of the design. We put a "PHOENIX" graphic across the bottom, with this bird coming out of the flames and ashes. It was delivered to Herman within an hour, and he ran it (literally) over to Mr. Berman, who approved it.

Thank God and the Apache Trading Post for all their help!

THE BIRD THAT STARTED IT ALL: THE INFAMOUS AND
ELUSIVE PHOENIX FROM PHOENIX'S TOWN AND COUNTRY
MALL (DISCOVERED AFTER THE CRUNCH, OF COURSE).

John Eaves Alternate Version
5/96 Cochran's Rocket Logo

UNUSED *PHOENIX* LOGO, BY JOHN EAVES ("COCKY'S ROCKET").

▲

▶

THE CHOSEN LOGO BY EAVES.

PHX LOGO ♯1/96
ZEFRAME COCHRANE

▲

UNIFORM "PATCHES" FOR COCHRANE'S
FLIGHT CREW, BY DOUG DREXLER.
Courtesy of the artist.

ZEPHRAME COCHRANE

FIRST FASTER THAN LIGHT

EAVES'S FIRST PASS AT THE PATCH...

...AND HIS FINAL, APPROVED VERSION.

ZEFRAM COCHRANE

THAN LIGHT

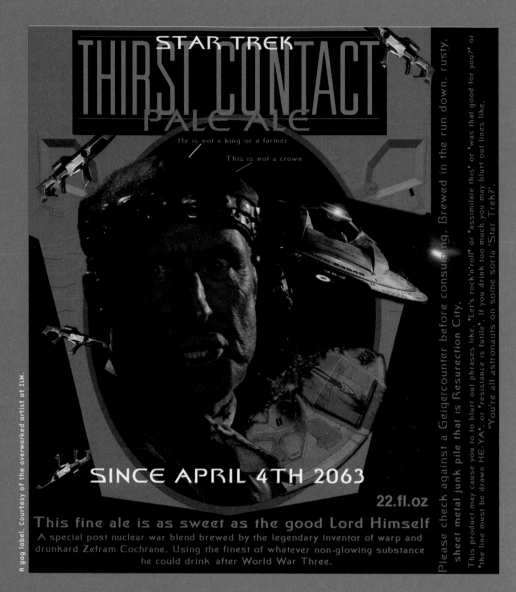

STAR TREK
THIRST CONTACT
PALE ALE

He is not a king or a farmer

This is not a crown

SINCE APRIL 4TH 2063

22.fl.oz

This fine ale is as sweet as the good Lord Himself

A special post nuclear war blend brewed by the legendary inventor of warp and drunkard Zefram Cochrane. Using the finest of whatever non-glowing substance he could drink after World War Three.

Please check against a Geigercounter before consuming. Brewed in the run down, rusty, sheet metal junk pile that is Resurrection City. This product may cause you to to blurt out phrases like, "Let's rock'n'roll" or "assimilate this" or "was that good for you?" or "the line must be drawn HE-YA", or "resistance is futile". If you drink too much you may blurt out lines like, "You're all astronauts on some sorta 'Star Trek'".

HEY, WAIT A MINUTE!
HOW'D *THIS* GET IN HERE?

Yet more work remained to be done on the *Phoenix*: the interior, which would appear in the warp-launch scenes featuring Riker, Geordi, and Cochrane. Set Designer Nancy Mickelberry and Eaves worked separately on concepts for the ship's interior design. For Eaves, the question was whether to give the *Phoenix* cockpit the look of an aircraft, such as the *Concorde*, or whether to go for a more "space-shuttle" look.

JOHN:

I decided to incorporate a bit of space-shuttle detail here and there, plus a few gyros and scopes. The design I came up with was seen as not being "future tech" enough, and the overall sketch was too complicated—too many panels, controls, setups. Nancy's design, on the other hand, was simple and

beautiful, with a lovely wrap-around console. Together we came up with a seating arrangement where Zefram sat forward of two passenger seats; if you view it from above and look down, the arrangement looks something like three bowling pins stacked in a triangle.

Finally, the construction department—Tom Arp, Jack Carroll, and their talented crew—took over and began building the set, while the scenic department— Mike Okuda, Shawn Baden, John Josselyn, and Anthony Fredrickson—went to work out the designs for switches, controls, and graphics. Discriminating film viewers, take note: the ever-whimsical Mike, an admitted *Buckaroo Banzai* fan, strategically placed a couple of *Buckaroo* "overthrusters" in the *Phoenix* cockpit. Find them, if you can....

The Endeavor

At long last, the *Phoenix* was done; the next item on Peter Lauritson's design list for John Eaves was a Federation starship, the *Endeavor*. If you can't remember seeing the ship in the movie, don't fault your memory: it wasn't there. Originally, the *Endeavor* was to have been a key ship in the opening battle against the Borg, and it was brought into being for the sole purpose of being gloriously destroyed. Eaves did about five "passes"—i.e., design sketches—of the ship, which reveal it to be in the *Reliant* and *Nebula*-class family.

However, the *Endeavor* became a "cutting-room floor" casualty when the script writers decided to replace it with the *Defiant*, in order to get Worf into the film and onto the *Enterprise*.

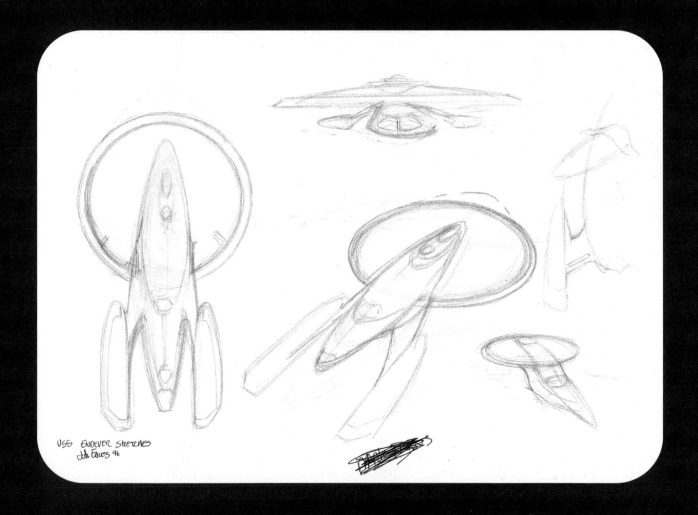

USS ENDEVER SKETCHES
Jhn Eaves 96

▲
EAVES'S FIRST — AND LAST — SKETCHES
OF THE CAST-ASIDE *ENDEAVOR*.

The Borg Sphere and Cube

First on Lauritson's list of Borg craft was the Borg sphere, the vessel in which the Borg travel back in an effort to change Earth's future. Spheres aren't new to science fiction audiences; both *Star Wars* and *Starman* utilized the shape.

JOHN:

Finding a new way to execute a spherical design that wasn't reminiscent of either film was difficult, but I did my darnedest to make it as different as possible. The details are extremely faceted low relief, combined with high relief to cause a series of multiple planes. We also left cylindrical openings at the north and south poles where all the detail comes to an edge, then cascades down into a half sphere. Looking down on it, you can see a "dome inside a dome." The ship is painted a rich, deep indigo with gold and silver details.

EARLY DRAWINGS OF
THE BORG SPHERE,
BY JOHN EAVES.
▼

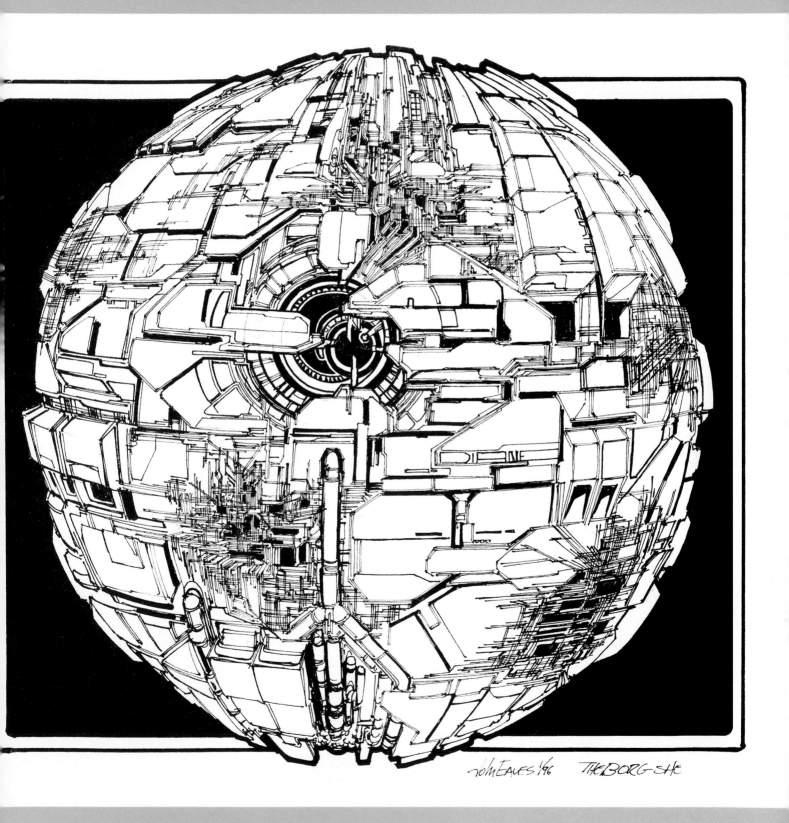

"BORG SPHERE" - FINAL   JohnEaves 1/96

TIME TRAVEL SHIP "STAR TREK BORG"

▲ NOTE THE MOVIE'S TITLE,
USED FOR A BRIEF TIME AFTER
RESURRECTION WAS DROPPED.

▶

THE STUNNING RESULT: A "BEAUTY
SHOT" TAKEN OF ILM'S MODEL OF
THE BORG SPHERE. Courtesy of ILM.

As for the Borg cube—well, originally the script called for it *not* to be a cube, but a tetragon. This caused some concern among the art department staff, who were unable to find the term "tetragon" in the dictionary. However, persistence and research finally paid off; the term, it was discovered, indicated an odd-shaped rectangle. So that's where the design began: variations on the tetragon.

JOHN:

The first one I did had beveled edges and deep canyons throughout; I was trying to get away from the familiar *Next Generation* series cube. (As always, we wanted to give the filmgoing audience much more than what they'd already seen on television.) I did three or four passes in the rectangular shape. As time went on, Rick Berman, Ron Moore, and Brannon Braga rewrote the scenes, returning to the original cube style of the Borg ship.

IT'S A BIRD, IT'S A PLANE, IT'S A...UM...ER...TETRAGON. WE THINK. AN EARLY EAVES SKETCH. ▶

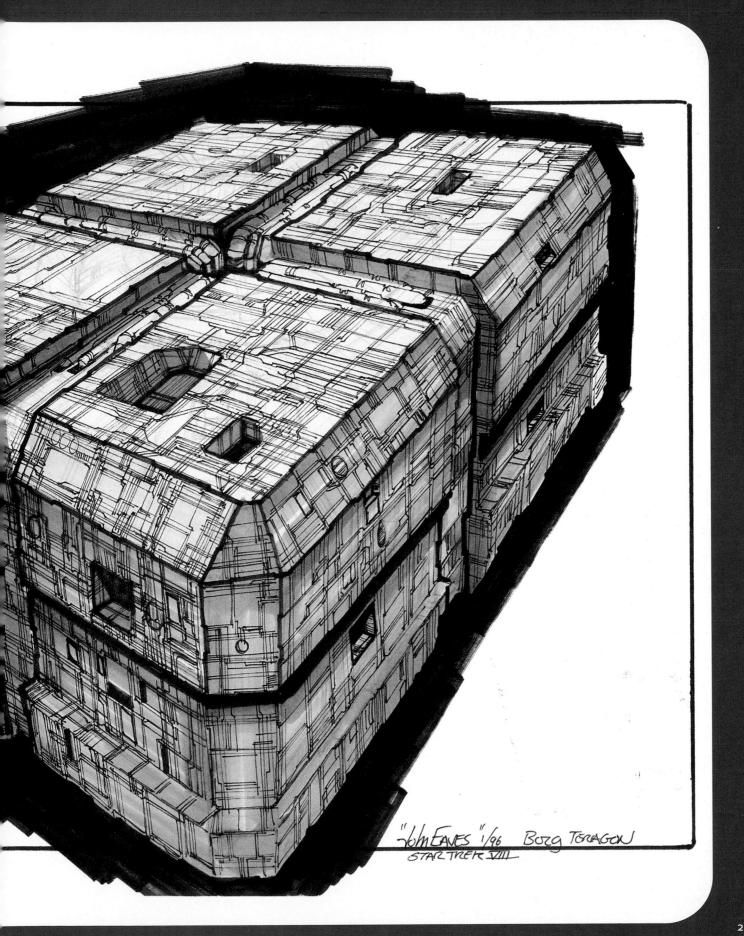

"John Eaves" 1/96   Borg Teragon
STAR TREK VIII

PORT FOR BORG SPHERE

TETRAGON SHOWING THE SPHERE'S EXIT PORT.

The original *TNG* cube was constructed of plastic model parts in multiple layers and lit from within; while it had a good amount of detail for television, the model would not photograph with sufficient scale for the big screen. A new design based on the cube shape was needed.

JOHN:

There's no mathematical pattern in the designs; instead, I did this odd offset where one section of detail would go one way, then angle off in a bizarre, nonsensical (to us nonassimilated types, at least) direction. Then I added insets and cutaway details, and a fine piping that went all over the ship. Some structures were left exposed, others were covered with pipe, and still others led into chambers.

NOW, **THERE'S A POLYGON WE'RE FAMILIAR WITH:** AN EARLY PASS AT THE BORG CUBE.

▶

John Eaves 2/96 Borg Ship

John EAVES 3/9
"FINAL" APPROVED

EST FASHION IN DESIGNER BORG SPACECRAFT

STAR TREK BORG

After a large number of sketches, the cube was approved and sent on to Industrial Light & Magic for construction. In order to get the greatest possible detail, Jeff Olson, Bill George, and John Goodson made the main body of the model from layers of brass etch, with modeled pieces placed sporadically throughout. Again, the colors reflected the dark tones of the sphere.

JOHN:

Because of the great intricacy of detail in the sketches, certain elements could be hidden—and were, in the Borg sphere. If you look very carefully at the lines, you can find the names of my wife, Diane, and my daughters, Olivia and Alicia. What's funny about this is that Playmates put out a toy Borg sphere—which just happens to contain the first initial of everyone's name.

Courtesy of ILM.

Courtesy of ILM.

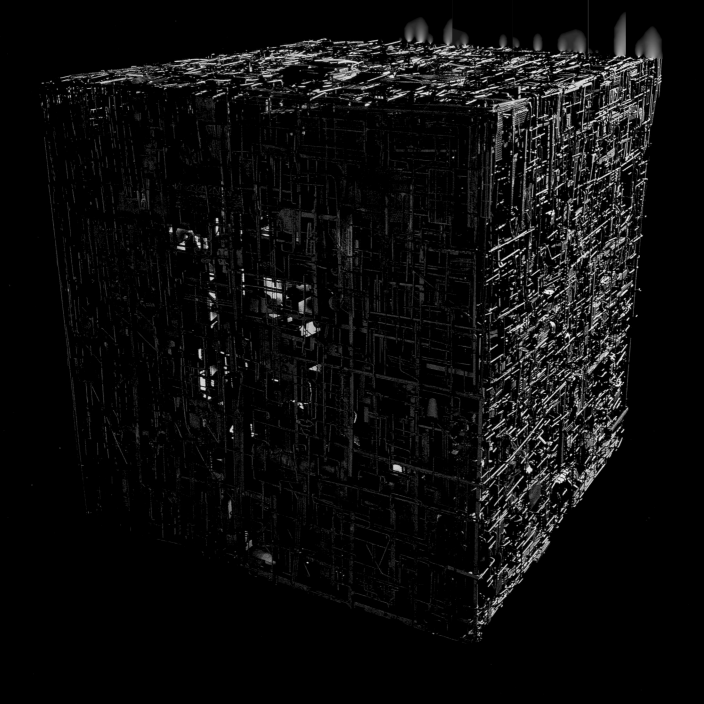

The Borg cube model used for
the *ST:TNG* television series.

◀ **Finally, a use for recycled paper clips:**
A close-up of the ILM model, showing the
cube's incredibly intricate details.

The Vulcan Lander
the T'Plana Hath

Early on, the new *Star Trek* film's title was changed from *Resurrection* to *First Contact*—and for good reason, of course, since the ending of the movie depicts a pivotal moment in *Star Trek* "history": the first encounter between Earthlings and an alien race. Once it was decided *which* aliens would make an appearance, the task of designing an appropriately Vulcan vessel began. (For all you trivia buffs: screenwriter Ron Moore christened it the *T'plana-Hath*, after the Vulcan matriarch-philosopher mentioned in *Star Trek IV: The Voyage Home* as originator of the quote, "Logic is the cement of our civilization with which we ascend from chaos using reason as our guide.")

Once John began researching Vulcan spacecraft, he discovered a surprising fact: Only two Vulcan vessels had ever appeared in *Star Trek*, one in an episode of *TNG*, and one on the silver screen, in *Star Trek: The Motion Picture*. And neither ship bore any similarity to the other. That left open an opportunity to go in a completely new direction.

JOHN:

I decided to make the ship more artistic than aerodynamic, and to take its design essence from the sea; if you looked down on the craft, you might feel you were looking at a starfish—with three limbs instead of five. Usually crafts—human crafts, at least—are designed with an even number in mind, for balance. Well, this structure has balance, only with an odd number of pieces, and with curves instead of straight lines. The main body of the craft is triangular; from it extend three arms containing the engines and propulsion systems. Those "arms" serve a double purpose—as landing legs. The bottom of the engines are also triangular, and the bottom of the landing foot also has an open-faced triangle. When the legs are in flight position, the open-faced triangle on the landing foot makes a thrust-ring around the bottom of the engine. When the legs deploy for landing, the fork that makes the thrust-ring drops down and

makes the landing platform with the main hatch situated in the center of the foot. In turn, each leg of the vessel has a hatchway.

Herman really liked it right away, so I sent it on to Mr. Berman, who called and said, "This is exactly the ship I want." I continued doing the detail sketches; Peter Lauritson and David Takamura were heavily involved with the final designs, in order to ensure the ship's functions were something the CGI modelers could make look good on the big screen.

◄

AN EARLY SKETCH OF THE VULCAN LANDER, *T'PLANA-HATH*.

►

AN EARLY LANDING SEQUENCE, BY JOHN EAVES.

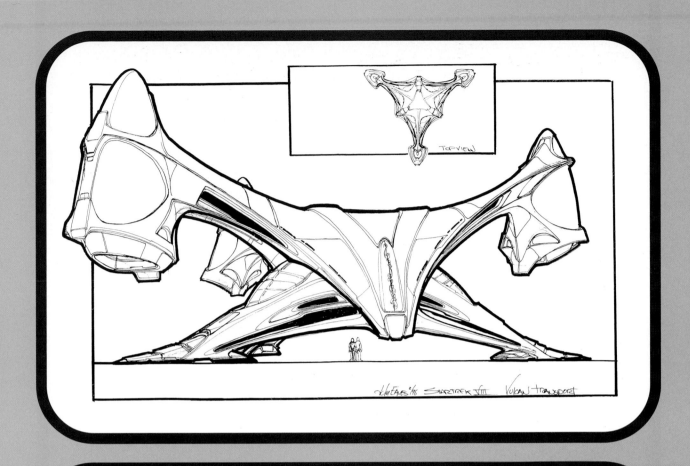

John Eaves '96   STAR TREK VIII   Vulcan transport

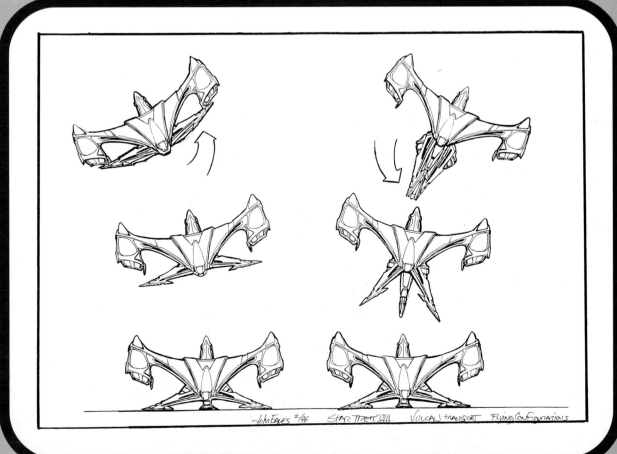

John Eaves ²/96   STAR TREK VIII   Vulcan transport   Flying Configurations

Although things went smoothly at the beginning, with the very first design being approved, problems arose.

JOHN:

I had trapped myself with this design: from a three-quarter or a top view I could draw it just fine. But I found it almost impossible to figure out how it would look in other angles, because all the bizarre compound curves had minds of their own—making accuracy insanely frustrating to achieve when I tried to put it on paper. It wound up being the hardest ship I'd ever drawn. I actually had to make a miniature of it just so I could have a reference to draw from. That little model ultimately became the study model for the CGI artists at Vision Arts and Pacific Ocean Post.

Courtesy of John Eaves.

The Vulcan
ship miniature,
TOP view...

...and **FRONT**.
▶

Courtesy of John Eaves.

Right around the same time, Peter Lauritson called Eaves to discuss another challenging aspect of the Vulcan ship. A full-size model had been made of the *T'plana Hath*'s landing foot from one of the detail sketches. It was to be built in the forest for live-action photography; later optical and matte paintings would be provided by Matte World. Lauritson needed sketches demonstrating how the set and painting would fit together for the shot. Cue the illustrator. . . .

JOHN:

Once the foot was constructed and Peter and David looked at the concept sketches from Matte World and me, they felt that the landing configuration didn't produce the best angle of the Vulcan ship. So they had me redesign the leg deployment so that the main body swiveled away from the landing claws, making the ship come into a forward-facing position with one foot squarely in front of the ship. If you looked down on the craft, it would appear to have six appendages rather then three.

It took a lot of work to make those legs come down. We had to change the way they were angled, because where the engines were concerned, the body tapered down to a point and was so long when the legs needed to move, that it looked like the ship was on "tiptoes"—that the legs were too high above position to accommodate the shape. Once we changed the angle, though, a lot of problems were ironed out, including the one I had making the miniature. (I thought it'd take me two weeks, max, but it wound up taking six and a half to flesh out the mechanics of the design and make the model accordingly.)

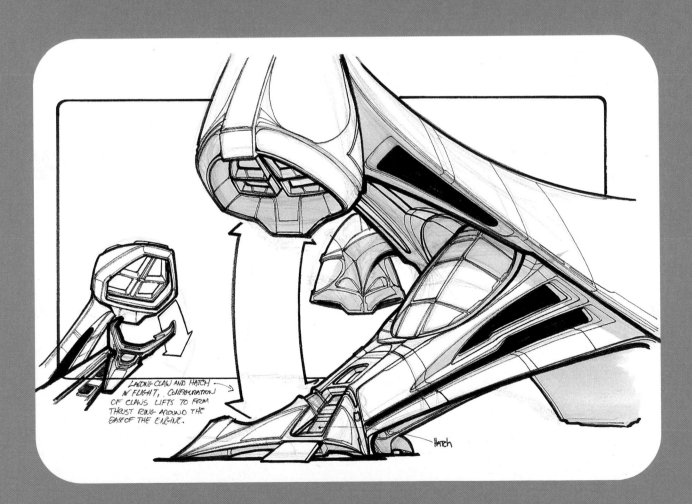

LANDING CLAW AND HATCH IN FLIGHT, CONFIGURATION OF CLAWS LIFTS TO FORM THRUST RING AROUND THE BASE OF THE ENGINE.

▲

DETAIL OF LANDING CLAW AND HATCH. SKETCH BY EAVES.

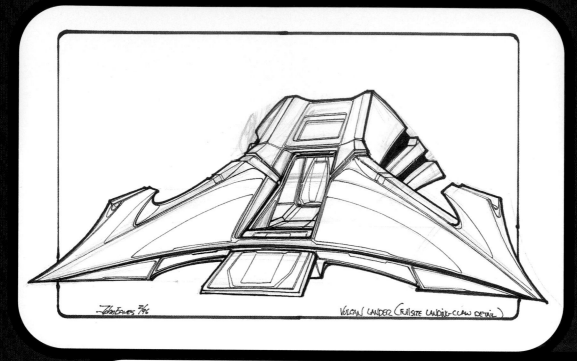

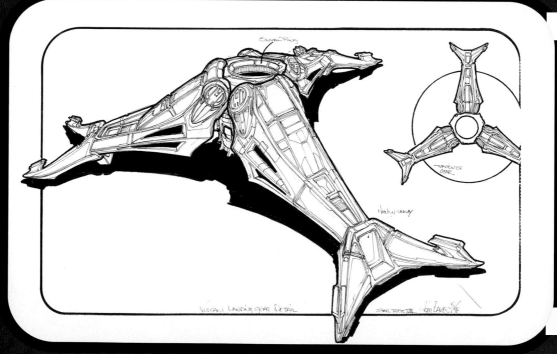

▲
THE REWORKED VERSION OF
THE LANDING GEAR.

▶
THE NEW, IMPROVED LANDING SEQUENCE.

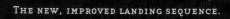

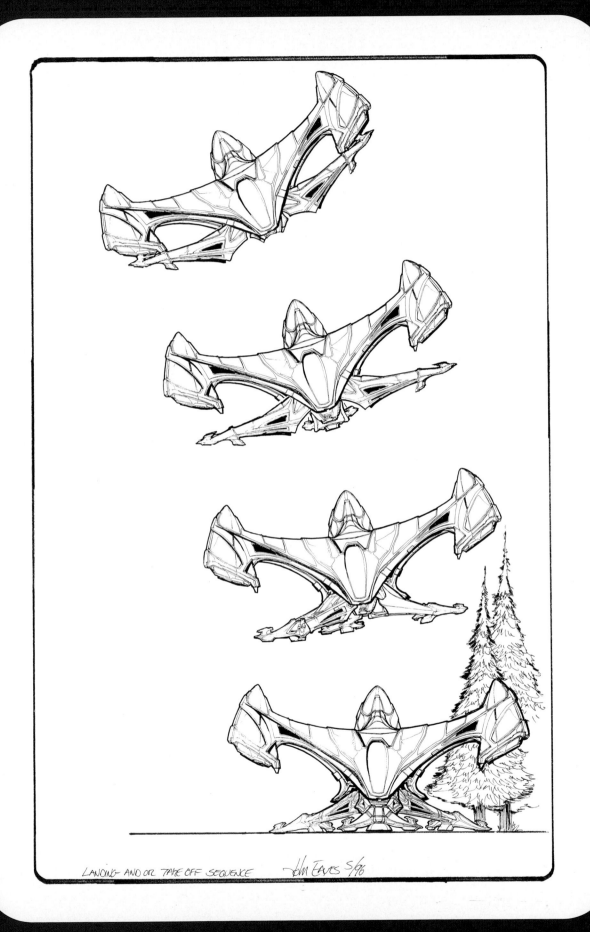

LANDING AND OR TAKE OFF SEQUENCE   John Eaves 5/96

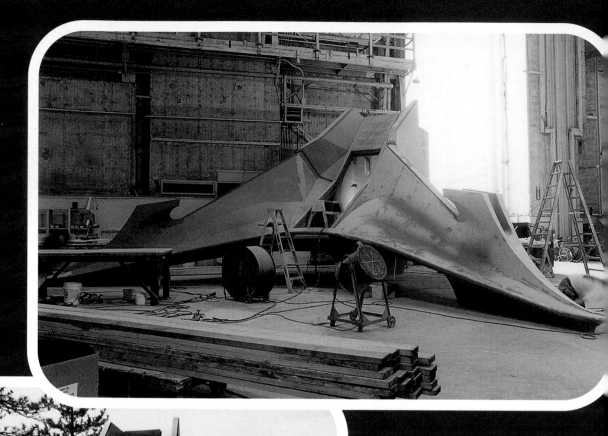

While the *T'plana-Hath*'s basic shape remained the same throughout the design process, modifications were made to the engines (reducing their number and simplifying them) and the exterior lighting. At one point, a sketch was done in which the ship's lights shot straight up like those of the Luxor Hotel in Las Vegas; but in the end, the designers at Pacific Ocean Post and those at Matte World produced the lights, which bathed the ship in secondary and "bounced" lighting.

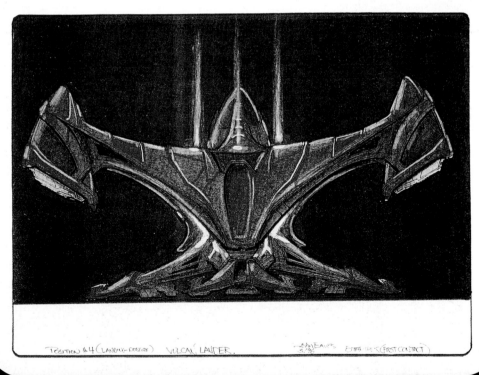

VARIOUS EXPERIMENTS IN LIGHTING THE SHIP'S EXTERIOR.
THE THIRD—AND MOST BRILLIANTLY LIT—APPEARED IN THE FILM.

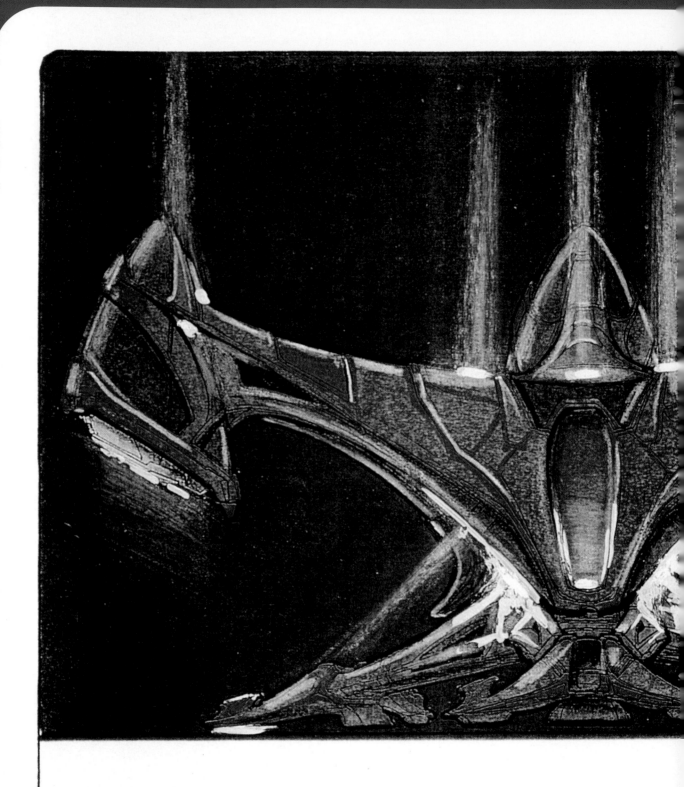

POSITION #4 (LANDING POSTURE) VULCAN LANDER.

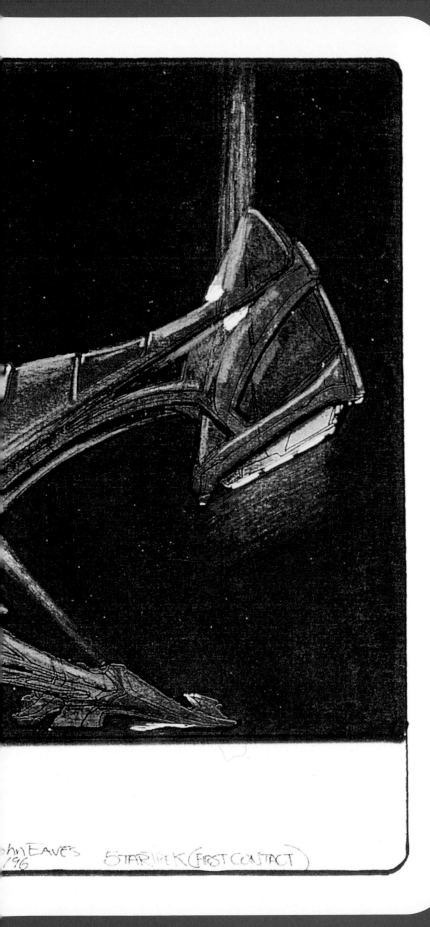

JOHN EAVES
'96   STAR TREK (FIRST CONTACT)

One problem facing our intrepid design crew was the ship's markings. The *I-pland-Hath* had to appear distinctly Vulcan enough to suit the strict scrutiny of *Star Trek* fans; at the same time, graphics whiz Mike Okuda wanted to keep the audience mystified as to the identity of the "first contact" aliens until the very instant the first Vulcan lowers his hood to reveal those unmistakable ears. Mike felt that the Vulcan logo of a circle pierced by a smaller triangle was simply too recognizable, and so instead, Vulcan calligraphy appears down one face of the craft. (This is the same "ancient writing" that was seen on Spock's burial robe in *Star Trek II: The Wrath of Khan* and *Star Trek III: The Search for Spock*.) Finally, Okuda decided that the inscription was also too much of a clue, so it was removed. Once again, Herman Zimmerman worked his magic with the color scheme, selecting from rich palette of purples and golds.

THE VULCANS ARE COMING, THE VULCANS ARE COMING
THE CGI VULCAN SHIP COMPOSITED ON A
LIVE-ACTION PLATE BY PACIFIC OCEAN POST

THE SAME, WITH DUST COMPOSITED
AS A RESULT OF THE "LANDING

The *Enterprise-E*

Corridor Set

"**S**ee what you can come up with," Herman Zimmerman had told Eaves, leaving the design for the *Enterprise* corridor–where many of the harrowing encounters between the Borg and the crew were to take place–wide open.

JOHN:

The shape is basically a horseshoe (I mean, I'm from Arizona; what other good shapes to design with *are* there?)–a wide U with a dropped notch in its center. Down that notch, I ran a section of overhead lights; then it returns back up and makes a little alcove on the top. We also had side panels with narrow, long displays that could be used for monitors or whatever else was needed, and handrails on the inner curves. Herman wanted the panels to be removable, so that when the Borg assimilate the ship, the old panels could be replaced with "Borg panels." Atop those "Borg panels" were "Borg alcoves," designed by Bill Hawkins. The alcoves were used to house inactive Borg, so that the corridors and decks were lined with Borg drones.

In addition, the very versatile corridors were used for hatches for lifeboats (aka the escape pods).

JOHN:

We made a section of corridor with all these hatches that folded up; they were vacuum-formed pieces. John Dwyer and Bill Dolan were the set dressers on the film, and John D. came up with this vacuum-formed piece he'd found that was–believe it or not–the hood off an old Camaro. And it made a *perfect* hatch.

We also wound up designing a lot of "ends," which are pieces that you can put at the back of a particular set, to create different areas of the ship. We could take a corridor and put a Jefferies tube end piece on it, or a hatchway. And we had a lot of corridor–two full quarter-circles of it, with a couple of T-intersections and walkways. You could walk for a good five minutes from the engine room set through Jefferies tubes without ever walking out of the set. There was also the big main door to engineering that Nancy Mickelberry had come up with. She put a second level of corridor above that, and you still had another story-and-a-half of warp core going up. The set was immense! Nancy and Herman worked together for a long time designing it (after all, it had to seem "Federation-style" and then "Borgified"). The set had many neat areas, many of which never made it into the finished film.

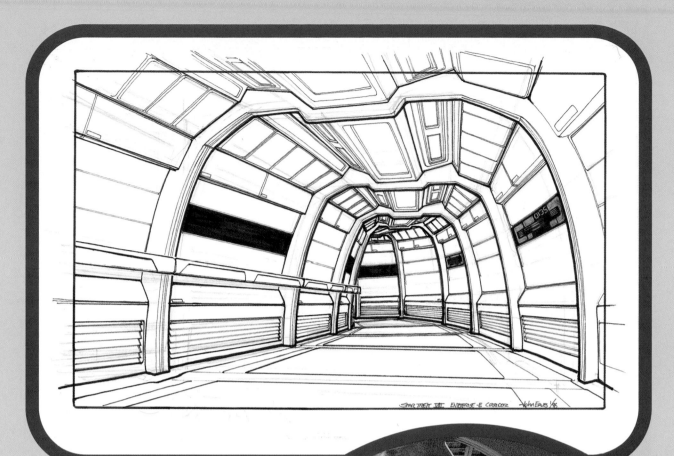

▲
THE *ENTERPRISE*-E "HORSESHOE"
OF A CORRIDOR. SKETCH BY EAVES.

►
**YOU MEAN YOU DIDN'T KNOW
STARSHIPS WERE MADE OF WOOD?**
THE SET BEGINS TO TAKE SHAPE.

Courtesy of John Eaves.

▲

ONE WAY TO COOL OFF A BORG-HOT SHIP.

◄

COME TO THINK OF IT, WHERE
DO THEY PUT THEIR TRASH?

Courtesy of John Eaves.

◀ Lights...

▼ Carpets...

Courtesy of John Eaves.

ACTION!

BILL HAWKINS'S BORG ALCOVE.

Courtesy of Bill Dolan.

▲
A COUPLE OF CORRIDOR "ENDS."
◄

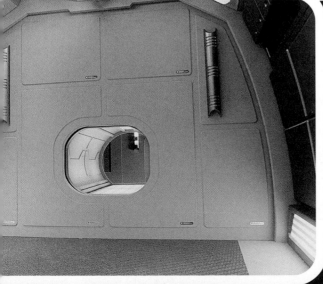

16 ENGINEERING

THE DOORS TO ENGINEERING.

The construction of Zimmerman's and Mickelberry's engineering set — pre-Borgification.

Courtesy of John Eaves.

Courtesy of Bill Dolan.

AND THE FINAL STUNNING SET. ▶

Courtesy of Bill Dolan.

245

The Airlock Set

The airlock provided the setting for Picard, Worf, and Hawk's exit from the ship onto the actual saucer, in an effort to stop the Borg from summoning reinforcements. According to the plot, the only way for our heroes to get down to the deflector dish is to exit the top of the saucer and walk (with the aid of magnetized boots) to the ship's underbelly. Located adjacent to the bridge, the set consisted of a suit-up room, then the airlock itself.

Eaves's version of the airlock set had a gridded floor and a rectangular room with doubled edges; the suit-up area had fold-up benches, and a glass wall with equipment—giant air tanks and control panels—behind it. At the same time, Bill Hawkins was also making airlock designs.

JOHN:

Bill's design, which wound up being used, was really cool; he made a little suit-up room with phaser-rifle racks all over the walls. From there, you entered a decompression chamber through a small, offset circular door; then it was onward and outward into space.

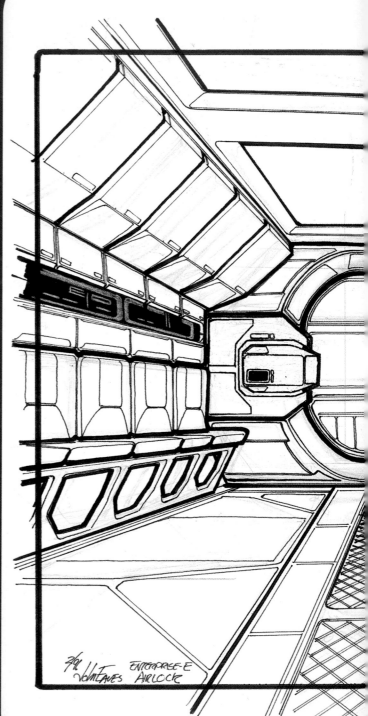

EAVES'S AIRLOCK SKETCH. ▶

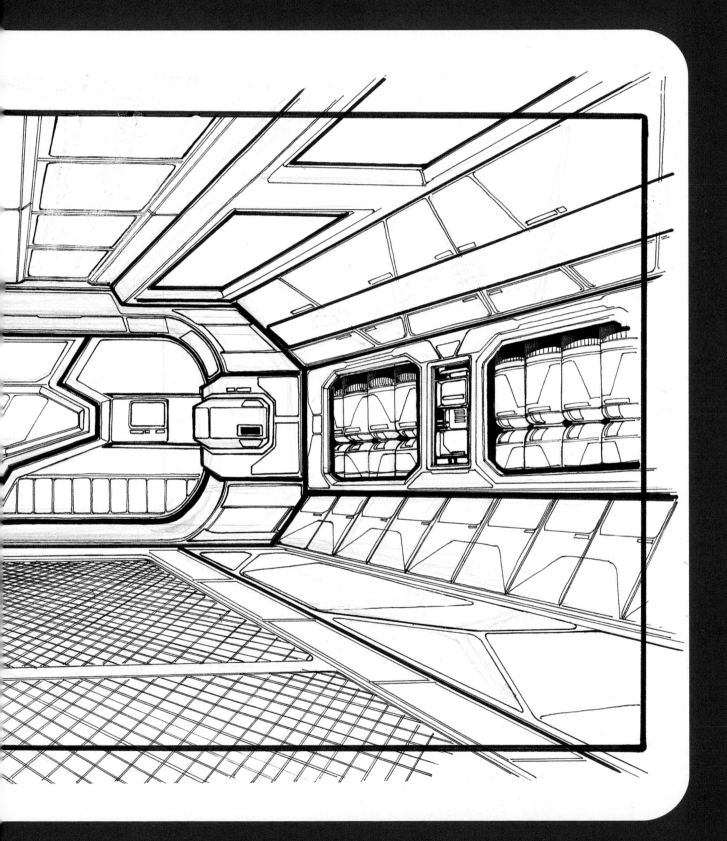

Quantum Torpedo Launcher

If you don't remember this one either, it's also because you never had a chance to see it. At one time, the script called for the crew to wage a battle against the Borg, by firing quantum torpedoes back at the deflector dish. As the power wasn't working, the crew were forced to go out on the saucer's exterior, manually pull one of the torpedo launchers from its cove, and fire it at the deflector.

JOHN:

We designed the launcher so that it would emerge from its bay for maintenance, at which point the crew attempts to physically position it backwards in order to fire manually at the Borg. We created a removable hatch, from beneath which the launcher emerges; and there's a cove that Picard crawls down into so that he can fire the torpedo without getting hit by Borg crossfire. We also drew this little communications array above the deflector dish—we thought that the torpedo could nick that area of the ship, disabling the Borg's uplink array, and still not destroy most of the ship.

Eaves did a series of three drawings: one showing how the torpedo came out of its launcher, one showing how the launcher controls worked, and a third showing how the torpedoes fit into the launcher and where Picard would hide. It was decided to come up with a new type of torpedo, as well—a deadlier, more vicious-looking version of the Mark V torpedo that had been seen in previous *Star Trek* films.

The newer, nastier torpedoes were drawn and ready for action—but never appeared in the finished film, although they are mentioned in the dialog. As time went on, the scriptwriters realized that this scenario would more than likely cause too much destruction to the *Enterprise* no matter how they were fired, so the scene was radically revised.

THE NEVER-SEEN ▶
TORPEDO LAUNCHER,
WITH LAUNCH SEQUENCE.

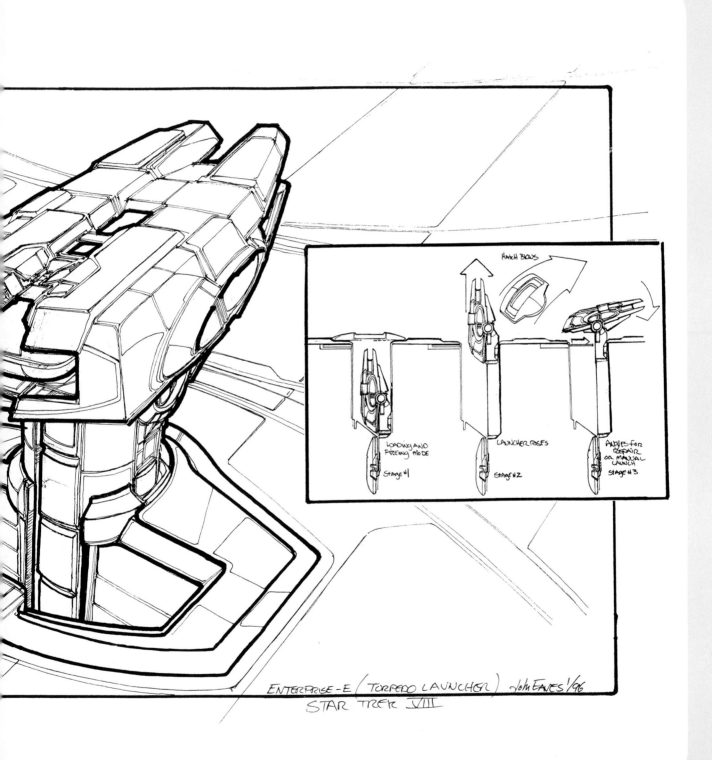

HATCH BLOWS

LOADING AND
FIRING MODE
STAGE #1

LAUNCHER RISES
STAGE #2

ARISES FOR
REPAIR
OR MANUAL
LAUNCH
STAGE #3

ENTERPRISE-E (TORPEDO LAUNCHER) John Eaves!/96
STAR TREK VIII

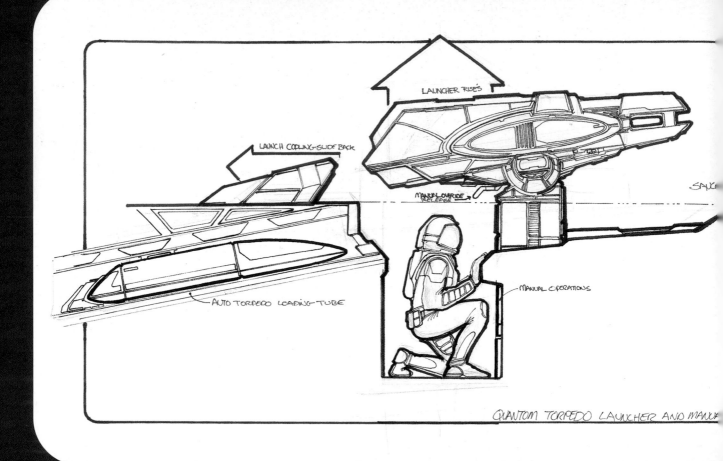

LAUNCHER RISES

LAUNCH COUPLING SLIDE BACK

MANUAL OVERRIDE RELEASE

SPACE

AUTO TORPEDO LOADING TUBE

MANUAL OPERATIONS

QUANTUM TORPEDO LAUNCHER AND MANUAL

▲

THE COVE WHENCE PICARD
WOULD HAVE MANUALLY LAUNCHED
THE QUANTUM TORPEDO.

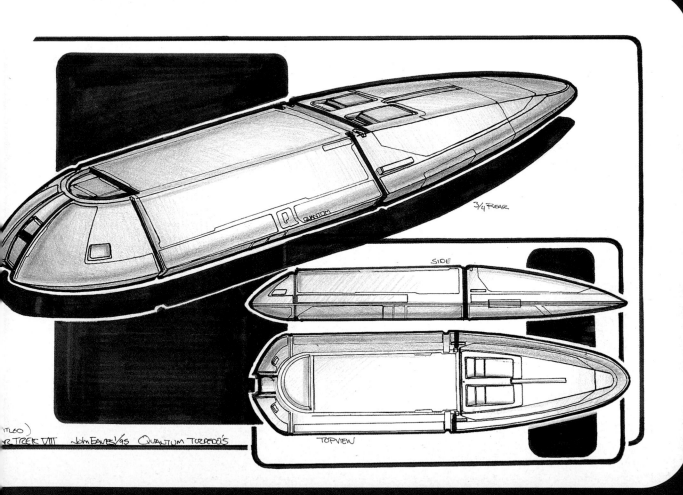

The leaner, meaner
Quantum torpedoes.

▼

3/4 REAR

SIDE

TOPVIEW

(UNTITLED)
STAR TREK VIII John Eaves 1/95 QUANTUM TORPEDO'S

Of course, the deflector dish remained the scene of a critical battle among Picard, Worf, Hawk, and the Borg, but the changes to the story meant changes to some details on the saucer dish. Linda King and Ron Wilkinson spent most of their time on the film working out the particulars of the deflector dish set, while back at ILM, John Knoll and Jeff Olson had the task of blending the set into the various opticals of the *Enterprise* miniature. However, when the set designs were finally approved, Olson received information about modification to the ship's exterior *almost* too late. He called John Goodson and gave him a mere twelve hours to make the changes. At this point, the model's principal photography had already begun; fortunately, none of the finished shots happened to show the model's deflector detail.

One of the artists sharing an office with Eaves, Joe Musso, was in charge of designing the battle sequence via storyboards of the deflector-dish fight scenes.

JOHN:

Joe must have done a thousand different story-boards working out this battle on the giant deflector-dish set; he started drawing them early when the launcher was still part of the plot, so he went through the whole script change.

Now, Joe is an amazing artist; he worked with Alfred Hitchcock, John Wayne, and many others. Everything he draws is the perfect angle, the perfect lens ratio, and here's his secret: He has a camera in his eye—honest! If you look carefully enough, you can see a little shutter in it.

A SAMPLE OF THE FABULOUS ▶
JOE MUSSO'S "DEFLECTOR
DISH BATTLE" STORYBOARDS.

Joe Musso also has a remarkable sense of humor (not to mention an infectious laugh), and when the two shared an office, they became somewhat famous—or rather, infamous—for their practical jokes. And, it seems, they played one joke too many. . . .

JOHN:

Well, one day, we both went into work in the office, and I noticed this subtle but terrible smell—like dirty socks or a dead rodent or something. I kept hoping it would just go away, but as the day went on, it got worse and worse. Joe and I didn't say anything to each other about it, because neither of us wanted to say the wrong thing, so we both maintained silence. But we kept giving each other these funny little glances, and I knew we were both thinking the same thing: "If it isn't me, it must be the other guy."

We suffered like this for two whole days, until finally everyone in the office just cracked up. It seems that Bill Hawkins had left a bucket of Limburger cheese under the desk, to get even with us. And he certainly did—Joe and I suspected everyone who came into our office of needing a shower.

Precisely *what* prompted Hawkins's revenge, Eaves will not say. But he does admit freely to being the source of some infamous "memos from Herman."

JOHN:

No one was safe in the office. Whenever Herman was out of the office, we'd pick someone who was doing a project for him, and send that victim a "special" note, supposedly from Herman.

For example, unsuspecting Set Designer Les Gobruegge, who was working on the *Enterprise*-E bridge set at the time, received a memo from "Herman" which said, in essence, that the new *Enterprise* marked a return to the days of the luxury liners. Therefore, Les needed to design some "refreshment caddies" and "stewardesses" that were to come onto the bridge and offer coffee to the crew during stressful situations.

JOHN:

And of course we marked it "URGENT—NEED DRAWINGS ASAP!" Now, while Herman was gone, Les actually began to draw these neat little caddies, and Federation hostesses to boot. So when Herman returned to the office about two hours later, Les took him some sketches and said, "Here are your caddies and your stewardesses." And Herman said,

"My WHAT?"

Les and Herman went back and forth for a while until Les finally figured out what had happened to him. To tell the truth, I've always suspected him of being part of that Limburger fiasco.

Costume designer Deborah Everton was another victim. She had approached Rick Berman with the question, "Why are we only Borgifying humans? What if there are other alien races inside these Borg, such as Cardassians and Klingons, for example?" Berman liked the idea, Everton relayed to others in the art department trailer, moaning, "Me and my big mouth! I know I've made more work for myself!"

JOHN:

Well, after she told us that, it certainly seemed that she was a good candidate for a special memo from Herman. So we sent her one that said: "Mr. Berman and I really like your idea about Borgifying other alien races. In fact, he wants you to use not only other alien races, but animals as well. I need the sketches by three o'clock."

We were really hoping to see some sketches—dog Borg, cow Borg. Unfortunately, Herman returned well before three o'clock, and Debra caught on too soon to our little joke.

Everton's response?

Well, she put a list up on her door, of who was allowed inside her office and who was not. I'll let you guess which list Joe and I were on....

The costume designs of Deborah Everton, beautifully illustrated by Gina Flanagan

Courtesy of the artists.

259

Various
Enterprise-E
Details

JOHN:

We wanted the exterior bridge detail to match the sets they were building on the soundstage. The outer bridge detail reflects that "inner" shape; looking down on it from a bird's-eye view, you see a flat-ended teardrop shape reminiscent of the E's blueprints.

Inside (in our imaginations, anyway) would be the bridge and observation lounge, which comprised one set. The script called for the lounge to have big windows that looked out onto space facing the back of the ship. In the exterior detail, the flat end of the teardrop is where those windows are. There are four levels atop the saucer, with the bridge being on the highest level. Each level "steps" down to the next.

DECK#4   3 FOOT SPACER   DECK

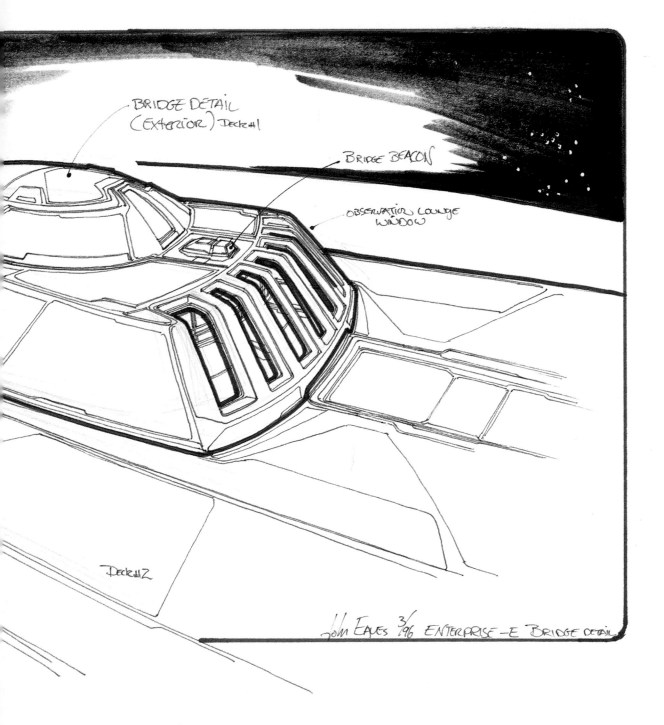

BRIDGE DETAIL
(EXTERIOR) Deck #1

BRIDGE BEACON

OBSERVATION LOUNGE
WINDOW

DECK #2

John Eaves 3/96 ENTERPRISE-E BRIDGE DETAIL

Moving back from the bridge detail, we go to the back of the first shuttlebay on the saucer. Eaves designed a docking bay, plus an observation tower that overlooks the ship's posterior. Had the set been built, a character sitting in the observation tower inside the *Enterprise*-E could look across the back of the ship, then swivel in his or her chair and see inside the shuttlebay.

SHUTTLEBAY DETAIL. ▶

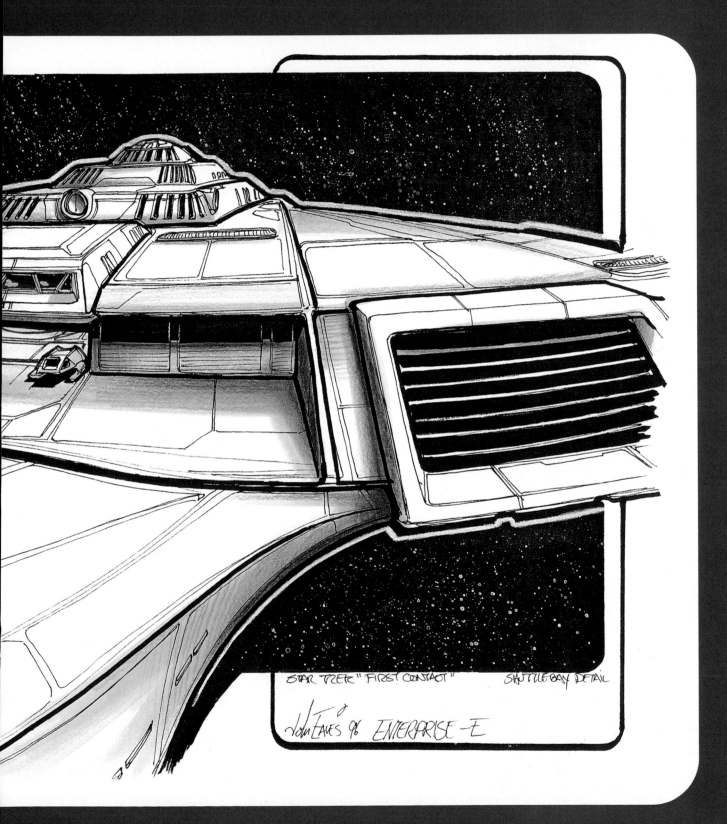

STAR TREK "FIRST CONTACT"   SHUTTLEBAY DETAIL

John Eaves 96 ENTERPRISE-E

The Deflector Dish Details

JOHN:

When it came to designing this area of the ship, I scooped out the body and inset the deflector in the resulting cove. When adding subtle detail around the dish, I borrowed from Rick Sternbach's design of the *Voyager*. Rick had modified the notched detail from previous starships to create a layered detail segmenting the body to the deflector cavity. I took that particular design as a starting point. Next came the torpedo launchers and the RCS [reaction control] thrusters. Rick was a great source of information; he knows the ships and Federation design so well, and did a wonderful job of doing the plans and filling in all the areas that needed it. Working with him was both an honor and a pleasure—not to mention great fun.

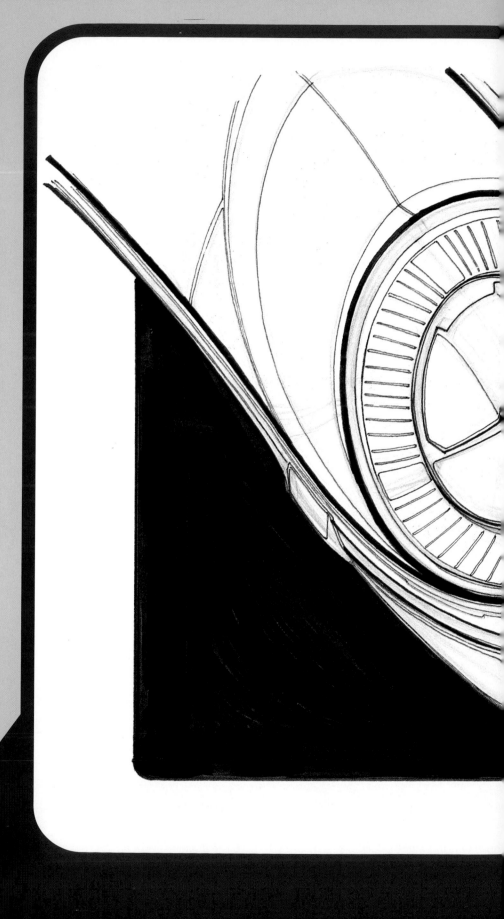

ENTERPRISE-E DEFLECTOR-DISH ▶ DETAIL. SKETCH BY JOHN EAVES.

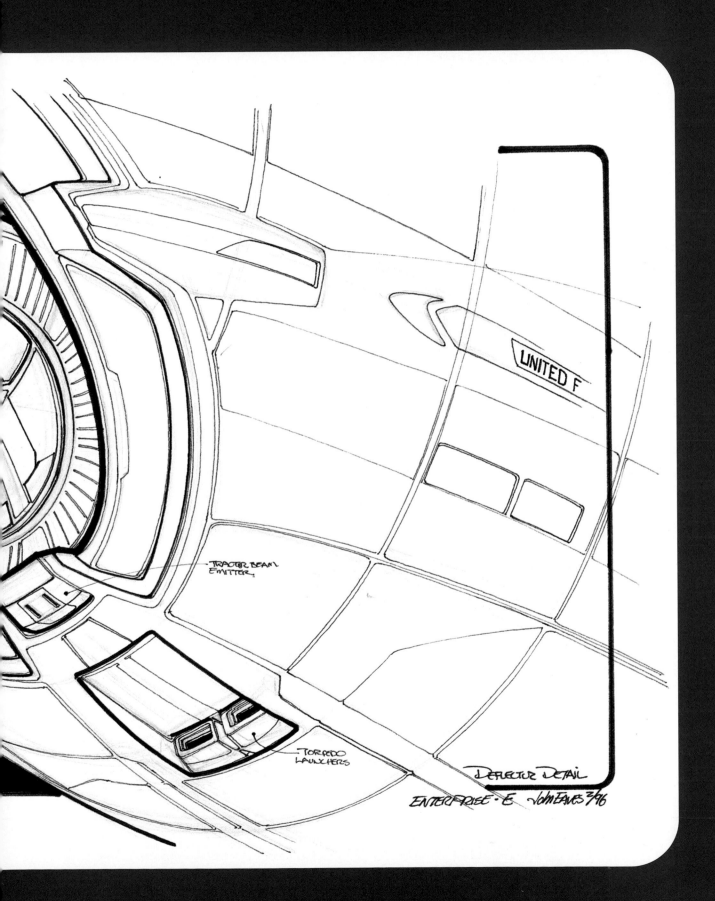

TRACTOR BEAM
EMITTER

UNITED F

TORPEDO
LAUNCHERS

DEFLECTOR DETAIL
ENTERPRISE · E   JOHN EAVES 3/96

JOHN:

Also, the traditional design for all *Enterprises* is the inner curve on the bottom back of the ship. Taking advantage of the ship's geography in this area, I incorporated the torpedo launcher and tractor-beam emitters. So there's a tractor beam on both the front and back of the ship's underbelly, along with torpedo launchers which provide optimum firing points.

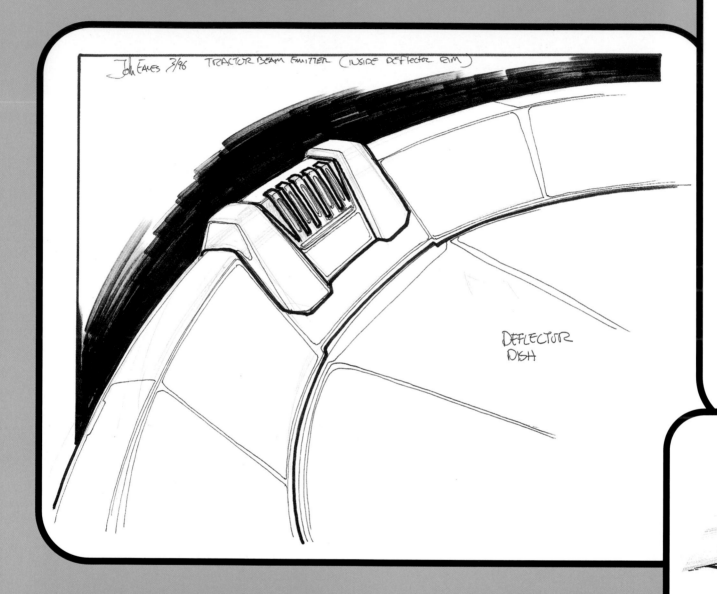

JOHN EALES 3/96   TRACTOR BEAM EMITTER (INSIDE DEFLECTOR RIM)

DEFLECTOR DISH

TRACTOR BEAM DETAIL. ▲

THE E'S NOT-SO-SEAMY UNDERBELLY. ◀

THE NACELLE DETAIL. ▶

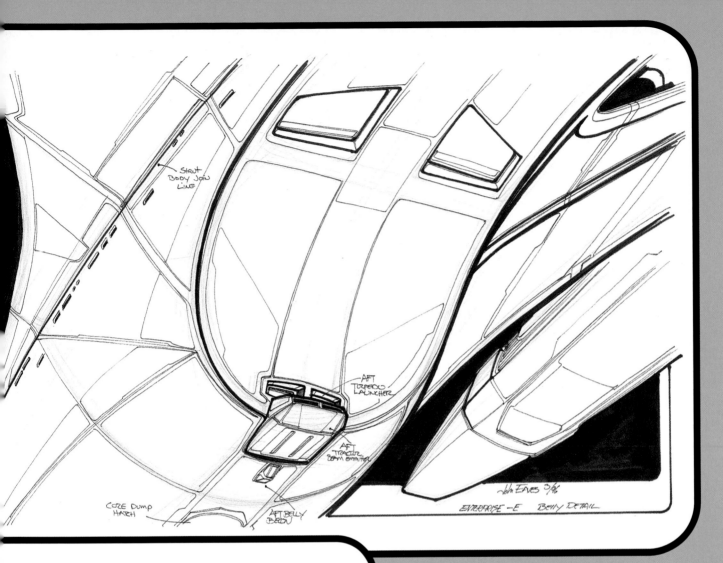

Strut
Body Join
Line

Aft
Torpedo
Launcher

Aft
Tractor
Beam Emitter

Core Dump
Hatch

Aft Belly
Beacon

John Eaves 9/96

ENTERPRISE - E   BELLY DETAIL

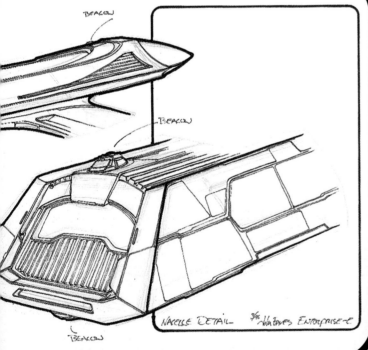

BEACON

BEACON

NACELLE DETAIL   9/96 John Eaves ENTERPRISE-E

BEACON

Let's continue onward to the nacelles, which underwent a number of changes.

JOHN:

There's an open cowling on top of the nacelle, so you can see where the warp drive's signature lighting originates. At one point, I had that cowling closed at both front and back with only the center open; however, Herman wanted the back open so the lighted area extended all the way to the end of the nacelle.

But when the model was constructed, the nacelle didn't appear balanced; ILM's John Goodson called and requested a return to the closed-end design. Zimmerman agreed; a cowled back it was.

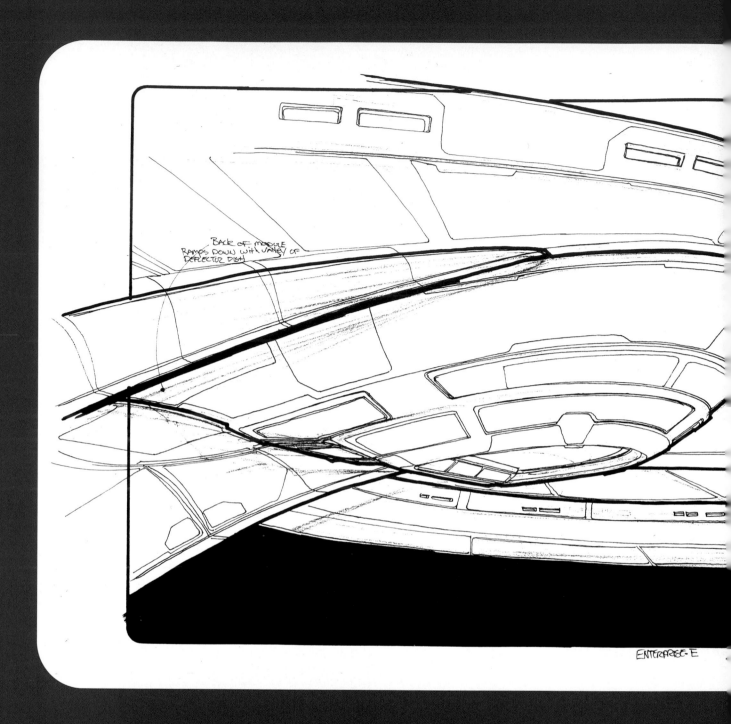

BACK OF MODULE
RAMPS DOWN WITH VALLEY OF
DEFLECTOR DISH

ENTERPRISE-E

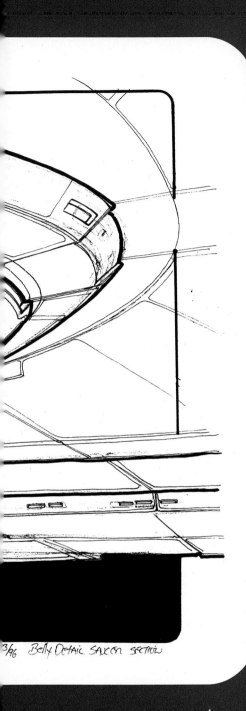

3/96 Belly Detail Saucer section

THE SAUCER'S UNDERSIDE.

JOHN:

From there, I did window insets on the saucer bottom, similar to the notched windows Andy Probert did on the bottom of the *Enterprise*-D saucer. Rick Sternbach also incorporated a few of those on *Voyager*, and went on to draw them on the E's saucer as well.

Other changes in the ship's design included the lighted tower on the saucer bottom. Since the *Enterprise*-E had no "neck" separating the saucer from the body, the deflector dish alcove tapers up to the saucer bottom—making the alcove the most advantageous location for the launcher, a massive magazine, and weapons array.

The phaser array, however, comes straight from the *Enterprise*-D and *Voyager* designs, and was already so futuristic in its technology that this particular *Star Trek* "tradition" was carried forward.

Yet the saucer bottom's shape is a definite break with tradition.

JOHN:

We tried something new. From profile, the area looks extremely flat. But when you flip over the bottom of the saucer and look at it, from the outer rim moving in, you'll see it has a beveled edge that goes to the phaser strip, then stair-steps a few times. I put a really deep section in the middle of the ship's curves—two decks' worth of groove. We actually put a ring of windows in there.

The saucer bottom is one of my favorite parts of the ship, because it's so unusual in terms of previous *Enterprise* design.

Other changes to the bottom area include a large "scooped" area which on the *Enterprise*-D served as a docking port. On the E, this area was changed into massive cargo doors, seen closed throughout *First Contact* (but, as Eaves points out, there's always a chance they might open up in a later film).

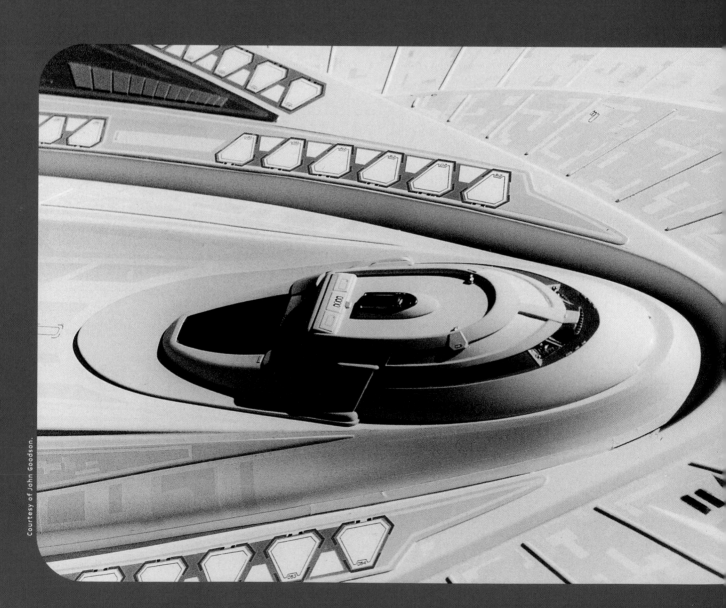

ILM MODEL OF THE
SAUCER'S UNDERSIDE. ▶

◀ CLOSE-UP OF SAUCER BOTTOM.

Courtesy of John Goodson.

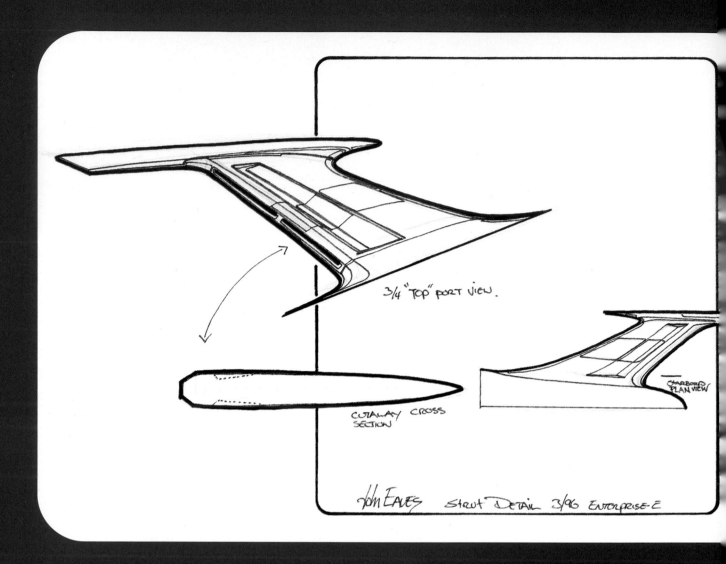

3/4 "TOP" PORT VIEW.

CUTAWAY CROSS SECTION

STARBOARD PLAN VIEW

John Eaves   Strut Detail 3/96 Enterprise-E

In keeping with the *Enterprise*-E's "sports car" look, the engine struts vee off the body at a forty-five degree angle, with a tether that tapers far forward; the effect is one of forward momentum, even when the ship is motionless.

JOHN:

I wanted that vee effect to curve with the inseam of the ship. I drew it the way I wanted it to look, but when it came to model making, the design had some problems; it wouldn't taper just right. John Goodson from ILM called me up and asked if the front could have the taper, and the back level out for a bit, then angle up. Seeing John's problem, I worked the angle out in sketches at the same time he worked with the model.

The struts were finally split, with insets along the leading edges. Ed Miarecki at ILM came up with the design for tapering them into the nacelles.

JOHN:

I drew that area vaguely, figuring that when it came time to make this part of the model, we'd discuss it. Jeff Olson and John Goodson would have some good ideas on how to solve the problem. They gave the modeling job to Ed Miarecki, who asked, "Should we do a nice bevel into the body with these straight edges on either side of the strut?" and did a sketch on the table while I was visiting ILM.

◄ STRUT DETAILS.

▼ ENGINE STRUTS AND NACELLES, TOP VIEW...

Courtesy of John Goodson.

...AND UNDERSIDE. ▶

Courtesy of John Goodson.

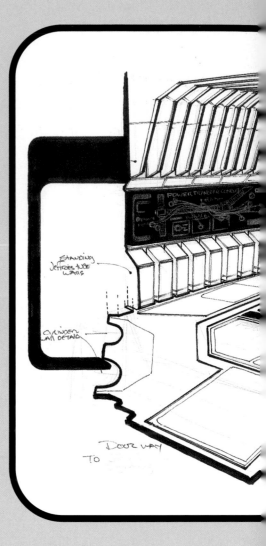

Speaking of collaborative efforts, that brings us to the exterior detail of the lifeboat hatches. As mentioned earlier, Eaves decided on a bevel-edged triangle shape for them. Alex Jaeger came up with the actual escape-pod designs; Eaves drew the detail on how the pods were physically laid out on the saucer, and Rick Sternbach came up with the number and placement pattern for them. Once again, we have to emphasize just how much of a collaborative effort a film of this magnitude can be; one single object on the screen—such as the model of the *Enterprise*-E—may represent the creative efforts of several talented artists.

Interestingly enough, even though Herman Zimmerman wisely commenced design work months in advance of *First Contact*'s official start, work on sets continued up until only a few weeks before the feature's release on November 22, 1996. Such work was inspired by the insightful comments of a Paramount executive who, knowing little of *Star Trek*, had seen the rough cut. On behalf of those for whom the latest film represented their "first contact" with *Star Trek*, she suggested that more explanation was needed of the Borg's horrific assimilation of the ship's crew.

JOHN:

So Mr. Berman, Herman, Peter, and all of us got together and came up with a new set—a Borg "chamber of horrors" adjacent to engineering, which explained how the Borg assimilated crew members and showed the nefarious ways in which they "consume" their captives. We used existing set pieces in order to save the production a lot of cash.

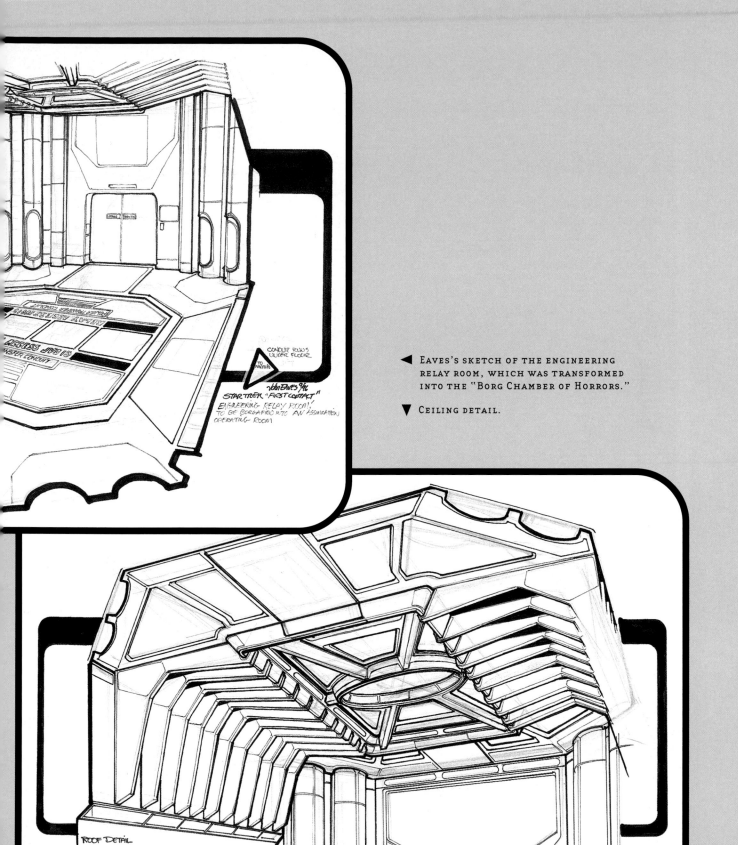

◄ EAVES'S SKETCH OF THE ENGINEERING
RELAY ROOM, WHICH WAS TRANSFORMED
INTO THE "BORG CHAMBER OF HORRORS."

▼ CEILING DETAIL.

Federation Props

At the same time that Eaves was working on ships and sets, he was also designing a number of props—both Federation and Borg—for prop master Dean Wilson. The first prop he designed was a fairly large "scanning device," used by our fearless Federation friends to examine Zefram Cochrane's ship for damage after a Borg attack.

JOHN:

It was an X-ray type of scope—basically, a framework with handles on it, and a mechanism plate in the center of it. This device was attached to the missile and moved around so our crew could see what was inside the missile. We also put controls on it so that you can adjust the depth—how deeply you're looking inside.

Two different sizes were made: a large one for the actual Titan missile, and a smaller one. From the art department, the sketches went to the "propper" effects department, where the actual props were built.

The second prop—or rather, group of props, since several were built—was the Federation phaser rifle, upgraded to a more ballistic, assault-type weapon.

JOHN:

I started with a design Dean Wilson, prop master, gave me of a laser-tag rifle he'd found. It was sleek and "Federation-looking" already. I took that shape and made it heavier in design, with an open-butt stock on the back. The gun body has a standard trigger handle, and a palm grip forward of the trigger. The actors held the rifle like a shotgun.

At one point, we were going to give the rifle an "extend-a-stock" feature for more marksmanlike appearance. But after the first prototype rifle was completed, Rick Berman handled it, and decided the extend-a-stock was unnecessary. So instead, we added straps to the rifles, because the characters had to go out in a zero-g environment and needed something to keep the rifles from floating off into space. "Propper" effects designed a retractable belt that would automatically feed back into the stock of the rifle when it wasn't shouldered.

The rifles also had to be opened in the film, to show their internal mechanics when crew members attempt to modify them. The updated design allowed for microchips to be removed or added in order to modify the rifle's function. (The circuitry "integrated" inside the chip used graphics established by Mike Okuda.)

Another required device was the magnifying/tooling window that Picard uses later in order to try to manipulate the rifle's internal mechanism; it was a clear "plate" that fit over the rifle and provided readouts necessary for calibrating the weapon.

Finally, as time went on, a second version of the same rifle was required.

JOHN:

Doug Drexler and I started doing variations on the same theme. Doug came up with four or five variations that looked really good; he altered the barrel and sloped it from the faceted design, so it looked more like a grenade-launcher barrel. He also put some plating on its side, making for a heavier "combat" model. I wound up doing about four or five passes as well; ultimately, a combination of our drawings were used to make two new styles of rifles.

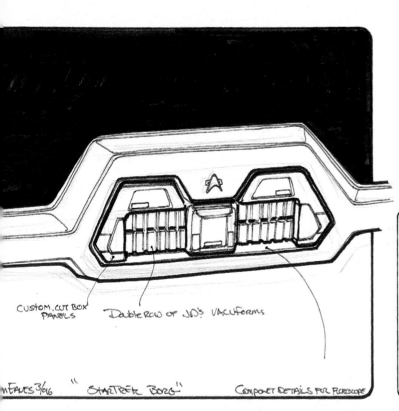

CUSTOM CUT BOX
PANELS

DOUBLE ROW OF JD's VACUFORMS

nEALES 3/96 " STARTREK BORG " COMPONET DETAILS FOR FLUROSCOPE

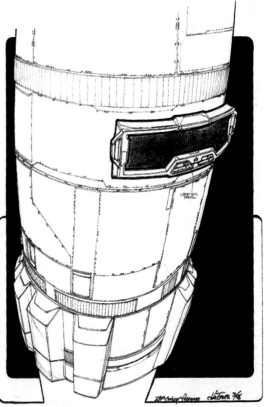

THE TWENTY-FOURTH-CENTURY
"FLUOROSCOPE" USED TO SCAN
THE *PHOENIX* FOR DAMAGE.

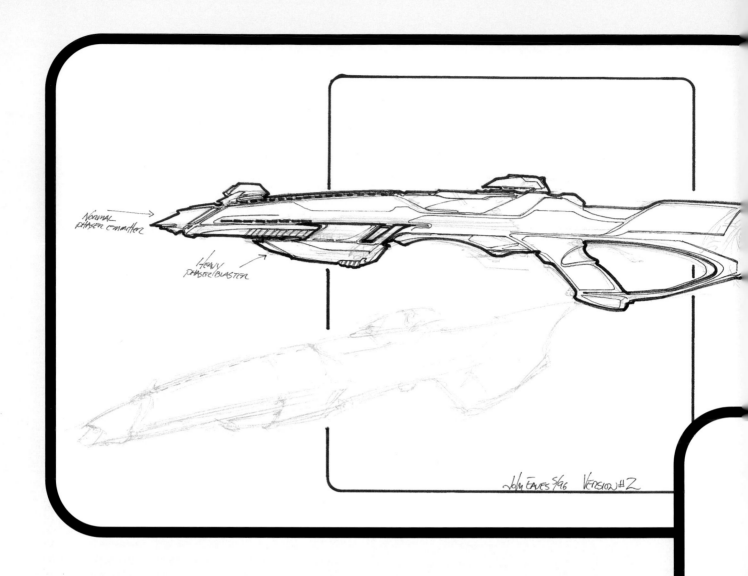

Nornial
Phaser emmitter

Heavy
Phaser/Blaster

John Eaves 8/96 Version #2

TWO OF EAVES'S EARLY PHASER RIFLE MODIFICATION DESIGNS. ▶

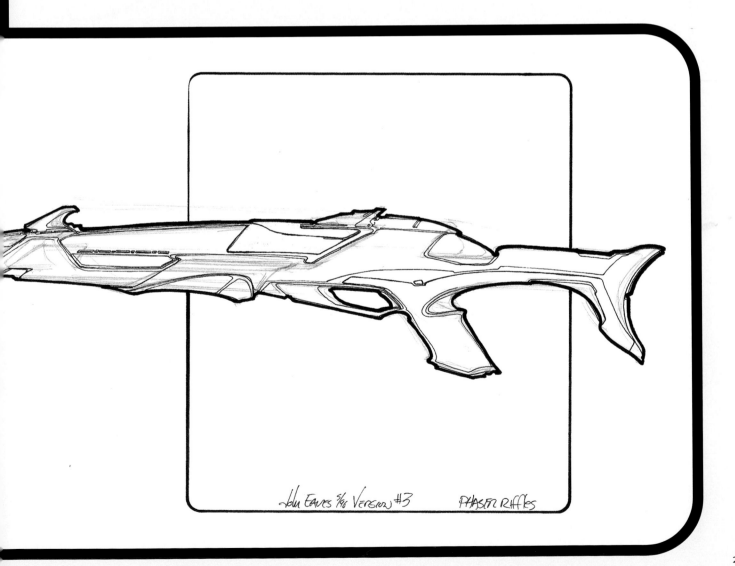

John Eaves 8/98 Version #3   PHASER RIFFLES

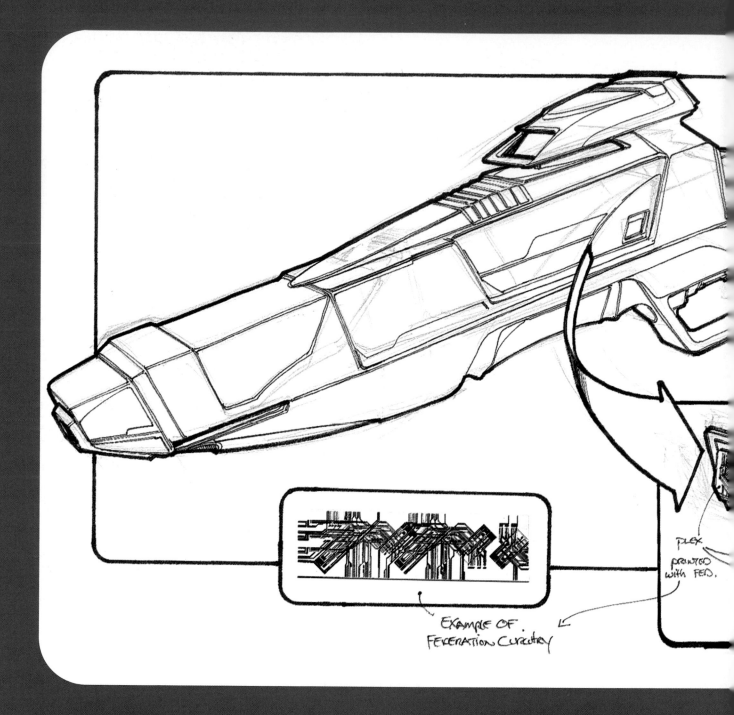

EXAMPLE OF
FEDERATION CIRCUITRY

PLEX
PRINTED
WITH FED.

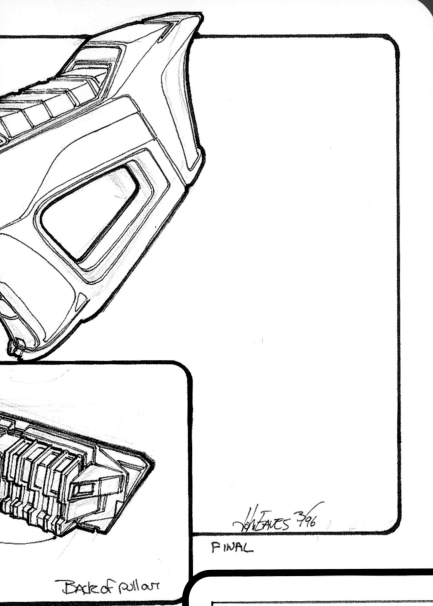

◄ THE FINAL VERSION.

JohnEaves 3/96

FINAL

Back of roll out

THE MAGNIFYING PLATE
USED FOR ADJUSTING THE
RIFLE'S INTERNAL MECHANISMS.
SKETCH BY EAVES.
▼

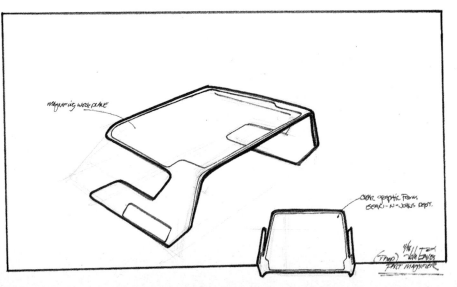

magnifying wedge plate

clear graphic from
Scan-n-Johns dept.

John Eaves 4/96

(Prop)

Part Magnifier

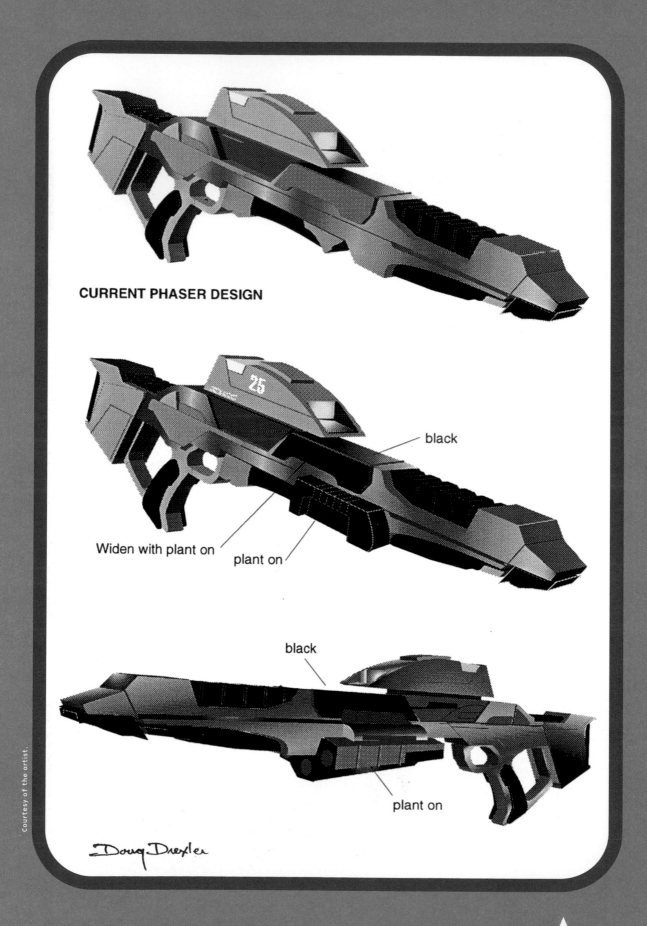

CURRENT PHASER DESIGN

black

Widen with plant on

plant on

black

plant on

Doug Drexler

CGI RIFLE MODIFICATIONS BY DOUG DREXLER. ▶

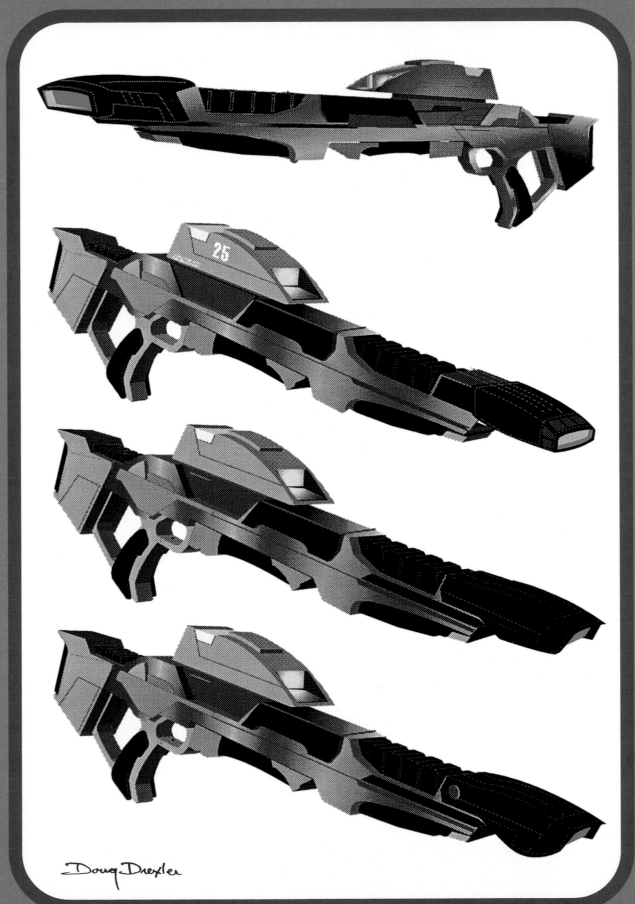

Doug Drexler

Borg Props

The very first thing Zimmerman set Eaves to work on was the Borg queen; at the same time, he set artist Ricardo Delgado to work on Borg concepts as well. Delgado, who excels in artistic creation that meshes the organic with the mechanical, was actually the first illustrator Zimmerman hired in 1992 to bring *Deep Space Nine* to life. At the time *First Contact* was being filmed, Delgado was busy designing dinosaurs at Disney, a job that came to him as a result of his brilliant comic book series *The Age of Reptiles*; he actually worked after hours and during lunch, conceiving sketch after sketch of the Borg and their grim habitat. Delgado's work is wondrously hellish and truly terrifying. His work is too beautiful to be forgotten—so here's a look at what the Borg were during the early stages of the film's gestation.

All Things Borg and Beautiful: The art of Ricardo Delgado

John — Here are my thoughts regarding the Borg stuff.

The concept for the Borg obelisk and the basic design in general for First Contact were rooted in ancient architecture. I felt the obelisk was a natural geometric progression from the cube, while the obvious reference to Egyptology would also make the audience wonder if this was the Borg's first visit to Earth.

The Queen's head design is an amalgamation of Nefertiti and a parasitic wasp, combined with the pre-existing notions of what the Borg look like. The wrist sickles are derived from dromeosaurs, carnivorous dinosaurs whose big toes were armed with huge sickle claws. My budding interest in pre-Romantic Celtic and Druid iconography explains the ancient Borg text covering the body.

Some of the drawings have a matte black/gloss black texture to them, as if the Borg had forged countless galaxies' worth of metals to achieve their carapace-like armor. And lastly, I thought the exposed skulls would look cool.

— Ricardo Delgado

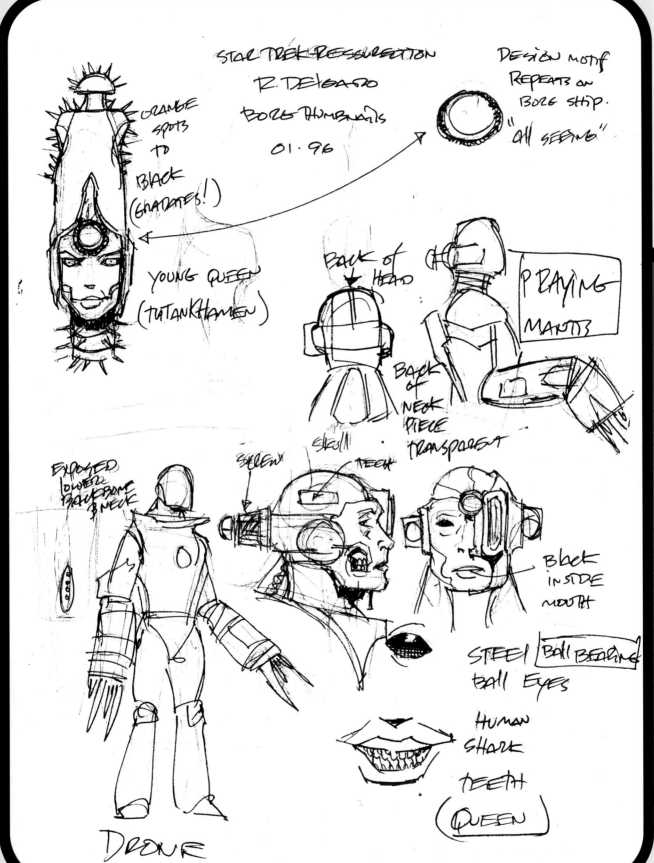

STAR TREK RESSURECTION
R. DELGADO
BORG THUMBNAILS
01·96

DESIGN MOTIF
REPEATS ON
BORG SHIP.
"ALL SEEING"

ORANGE
SPOTS
TO
BLACK
(GRADATES!)

YOUNG QUEEN
(TUTANKHAMEN)

BACK OF
HEAD

BACK
OF
NECK
PIECE
TRANSPARENT

PRAYING
MANTIS

SCREW

SKULL

TECH

EXPOSED
LOWER
JAWBONE
& NECK

BLACK
INSIDE
MOUTH

STEEL BALL BEARING
BALL EYES

HUMAN
SHARK
TEETH
(QUEEN)

DRONE

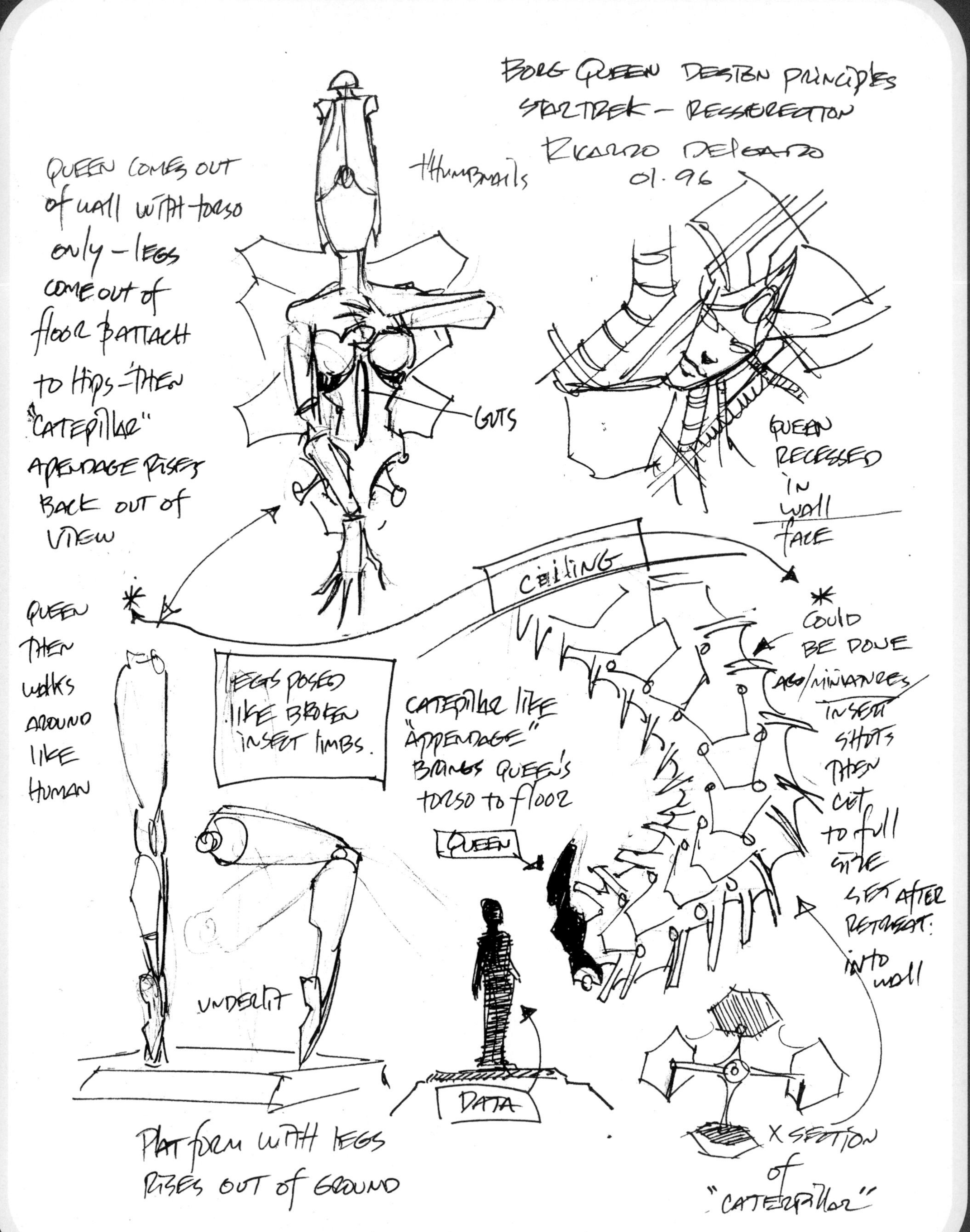
BORG QUEEN DESIGN PRINCIPLES
STARTREK - RESSURECTION
RICARDO DELGADO
01.96
THUMBNAILS
QUEEN COMES OUT of wall WITH torso only - LEGS COME OUT of floor & ATTACH to Hips - THEN "CATEPILLAR" APENDAGE RISES BACK OUT of VIEW
GUTS
QUEEN RECESSED IN WALL FACE
CEILING
QUEEN THEN WALKS AROUND LIKE HUMAN
LEGS POSED LIKE BROKEN INSECT LIMBS.
CATEPILLAR LIKE "APPENDAGE" BRINGS QUEEN'S TORSO TO FLOOR
QUEEN
* COULD BE DONE AS/MINIATURES INSERT SHOTS THEN CUT TO FULL SIZE SET AFTER RETREAT INTO WALL
UNDERLIT
DATA
PLATFORM WITH LEGS RISES OUT OF GROUND
X SECTION of "CATERPILLAR"

Courtesy of the artist.

ENTERPRISE-E

STAR TREK VIII
BORG OBELISK CONCEPT
RICARDO DELGADO

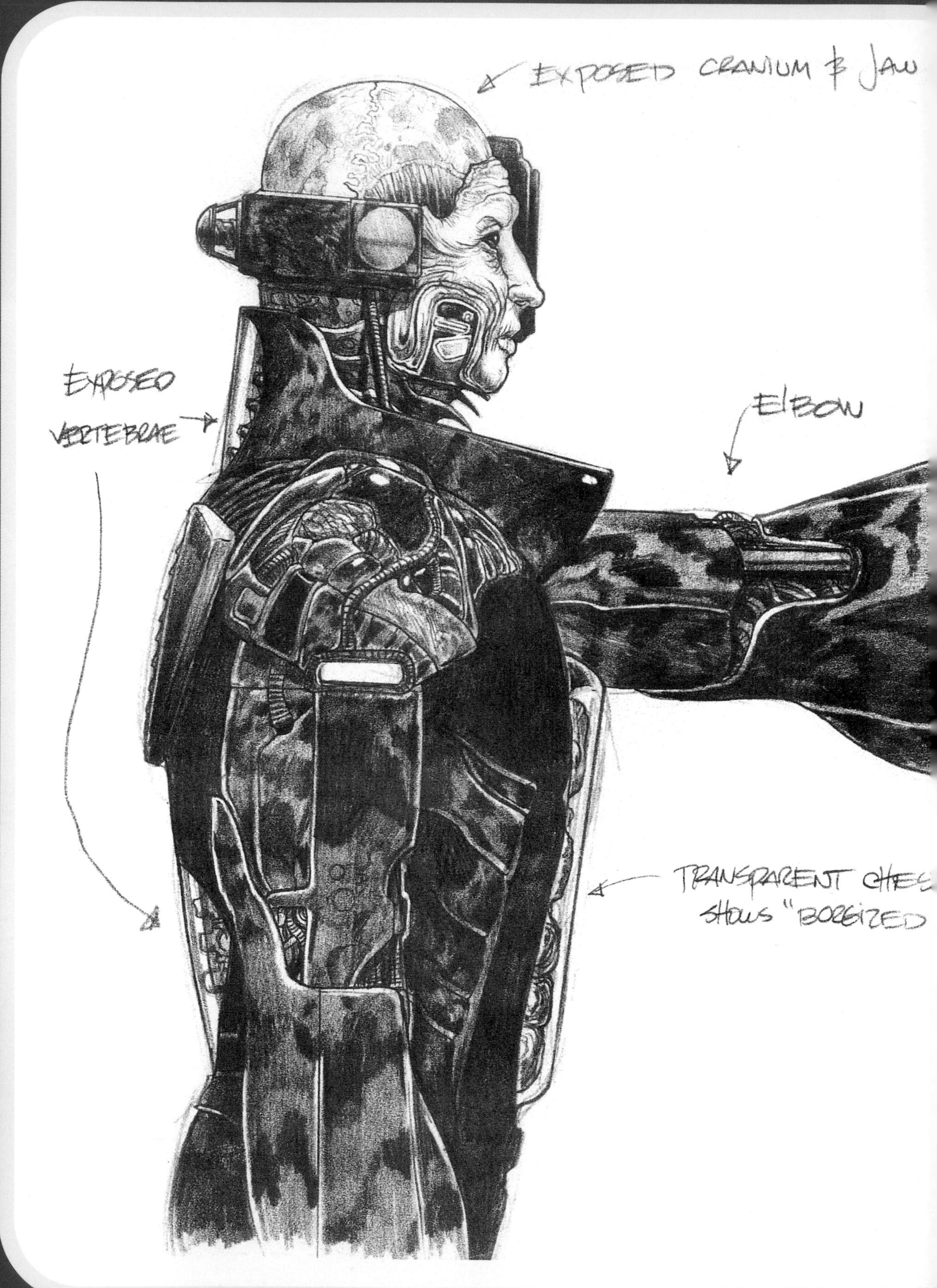
EXPOSED CRANIUM & JAW
EXPOSED VERTEBRAE
ELBOW
TRANSPARENT CHES
SHOWS "BORGIZED

Courtesy of the artist.

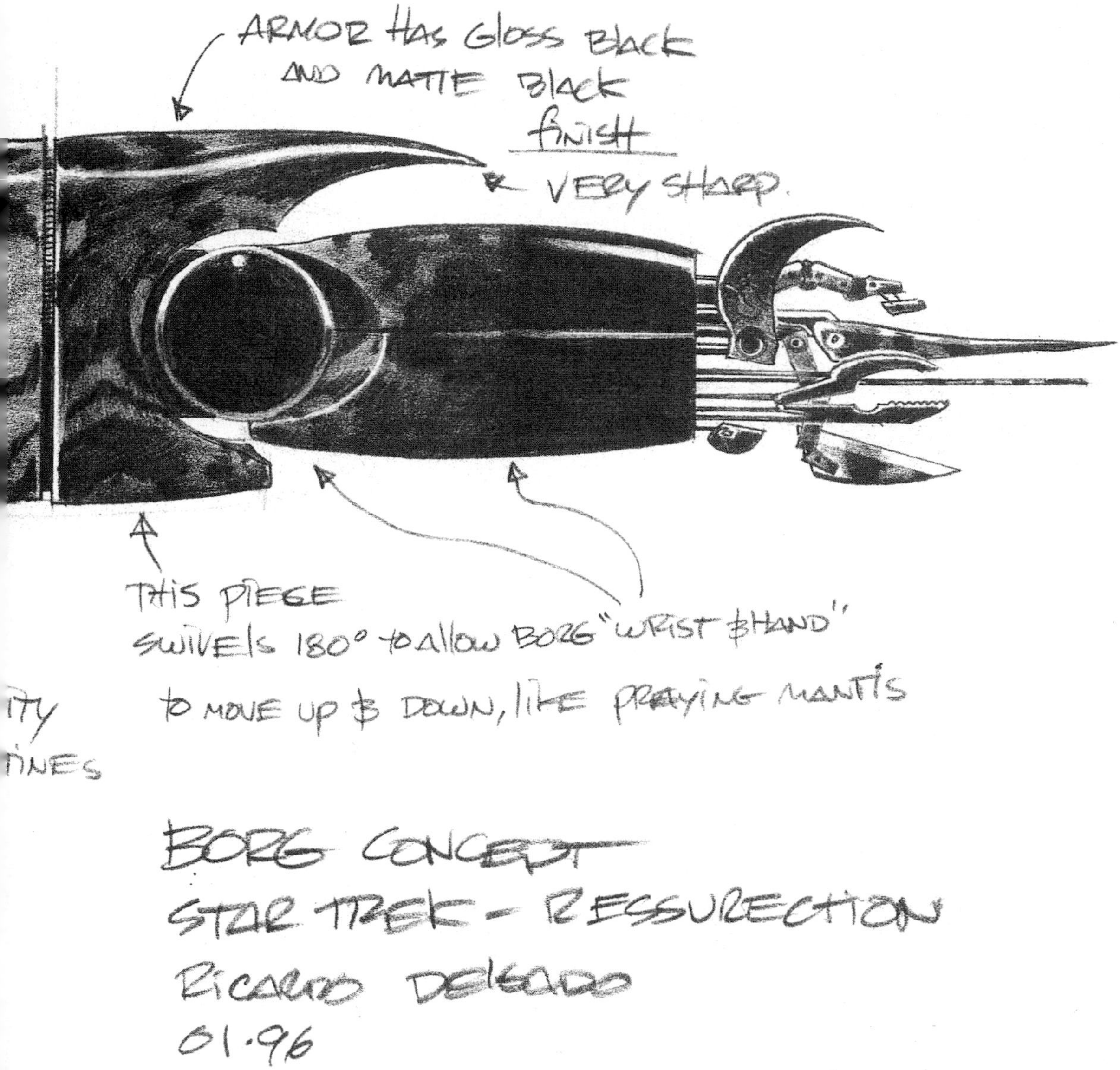

ARMOR HAS GLOSS BLACK
AND MATTE BLACK
finish
VERY SHARP.

THIS PIECE
SWIVELS 180° TO ALLOW BORG "WRIST & HAND"
TO MOVE UP & DOWN, LIKE PRAYING MANTIS

BORG CONCEPT
STAR TREK - RESSURECTION
RICARDO DELGADO
01·96

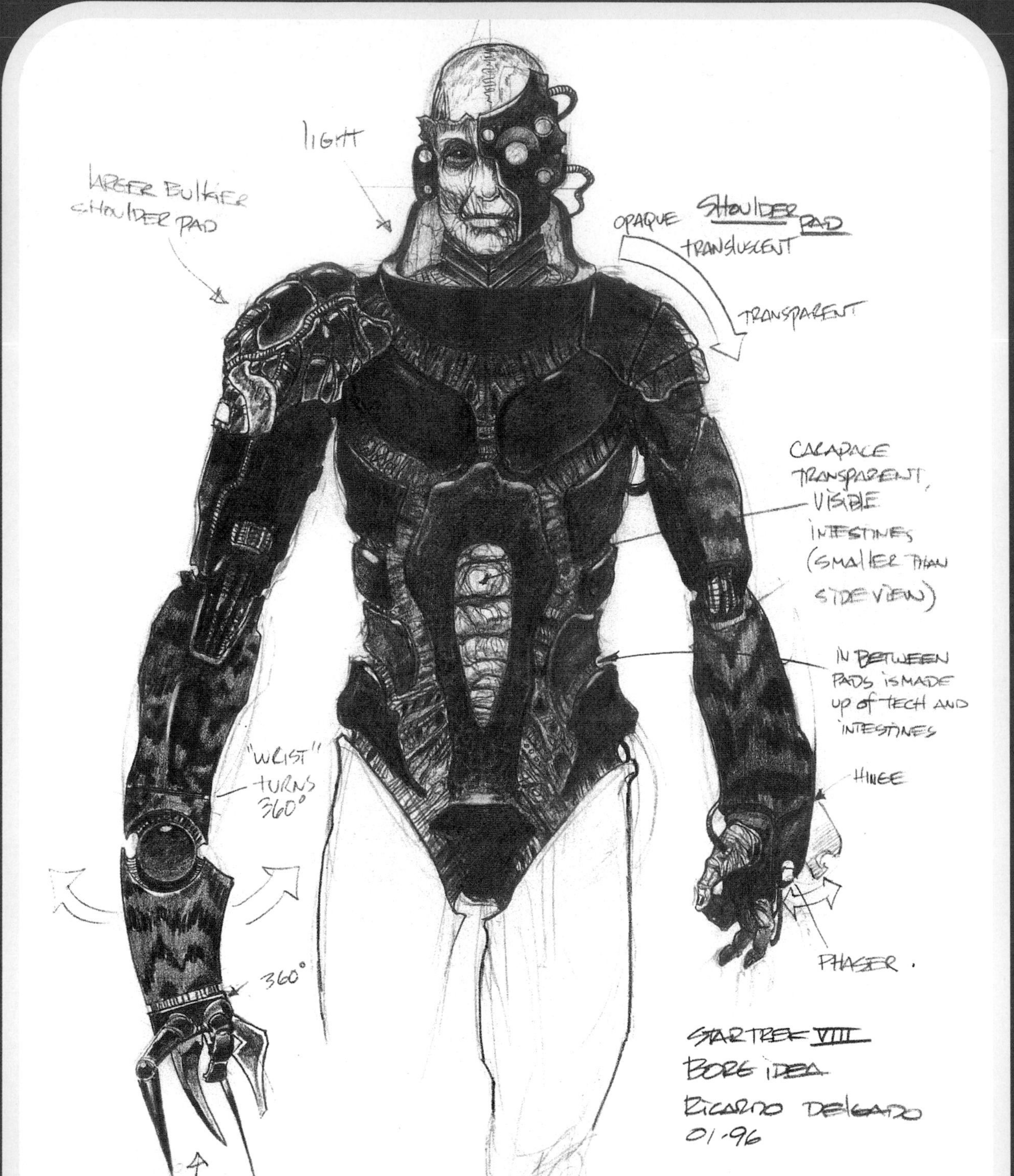

LIGHT
LARGER BULKIER SHOULDER PAD
OPAQUE SHOULDER PAD
TRANSLUSCENT
TRANSPARENT
CARAPACE TRANSPARENT, VISIBLE INTESTINES (SMALLER THAN SIDE VIEW)
IN BETWEEN PADS IS MADE UP OF TECH AND INTESTINES
HINGE
PHASER.
"WRIST" TURNS 360°
360°
STAR TREK VIII
BORG IDEA
RICARDO DELGADO
01-96
"FINGERS" MOVE INDEPENDANTLY

Courtesy of the artist.

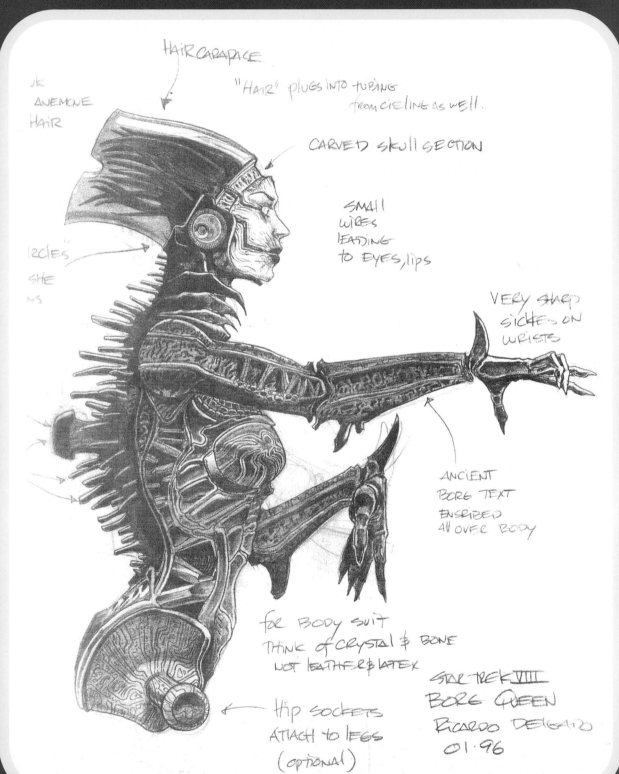

HAIR CARAPACE

"HAIR" PLUGS INTO TUBING
from CIELINE as well.

JK
ANEMONE
HAIR

CARVED SKULL SECTION

SMALL
WIRES
LEADING
TO EYES, lips

ICICLES
SHE
NS

VERY SHARP
SICKLES ON
WRISTS

ANCIENT
BORG TEXT
ENSCRIBED
All OVER BODY

for BODY SUIT
THINK of CRYSTAL & BONE
NOT LEATHER & LATEX

STAR TREK VIII
BORG QUEEN
RICARDO DELGADO
01·96

HIP SOCKETS
ATTACH TO LEGS
(optional)

Row of lights

HEADPIECE
POPS OUT OF
SUPPORT STRUCTURE

STAR TREK VIII
BORG QUEEN THRONE

RICARDO DELGADO
02·96

light

Sadly, Delgado was unable to continue his work for the feature, due to the demands of another project. The task of creating a look for the sinister and seductive Borg queen then fell to Debra Everton, who with her illustrator, Gina Flanagan, did all the costumes for *First Contact*. (With one exception, that is: the elegantly austere new uniforms seen in the feature came courtesy of veteran *Star Trek* costume designer Robert Blackman.)

Everton and Flanagan were newcomers to the set at this point, and were working so feverishly on all the characters' costumes that no sketches of the queen existed when Herman Zimmerman needed a design for the mechanical device that would connect the Borg queen's head to her body.

JOHN:

There's a scene in the film where the Borg queen speaks, but you don't know where her voice is coming from. Data (who is strapped to a table) hears her voice, and finally sees her disembodied, talking head floating on a mechanical rig. Visually, he follows her head until he sees the body waiting in a framework with hoses all around it. Her head finally plugs into her body, and the mechanical framework opens, and she steps out in all her sinister glory. The connecting rig—that's what Herman needed drawings for.

First, I came up with a heavy wire setup and framework; looking at the body from the front, it's standing in an arms-out, thumbs-in, palms-out pose. If you were able to step around that body, you'd see a very thin framework holding it up.

Since I needed a body for the sketches, I drew up a "mock" version of the queen to use until Debra's queen was done. I decided to give her a bodysuit so that it'd be easier for the viewer to distinguish her from the device. Part of my inspiration for the black bodysuit came from a Japanese animated film called *Black Magic 66*, which features a sleek female robot with some great-looking plating on her, sort of a Catwoman from *Batman Returns* look overlaid with a lot of mechanics.

It wasn't decided until quite late whether the Borg queen would have hair or not, so in my sketch I put in some wiry, resistor-looking hair for her. I only did two passes on the Borg queen, and they wound up being too *Alien*-ish in concept, the way the pipes and framework looked. My drawings wound up being used as a rough guideline for the final Borg queen rig, which was designed by Dean Wilson and his crew on the spot.

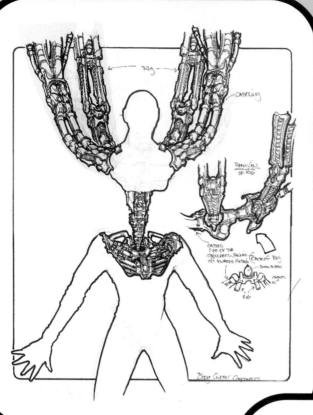

◀ The Borg queen's
mechanical rig,
by John Eaves.

▼ Some assembly required:
a "temporary" queen.

And another
"Queen for a day." ▶

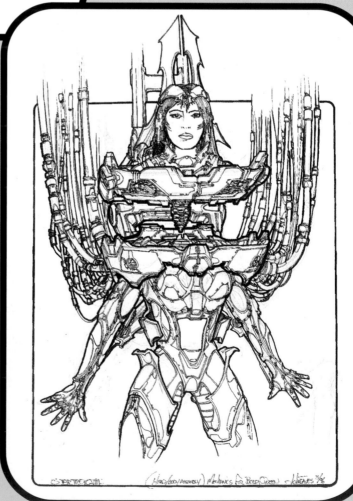

STARTREK VIII   (HEAD/BODY ASSEMBLY) Mechanics for Borg Queen   —JohnEaves 3/96

ALEX JAEGER'S STORYBOARDS FOR THE QUEEN ASSEMBLY.

RESISTANCE IS FUTILE!

▲
THE "POPULAR QUEEN": ALEX JAEGER OFFERED UP THIS VERSION OF THE BORG
QUEEN FOR PARAMOUNT'S CONSIDERATION, USING FELLOW ILM WORKER MARRIANE
HEATH TO POSE FOR THE PHOTO. THE FINAL COMPUTER-GENERATED DESIGN WAS
NOT CHOSEN FOR THE FILM (DEBORAH EVERTON WAS ALREADY WORKING ON HER DESIGN),
BUT SO MANY POSTERS OF JAEGER'S CGI QUEEN POPPED UP ALL OVER ILM AND THE
PARAMOUNT LOT THAT IT WAS DUBBED THE "POPULAR QUEEN."

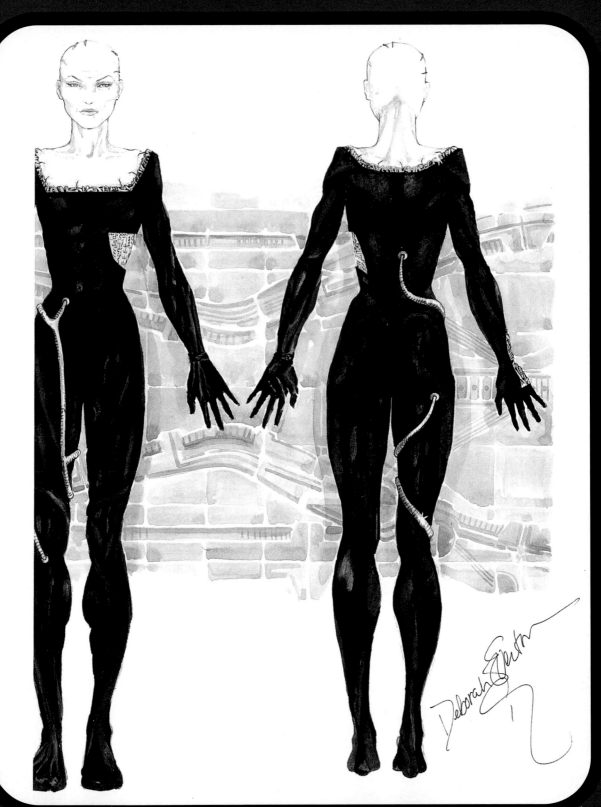

ELEGANT AND SINISTER SIMPLICITY: EVERTON'S BORG QUEEN DESIGN.

EVERTON'S DRONES. ▶

Deborah Everton

Gina Flanagan

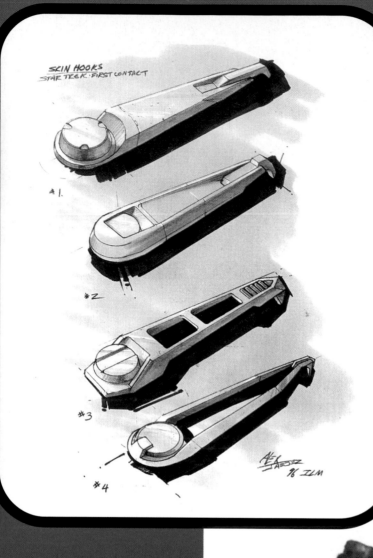

SKIN HOOKS
STAR TREK: FIRST CONTACT

#1.

#2

#3

#4

Alex Jaeger
96 ILM

◄ ALEX JAEGER'S SKETCH OF THE
BORG QUEEN'S "SKIN HOOKS"

▼ **HOOKED ON YOU:**
JAEGER'S CGI SKIN HOOKS IN USE.

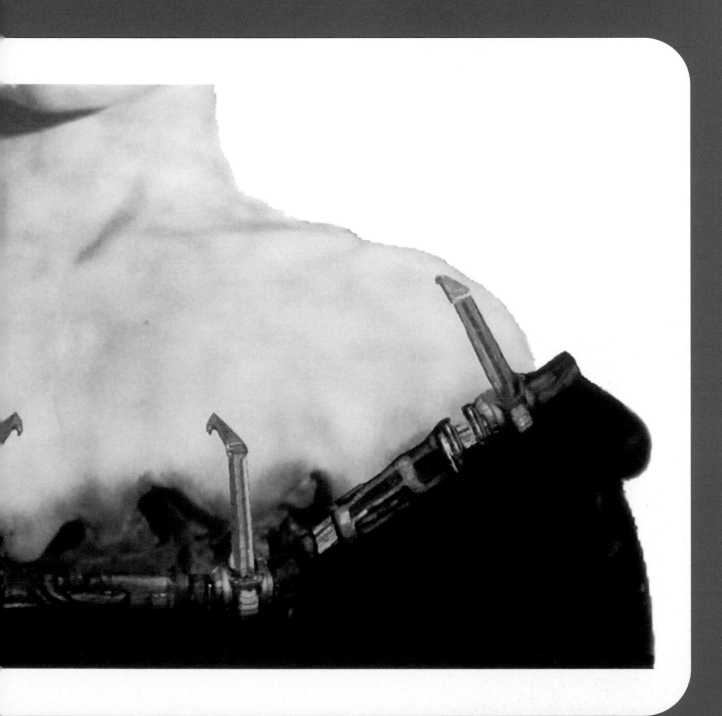

MAJOR MELTDOWN: USING A PHOTO OF FELLOW ILM WORKER KATIE
MORRIS, JAEGER USED HIS COMPUTER TO GENERATE IMAGES THAT
COULD BE USED AS A GUIDE FOR THE BORG QUEEN'S "DISSOLUTION"
ON-SCREEN. PRODUCER JEFF OLSON SUGGESTED JAEGER LOOK AT
TIME-LAPSE PHOTOGRAPHY OF ROTTING FRUIT FOR INSPIRATION.

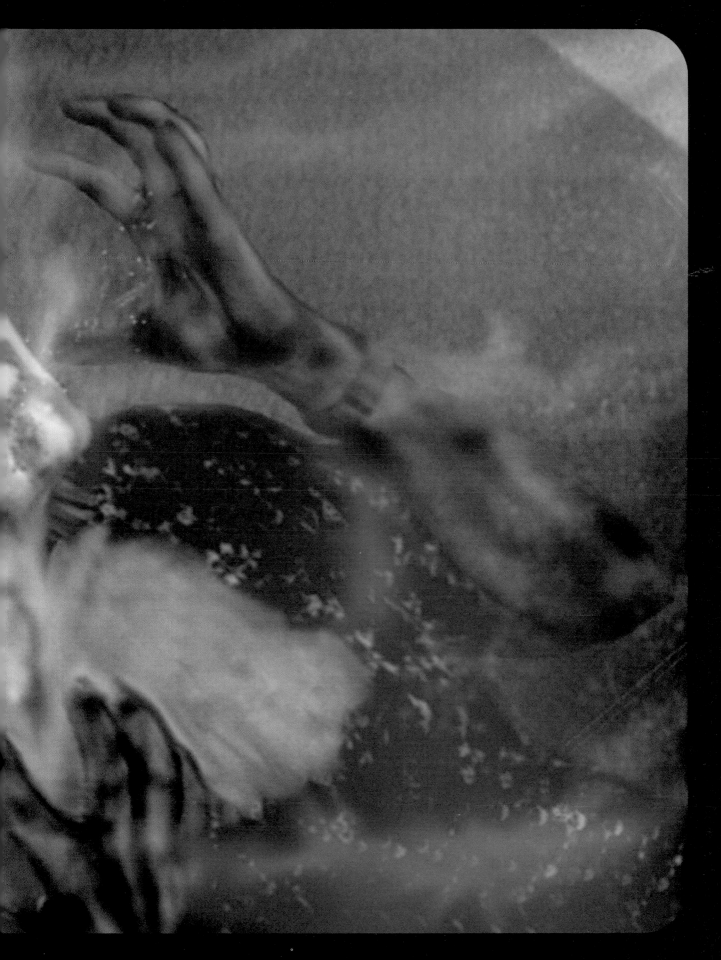

ALEX JAEGER ILM ART 1996

6.

7.

8.

9.

10.

11.

ALEX JAEGER ILM ART 1996

The opening pullback for *Star Trek: First Contact,* by Illusion Arts:

ONE OF THE LONGEST CAMERA PULLBACKS (THIRTY-FIVE SECONDS) IN CINEMATIC HISTORY WAS CREATED BY THE ILLUSION ARTS TEAM OF SYD DUTTON AND BILL TAYLOR, WHO ALSO CREATED MATTE SHOTS FOR *STAR TREK V: THE FINAL FRONTIER*, *STAR TREK GENERATIONS*, AND THE *ST:TNG* TELEVISION SERIES. THE PULLBACK BEGINS INSIDE PICARD'S EYEBALL, THEN SLOWLY REVEALS HIM TO BE A CAPTIVE INSIDE THE VAST CHAMBERS OF THE BORG CUBE.

IRONICALLY, INSPIRATION FOR THE BORG SHIP'S INTERIOR CAME FROM THE INTERIOR OF THE ROYAL BOTANICAL GARDENS IN KEW, ENGLAND. SYD DUTTON DECIDED TO USE SHAPES AND PATTERNS FROM THE 1845 CAST IRON STRUCTURE FOR THE BORG HIVE. DUTTON'S CONCEPT WAS COMBINED WITH THAT OF ILLUSION ARTS ILLUSTRATOR MIKE WASSEL TO CREATE A "CHAMBER INSIDE A CHAMBER."

THE FIRST THIRD OF THE SHOT CONTAINS LIVE-ACTION ELEMENTS FILMED AT PARAMOUNT, INCLUDING TWO SEPARATE SHOTS OF PICARD STRAPPED IN THE BORG CHAMBER. THE FIRST IS A CLOSE-UP USING A 50MM MACRO LENS THAT PULLS BACK FROM PICARD'S EYE TO A MEDIUM SHOT; THE SECOND IS A LONGER PULLBACK USING A 35MM LENS THAT EVENTUALLY REVEALS THE ENTIRE SET PIECE. SINCE IT WAS NOT POSSIBLE TO USE A COMPUTERIZED MOTION-CONTROL SYSTEM TO MOVE THE CAMERA, IT WAS NECESSARY TO MANIPULATE BOTH OF THE SHOTS DIGITALLY IN ORDER TO TIE THEM TOGETHER. THE MOVE WAS ALSO EXTENDED WITH A DIGITAL ZOOM SO THAT THE CAMERA COULD APPEAR TO START INSIDE THE IRIS OF PICARD'S EYE.

THE REMAINDER OF THE SHOT IS ENTIRELY COMPUTER GENERATED. THE FIRST PORTION OF THE SHOT CONTAINS ILLUSION ARTS' ROBERT STROMBERG'S PAINTING; THE SECOND SECTION IS A TUNNEL CREATED AS A 3-D COMPUTER MODEL BY FUMI MASHIMO. THE FINAL PORTION BEGAN AS A 3-D SHAPE, WHICH WASSEL CREATED WITH FORM-Z AND RENDERED IN STRATOPRO WITH A PRELIMINARY TEXTURE MAP.

ATMOSPHERIC EFFECTS THAT CONTRIBUTED TO THE SENSE OF SCALE IN THE SHOT WERE RENDERED SEPARATELY SO THAT THEY COULD BE ADJUSTED IN THE FINAL COMPOSITING IN AFTER EFFECTS.

—ADAPTED FROM TEXT PROVIDED BY ILLUSION ARTS. COURTESY OF ILLUSION ARTS.

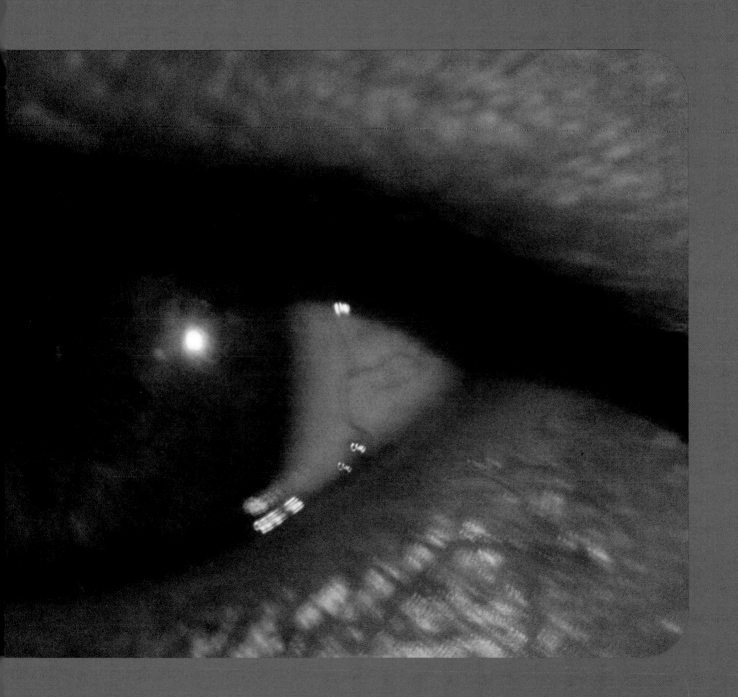

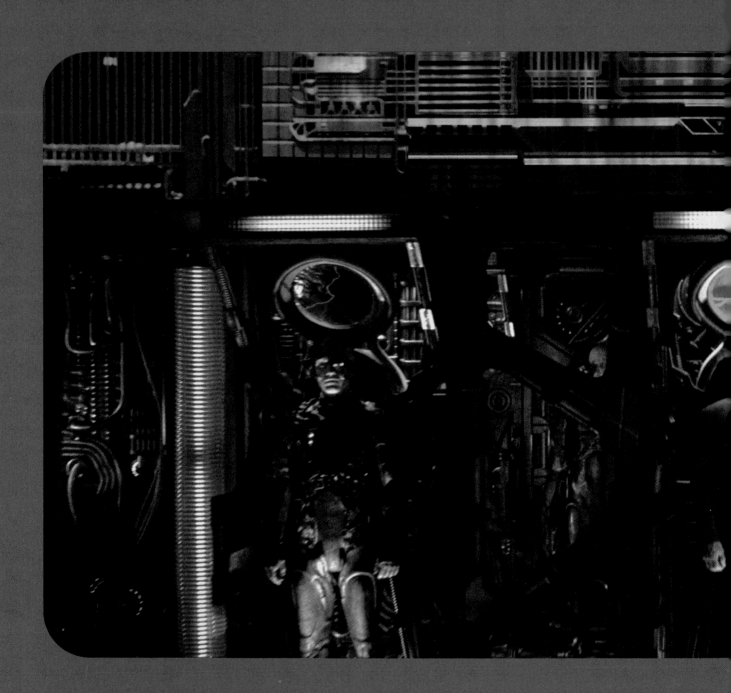

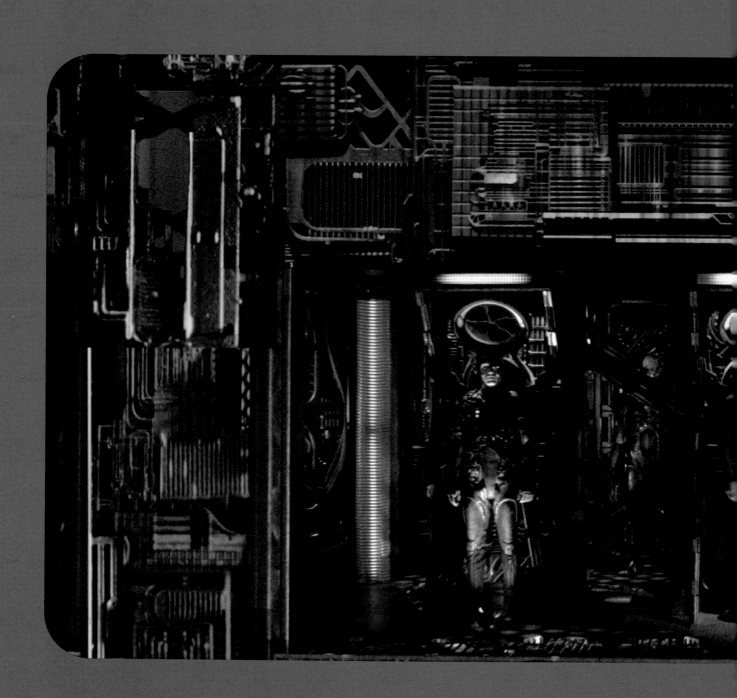

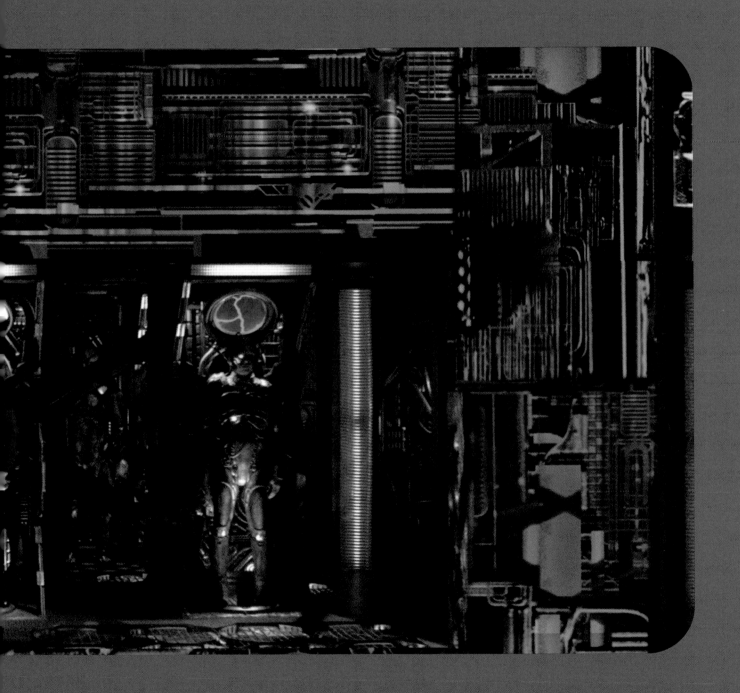

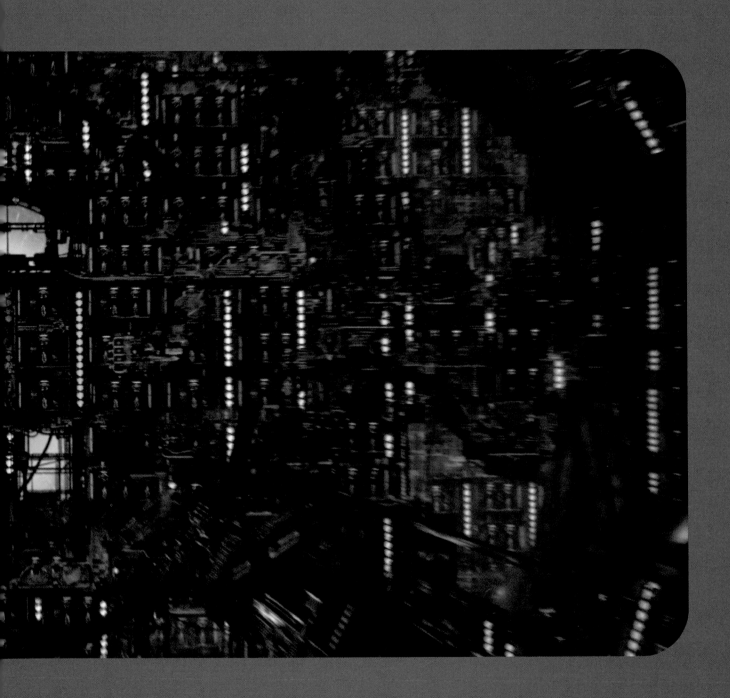

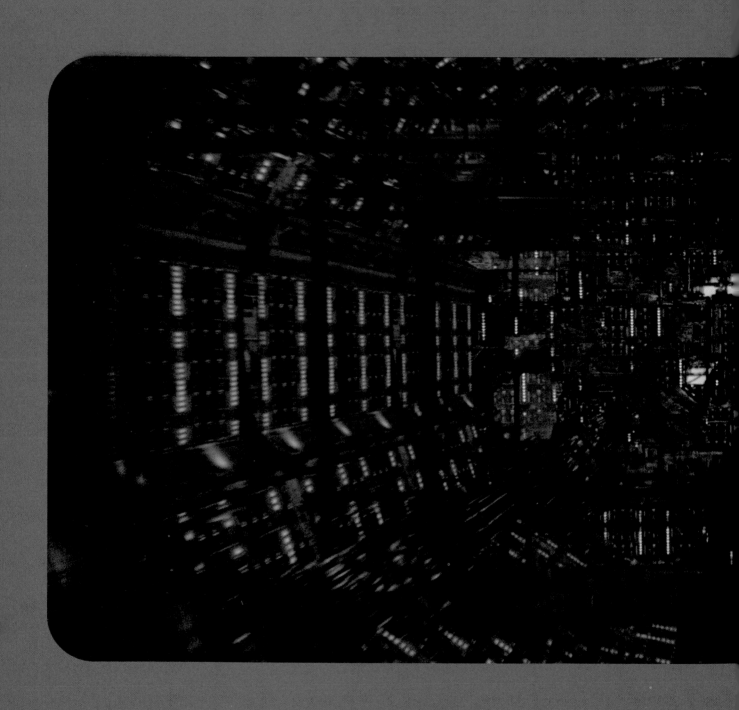

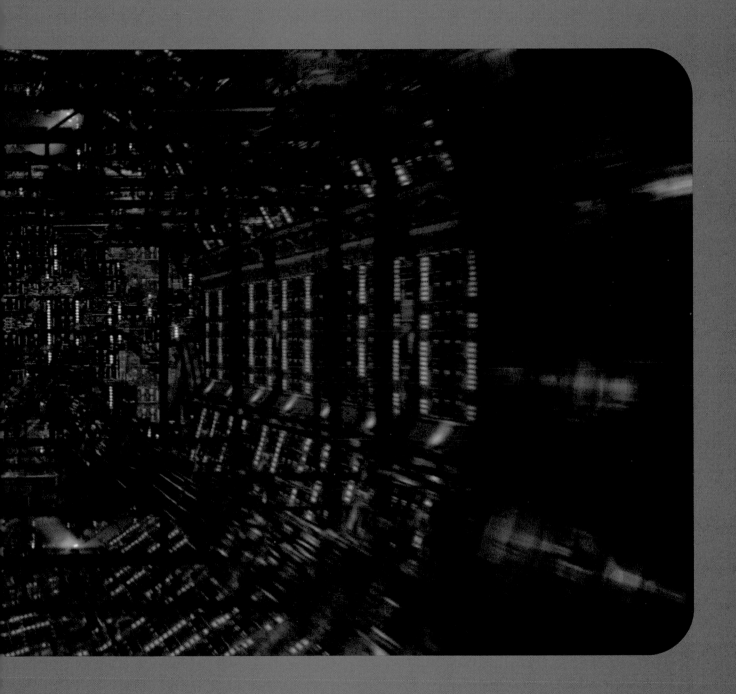

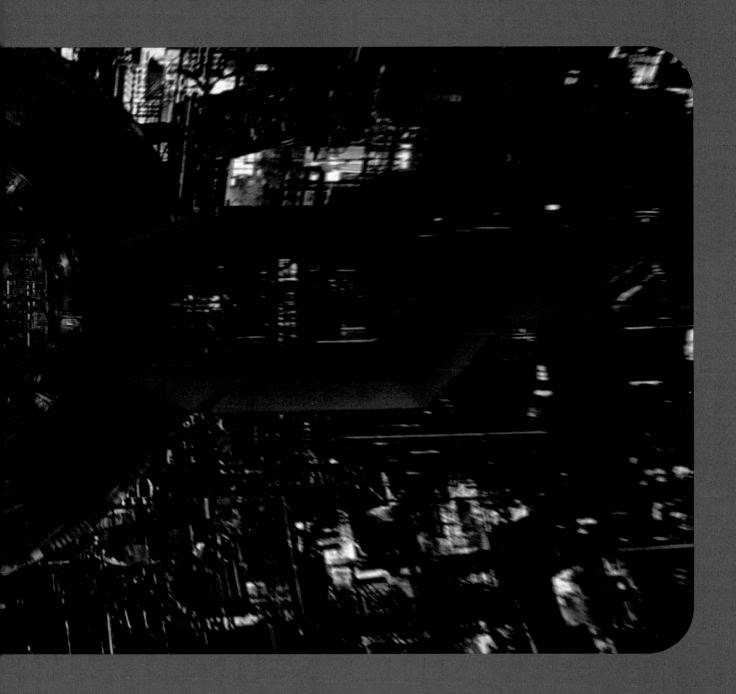

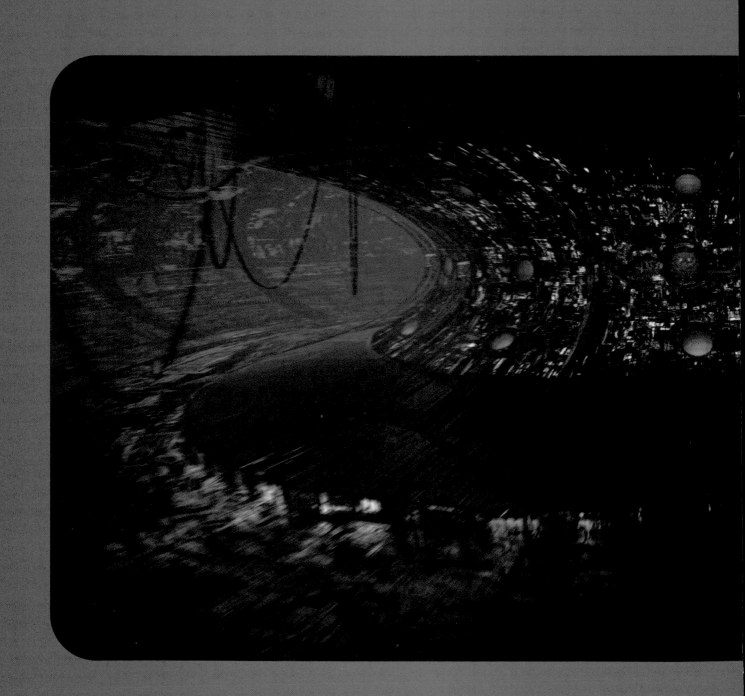

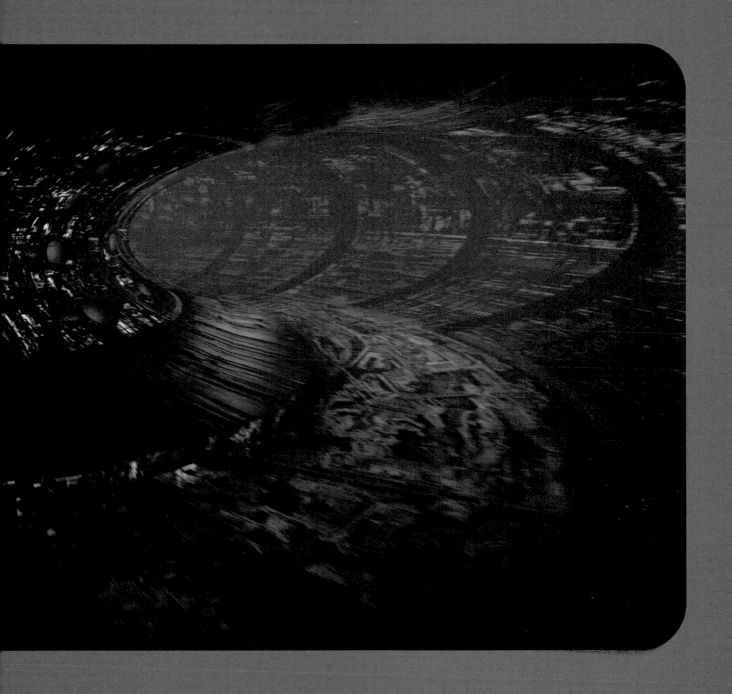

Other Borg props included the spires used in the "Borgification" of the *Enterprise*-E's deflector dish. The spires were rod-shaped devices that the Borg erected around the dish's center in order to alter the signal for their nefarious purposes.

JOHN: My spire design consisted of these big, heavy pipes with tubes coming off them, a design that was to be molded and repeated around the saucer's circumference.

Nancy Mickelberry was working on the spires at the same time. Now, Dean Wilson had brought in some clear tubular hummingbird feeders, and Nancy decided to incorporate them into her design—which was very clean, sharp, and angular, and also very in keeping with Borg architecture. Her design was sleek and scary; Herman especially loved the devices she drew, so she did blueprints and they built a series of hummingbird-feeder spires that encircled the deflector dish. The clear tubes were illuminated by orange and yellow lights that pulsed in a sequence for a few fleeting moments before Picard and Worf blow the array to bits.

The hummingbird-feeder spires were carried to the deflector dish in special "Borg backpacks," designed by Eaves. The backpack appears in a scene where one Borg removes a spire from the backpack his fellow drone is wearing, then uses it to help construct a "multiplexing beacon."

JOHN: The backpack is a harness with an open-faced center. All these tubes crisscross in the back of it, so you can pull the rods out from either the right or left side.

Eaves also designed the unsettling "framework" for Data's arm—a clamp that the actor's forearm fit inside, during the scene in which the Borg queen gives Data actual flesh so that he can feel what it's like to be human. Dean Wilson modified the design to give the device a more open feel and allow the camera to get a broader angle.

JOHN:

You can see the mechanics of Data's arm on either side of this clamp. And when the lid opens up, you can see little blades cutting away his artificial skin, peeling it back . . . and then replacing it with a piece of real skin.

My drawing for this prop wound up being fairly close to the final version—of course, allowing for the interpretation and extra detail the prop department came up with. It ended up being a very pretty—and eerie—piece.

EERIE BUT ELEGANT:
THE MECHANICAL "CLAMP"
FOR DATA'S ARM. ▶

BORG BACKPACK.
▼

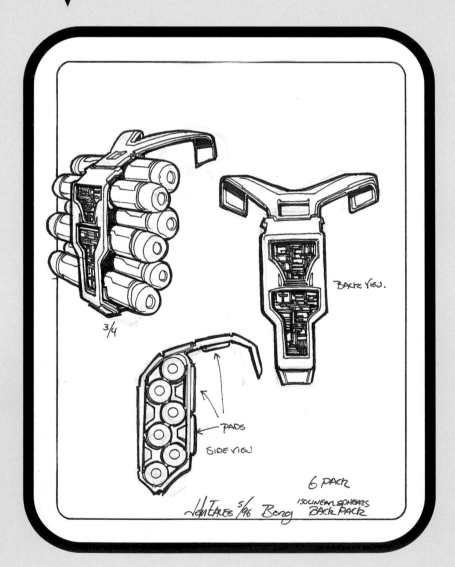

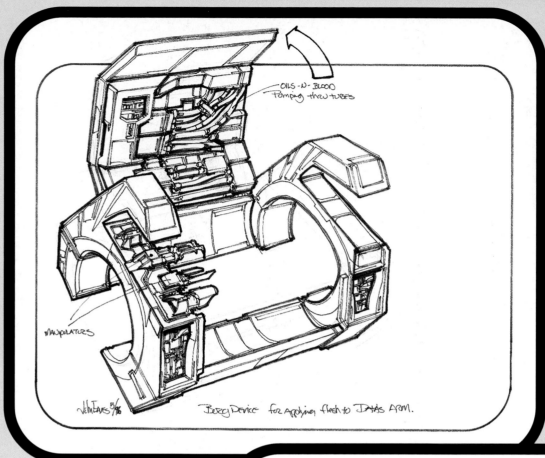

OILS-N-BLOOD
Pumping thru tubes

MANIPULATORS

John Eaves 5/96   Borg Device for Applying flesh to Data's Arm.

Pretty? Perhaps this is one of those "eye-of-the-beholder" instances. But "eerie" certainly seems apt, especially when it comes to describing the next few props on Eaves's to-do list. For example, there's the "Borg eye-piercing assimilation device," a charming little piece used in the very beginning of the film, when it punctures Picard's pupil.

JOHN:

[with disturbingly malicious glee] **I came up with a real wicked sewing-needle instrument; you hold it like a big fat pen. At the end, it has an intricate open-ended double needle, inscribed with Borg script.**

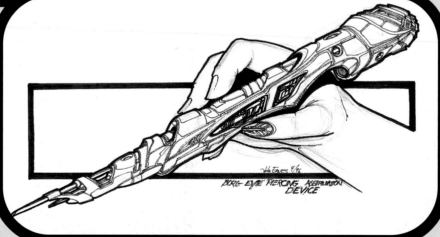

John Eaves 4/96
BORG EYE PIERCING ASSIMILATION DEVICE

▲

PICARD'S PUPIL-PIERCER, IN THE HANDS OF THE BORG QUEEN. (ONLY THE NEEDLE MADE IT INTO THE FINISHED FILM.)

And then there were the innocuously termed "Borg forearm pieces"—designed to stab, pierce, hack, buzz saw, and flay human flesh. Amazing, what such apparently nice people can hide in the dark depths of their creative imagination. . . .

JOHN:

I did some passes, and Deborah Everton had Todd Masters (who worked off the Paramount lot) do a lot of design work. Todd came up with some really bulky, menacing instruments with blades and knives and saws and hooks that articulated out of the Borg arms. His design followed the look of the Borg in the *Next Generation* series in terms of their size, but they were equipped with "feature details"—and they went from sketch to prop just as fast as he could render them.

Debra also had Todd and me try our hand at Picard's space helmet. I did a rough sketch showing three-quarters, side, and front views. From there, Todd went on to add his own artistic additions to the design. He offset some of the helmet's framework and added side windows to allow greater visibility.

Eaves's last drawing was done for a scene filmed a mere five weeks before *First Contact* opened in theaters. Why so late? Because, in late October, audiences at a test screening gave the film a score higher than any other *Star Trek* movie—and their enthusiasm gave Paramount the confidence to devote additional time and money to fine-tuning its project.

JOHN:

This is when the Borg "assimilation chamber of horrors" came into play. This last drawing for Herman is of a wounded Borg. He's lying lifeless on the floor, and beneath his damaged Borg armor, a Federation logo is visible; he's one of the *Enterprise* crew members that were assimilated. This adds to the sense of horror at what happens when the Borg assimilate humans.

Courtesy of the artist.

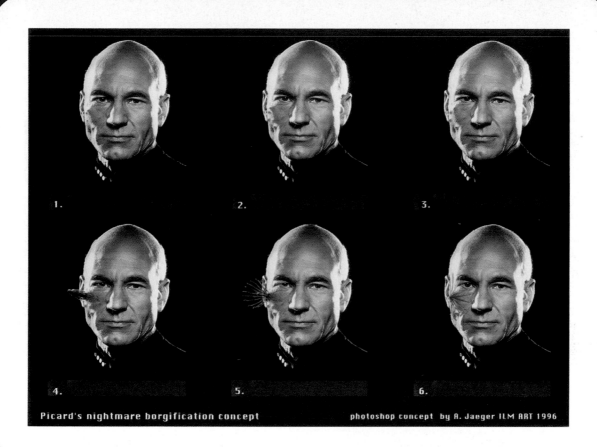

Picard's nightmare borgification concept

photoshop concept by A. Jaeger ILM ART 1996

▲
PICARD IN BLOOM: A HEAD SHOT OF PICARD, ALTERED VIA COMPUTER TO SHOW THE SEQUENCE OF FACIAL CHANGES DURING THE "CHEEK POPPER" SCENE. JAEGER CITES AN ICE-CUBE HOLDER ("WITH THOSE FINGERS THAT EXTEND AND GRAB") AS INSPIRATION. THE WOUND ON PICARD'S CHEEK IS A TWO-DIMENSION COMPUTER "PAINTING."

THE CINEMATIC RESULT.
▼

A hapless ILM employee (Jeff Mann) encounters a real pain in the neck (fellow ILMer Jon Rothbart). CGI "Borgification" by Alex Jaeger. ▶

▲

The *nearly* final result for the big screen. The CGI shots were created by ILM's Steve Braggs, using images designed by Jaeger as his guide.

▼

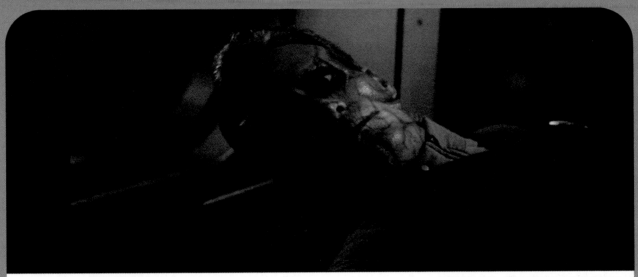

STAR TREK FIRST CONTACT   CONCEPT ART, ALEX JAEGER ILM ART 1996

LAST FRAME OF I.L.M SHOT
NOTE: COLOR CHANGE AND TRAILS LEFT BY THE TUBES MOVING UNDER THE SKIN.
SMALLER TUBES MOVE FASTER, LARGER TUBES MOVE SLOW AND PULSATE.

JAEGER'S COMPUTER-GENERATED
"BORGIFIED EARTH."

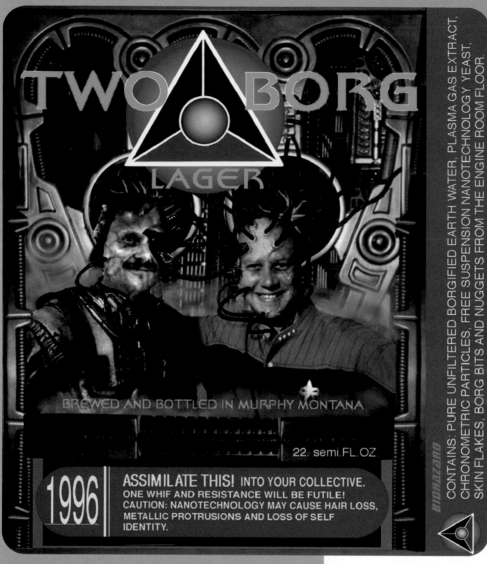

CONTAINS: PURE UNFILTERED BORGIFIED EARTH WATER, PLASMA GAS EXTRACT, CHRONOMETRIC PARTICLES, FREE SUSPENSION NANOTECHNOLOGY YEAST, SKIN FLAKES, BORG BITS AND NUGGETS FROM THE ENGINE ROOM FLOOR.

TWO BORG
LAGER

BREWED AND BOTTLED IN MURPHY MONTANA

22. semi.FL.OZ.

1996

ASSIMILATE THIS! INTO YOUR COLLECTIVE. ONE WHIF AND RESISTANCE WILL BE FUTILE! CAUTION: NANOTECHNOLOGY MAY CAUSE HAIR LOSS, METALLIC PROTRUSIONS AND LOSS OF SELF IDENTITY.

BIOHAZARD

▲
HEY, WAIT A MINUTE, HOW DID
THAT GET IN HERE (PART II)?
MORE WIT FROM THE STAFF AT ILM.

▶
BORG SPIRES SKETCH BY JOHN EAVES.
(NOT USED IN THE FILM.)

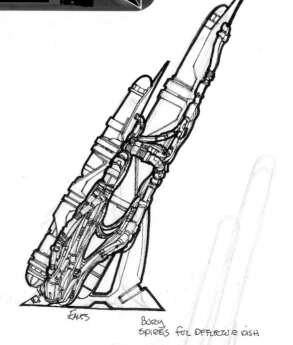

EAVES

BORG
SPIRES FOR DEFLECTOR DISH

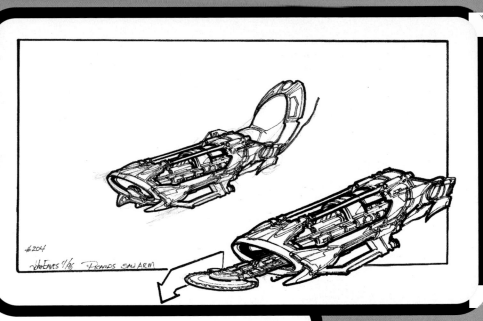

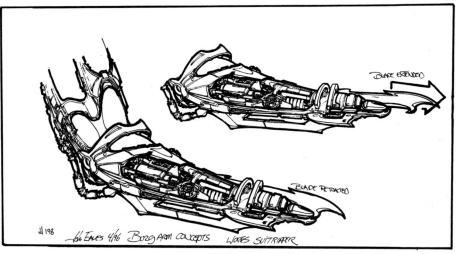

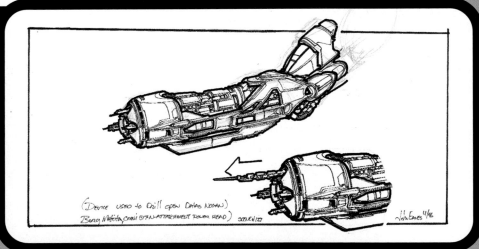

EAVES'S DESIGNS FOR THE BORG'S SINISTER DEVICES:
TOP: THE SAW ARM THAT MENACED PICARD.
MIDDLE: THE "SUITRIPPER" USED AGAINST WORF.
BOTTOM: AND THE "SKULLDRILLER" USED AGAINST DATA.

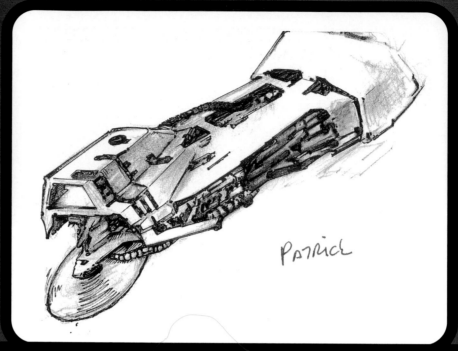

PATRICE

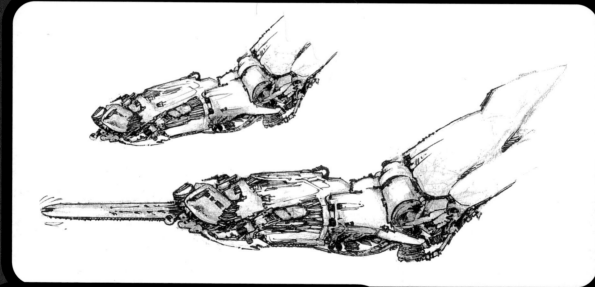

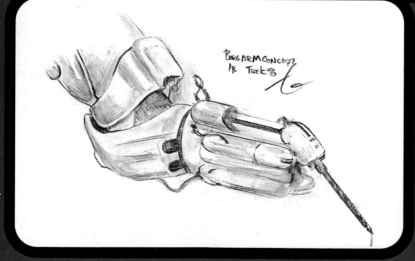

BORG ARM CONCEPT
1B TREK 8

TODD MASTERS'S TAKE ON

THE SAW ARM (TOP)...
THE "SUITRIPPER" (MIDDLE)...
AND "SKULLDRILLER" (BOTTOM).

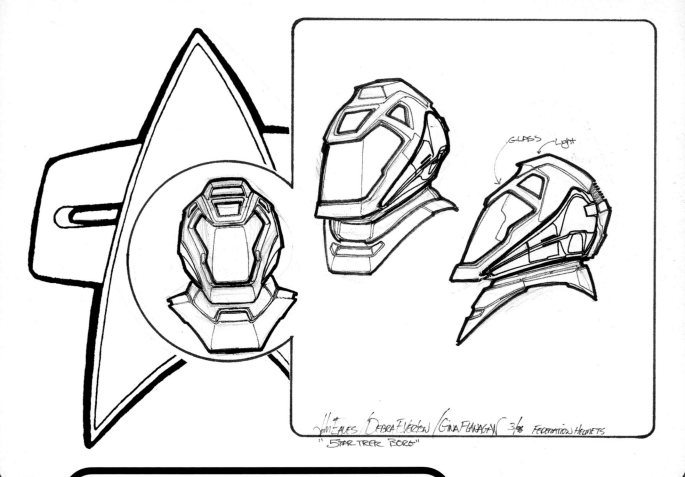

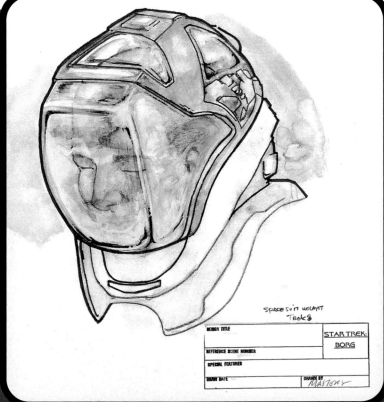

The "saucer walk" helmet, a collaboration by Everton, Eaves, and Flanagan.

Todd Masters's revision of the helmet.

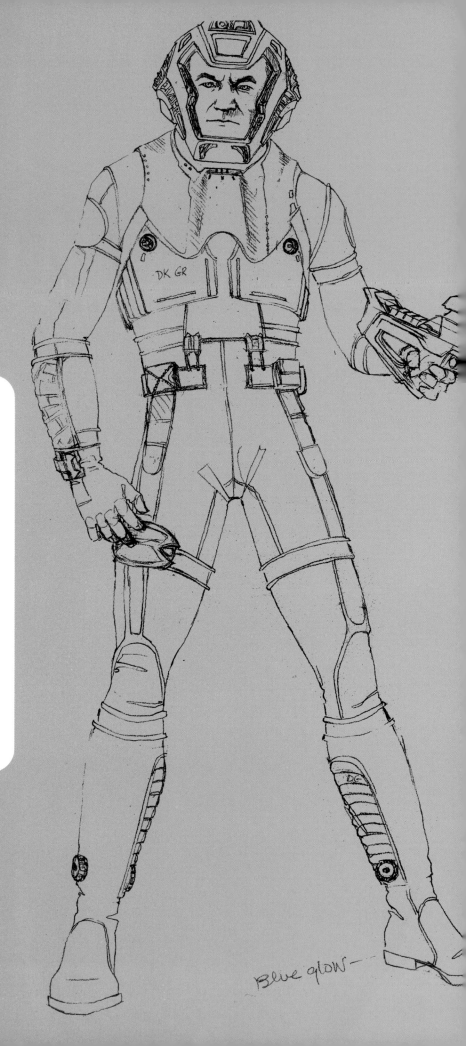

AN EARLY SPACESUIT DESIGN BY EAVES. ▲

DEBORAH EVERTON'S SPACESUIT, WHICH ▶
WAS USED IN THE FILM. FRONT VIEW...

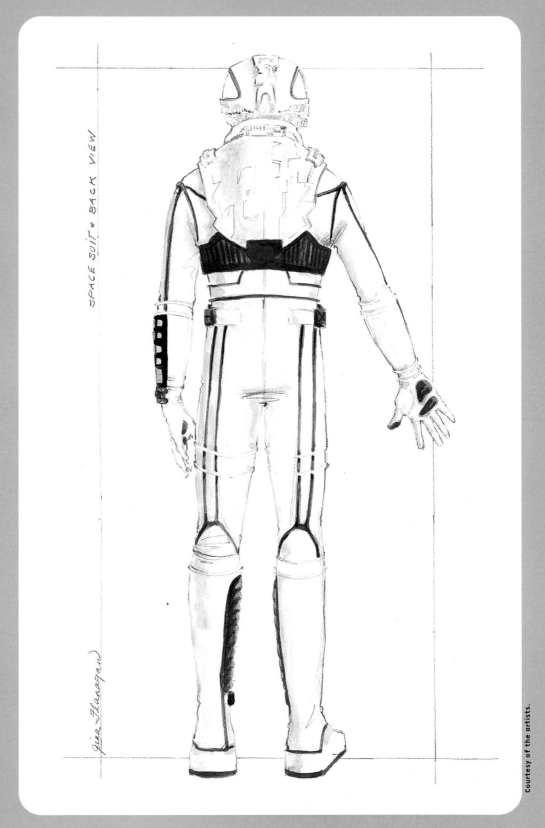

SPACE SUIT * BACK VIEW

Gina Flanagan

Courtesy of the artists.

...AND BACK. ▲

At long last, artwork for *First Contact* was completed—and *Deep Space Nine* was returning from hiatus—so the move from the feature trailer back to the *DS9* art department began.

JOHN:

It was a great privilege to work on the film with Herman and all the greatly talented artists and craftspeople on the film. It was an experience I'll always remember.

So this scrapbook ends. But *Star Trek*'s story continues, with the knowledge that new images, new characters, new tales are constantly being created, and will again be gathered together and shared with family and friends....

JOHN EAVES

THE ILLUSTRATED ILLUSTRATOR. ▲
BY CLARK SCHAFFER.

ACKNOWLEDGMENTS

As in any large project there are many friends, artists and companies that have contributed so generously, either directly or inspirationally in the creation of this book. My idea was to thank everyone that I could think of, but there would be no pages left for the rest of the book. So to all those that are listed and especially those that are not, this book's for you.

First and most of all, I want to thank the almighty God, His Son and Spirit, for blessing my paths, and for making my dreams come true. Thanks to my parents, Jim and Fran Eaves, without your love and guidance, I wouldn't be where I am today. Dad, you're my hero, and Mom, you're my guardian angel. To my sister Christi, thanks for all your great ideas and good advice. Thanks to my best friends Mark Zainer and Nelson Broskey.

I want to thank the following artists who have inspired me with their talents and imaginations. Robert T. McCall, you're an incredible talent, your artwork has been my cornerstone, and my guiding force. Steve Berg, my friend, who is the most gifted and talented artist I've ever seen, your work is genius, and a source of inspirations. Thanks to Ed (Capt. Walker) Verreaux, a great artist whose imagination is as endless as his talents, when I grow up I want to be just like you! To Joel and Ethan Coen, I want to give special thanks for the mastery of storytelling and imagery that they put on film. Kimalyn Eaves, who is the master of her medium, your mastery of fabric and costumes is truly magical. Thomas Kinkade, a painter of light, every piece of art you create is a masterpiece.

A very special thanks for all those talented individuals that I've been fortunate to learn from and work with over the years. Thanks to Grant McCune for giving me my first job in Hollywood at Apogee FX, you're a great friend and I miss working for you. Thanks to Richard Lewis and Steven Spielberg for giving me my first illustration job at Amblin. To Phil Edgerly, thanks for introducing me to the world of *Star Trek*.

Herman Zimmerman, who I am fortunate to call my friend, and who so kindly brought me into the *Star Trek* family; thanks for all the guidance and wisdom you've shared with me. To my good friend Greg Jein, who used to set my chair on fire, thanks for allowing me to work for you, I'm still your biggest fan. To all my friends at the following companies: Grant McCune Design, Boss Films, DreamQuest Images, Fantasy II FX, the Chiodo Bros, ILM and Lucasfilms Ltd, Sci-tec Publishing, Digital Domain, Digital Muse, Area 51, Cresenda Records, Illusion Arts, Acme Models, and Renfield Productions. Thanks to all at Matte World, Image "G," Paramount Pictures, Viacom and everyone at *Deep Space Nine* and *Voyager*.

Thanks to Rick Berman, and Gene Roddenberry.

—John Eaves
December 1997